BAPTISM BY FIRE

A SAWYER GRANT THRILLER

DREW COLE

Glint Storytelling
GROUP

JOIN MY COLE STORIES CLUB

Drew Cole's readers club members get free books, free behind-the-screen updates, and unique items to accompany the books.

Members are always the first to hear about Drew's new stories.

See the back of the book for details on how to sign up.

PART ONE

ONE

Janeen didn't know that the uncomfortable moments she was spending at the Lahaina Intermediate were the last normal ones of her life.

The bass made Janeen's teeth hurt. She was surprised at how loud it was. How could anyone talk?

The dance floor was filled with kids she barely knew—some standing in groups, some dancing, some just looking at their phones. Flashing lights made the ceiling look like something intergalactic. It was cool.

It was dark. The main lights of the cafeteria were barely on, if at all. And the fog machine didn't help matters, filling the floor with a haze. She thought the fog might have had a smell, but it was eclipsed by the various perfumes and colognes that filled her nose. Some of it was way too strong, but it all blended together.

Janeen felt somewhat relieved watching a couple of her classmates stumbling and laughing as they did. It was hard even for them to navigate the floor.

Imagine how hard it was going to be for me. This is my first dance at this Lahaina Intermediate.

She'd catch glances of some girls that she'd met weeks before. They only managed polite nods toward her. Some didn't look at all. And Malia gave her disapproving looks. The same looks she'd given Janeen since the first day.

She stayed on the outside of the dance floor. Her hands went from folded in front of her, to occasionally pulling on her dark blue dress. It was too long. She looked down at it. It was way past her knees. Her dad made sure of that. It was also too dark. Everyone around her seemed to be wearing a dress lighter colors to go along with the tropical paradise theme of their lives.

Janeen was out of place.

The next song was something slow. Something in Hawaiian.

She decided to leave the edge of the floor to venture to grab something to drink. Hopefully someone had spiked it.

As she started to move away from the floor, she stopped when a hand touched her shoulder.

"Dance?"

Her throat instantly went dry.

The boy was cute. His hair was disheveled, but she thought that was a choice. He was wearing a white dress shirt with a black tie. The top button was undone giving him a relaxed look. But Janeen also thought that was a choice.

"Akamai, remember?" He extended his hand. "We met in Algebra."

She shook it. "I didn't, don't take Algebra," she said.

She sounded like an idiot.

"I know!" He smiled. "You came into Algebra thinking it was English. I'm the one that told you what was up." He hadn't let go of her hand yet.

Janeen laughed with embarrassment and recognition. "Yeah, yep. Thanks for letting me not get too far into class."

"Ha, sure. I would have been curious to see you pulling out a copy of *Great Expectations* and trying to understand why the notes on the board didn't make sense."

She laughed, still holding his hand.

He smiled. She saw kindness. It was good enough.

Akamai moved to the dance floor. He had yet to let go of her hand.

She felt nervous, but a different kind than she'd felt on the floor to this point. He was cute. He was nice.

And he was the only one who'd really talked to her tonight.

They began to dance alongside other couples. His hands were gently on her hips; Janeen kept hers on his shoulders. Akamai was just a little shorter than she was. Not enough for it to be awkward, but it was noticeable.

The Hawaiian melody rang in the air, slow and steady. Janeen didn't understand the words, but this was the first time she'd felt comfortable tonight. Looking at Akamai, a boy who may end up being her friend, she felt alright.

But it didn't last.

Malia approached them from the right of the floor. Janeen caught a glimpse of her bright red dress out of the corner of her eye. Instantly, she became anxious.

"Hey, haole," Malia said in perfect Hawaiian accent.

Akamai said, "Malia, why don't you—"

It didn't matter. "Hey, haole, what's up?" Malia tilted her head slightly as she spoke.

Malia looked perfect, like she had stepped out of a Hawaiian model magazine (if there was something like that). Her hair as black as night was pulled into an updo.

Perfect. Her dark complexion offered the perfect backdrop to her bright lipstick that matched the dress.

But her eyes were filled with hate.

"I don't know what that means," Janeen said.

That was a lie. She knew what it meant. It was a derogatory term for people from the mainland.

She hoped she sounded defiant and that her voice hadn't shaken but she couldn't tell. Janeen still hadn't taken her hands off of Akamai's shoulders.

"It means," she paused, looking at her other equally dazzling classmate that Janeen didn't know, "that you should have sat this one out."

"Shut up, Malia," Akamai said. He motioned with his head for her to leave.

"Why you wasting your night with mainland trash, Akamai?" Malia wasn't looking at Janeen at all now, just at Akamai. "If her dress was any longer she'd be able to sail back home with it."

Instantly, Janeen felt like a spotlight had turned onto her. She was out of place.

Janeen let go of Akamai's shoulders and moved toward the closest exit.

/ TWO

He could think of worse places to do a job, and Bob wasn't complaining. The breeze in the night air was delightful with that flowery smell. He'd only been to Maui one other time, with his third wife on their honeymoon.

The trip lasted longer than their marriage.

He kept staring up at the moon in the sky and listening to all the different noises of the night. The crickets. The rustling of the trees in that perfect breeze. Despite how much he'd been smoking that day, he could still taste the pineapple he had gotten at a fruit stand.

These spoiled brats had no idea what it was like to have a real life. He spat in the direction of Lahaina Intermediate School. He wished he could reach it. Bob was far enough away to keep out of sight, but the bass was so loud it was almost rattling his windows.

Janeen. Or was it Janice. He couldn't exactly remember. All he knew was that she had a blue dress on, and she was whiter than rice and tall.

And he had a nice Hawaiian bed prepared for her in his trunk.

Bob was pretty tall, himself. This was gonna be a cake walk. He'd put on a little weight, but his bulky frame carried it well. And he had a lot of muscle under the girth. As much pushin' as cushion.

He had taken the precautions. The car he *borrowed* for this job was in need of a little TLC. Bob had put some blankets in the back, removed anything from the Malibu's trunk that could be used against him, like the tire jack—he'd had some problems in the past with those, and a scar to go along with the story

He took another couple puffs of his cigarette and patted the pocket of his brown overalls. Bob liked overalls for this type of job and he felt he was dressed right. The only drawback was that he smoked a lot when the jobs were a little tough, like this one. But he'd slow it down once the girl was in the car.

And after, maybe he'd even reward himself with another quick trip to that fruit stand.

THREE

When Janeen finally opened up the door to the dimly lit drop-off point outside of the school, she was overwhelmed with relief and also embarrassment.

She was sick of the transition. Sick of being from the mainland.

It was old.

As Janeen took in the plumeria-scented air, she surveyed the entrance. In no time at all, the adjacent parking lot would be filled with cars waiting to pick their kids up from the dance.

As she headed over to the parking lot, Janeen was glad to only notice a small cluster of cars close to the entrance. These most likely belonged to kids that had driven themselves. However, at the furthest end of the lot was a beat-up car. It was parked in the last stall. She squinted but couldn't see a driver.

Maybe a faculty member or something.

The ground didn't feel any easier on her heels out here, and she started to feel warm in the long dress. The air was breezy but the dress was just too long and heavy. She blamed her dad.

She pulled out her iPhone, and was about to call her dad to come pick her up when she stopped.

Akamai was calling her name. His voice seemed to be coming from one of the other exits. She'd left quickly enough from the dance floor to keep him at a distance.

Good thing. She lacked the strength to pretend she wasn't embarrassed and hurt. So she kept moving.

Sorry, Akamai, maybe if I wasn't the haole we could keep this up.

Janeen picked up the pace a little more toward Lahainaluna Road. She'd get clear of the parking lot before calling her dad to ask him to pick her up. He did tell her he was going to be interviewing a potential preacher to assume the lead role at a church that they'd been attending since moving.

That was her dad. When he wasn't leading at his job, he was leading at church. It took the board of the church about two seconds to ask him to help fill the pulpit with a new preacher. He said he had to do a quick interview tonight of someone else from the mainland that had asked about the job. Probably wouldn't go anywhere, her dad had said. But he wanted to give the guy a fair shake.

She wished that her dad and mom had tried to work things out. If her dad hadn't been relocating to Maui, she might have pleaded to stay with her mom. But both parents agreed to be liberal in how they allowed Janeen to pick. So, she decided to suffer in paradise. She'd see her mom regularly. They had the money, for sure.

But to be able to say she lived on Maui. What a dream!

Janeen passed all of the cars except for the junky one at the end of the lot.

Odd.

It certainly didn't look like it fit in with the others. It was beat up. Dents all over. The rear door on the passenger side looked like a spider web with the crack in it.

And it smelled—

She stopped moving.

As long as Janeen had lived here, the plumeria hit her every time she'd gone outside. But at the top of the parking lot, she smelled something else.

Cigarette smoke.

Her heart began to up its tempo as she stood motionless. She was about fifteen feet from the junker, but Janeen squinted, desperately trying to assure herself that no one was in the front seat.

There wasn't. It was empty. Just a cheap, green pine-tree air freshener dangled from the rearview mirror.

She was out of her mind. Just freaking herself out.

Get a grip, haole!

She pulled her phone out, and flicked it open to her dad's number. She wasn't going to go any closer to the road. In fact, she felt herself moving backwards toward the sound of the bass from the school. Maybe she could wait inside—

She heard footsteps first, and as soon as she initiated a call with her father, hands grabbed her by the shoulders. Her iPhone in the Hello Kitty case dropped to the asphalt and cracked, while simultaneously going to speaker on her dad's call.

As soon as she opened her mouth to scream, one of those hands let go her shoulder and draped across her mouth.

Ring.

All the energy she could muster to scream into the night

was blanketed by a hand reeking of cigarettes and rotten fruit.

She drew in a breath and didn't let it out as he pulled Janeen toward him. His body was against hers and for a moment she was certain she'd wet herself. She didn't—

Ring.

Please, God, don't let him rape me. God, I've never been with anyone—

Ring.

"Don't. Move. Janice."

Janice? Who is Janice? God please. Dad please pick up. Please please please please.

Ring.

The iPhone was still ringing and she was hoping her dad would pick up. The dial tone punctuated her breathless gulp as her assailant kept still.

From the ground, her dad's voice scratched upward.

"Babydoll, what's up, I'm meeting Pastor Grant about the church job, is everything good?"

Again, summoning what was left of her strength, Janeen screamed into the rancid smelling hand of her attacker.

She couldn't understand how, but he punched her.

Hard, in the back of the head. Really hard.

She was disoriented, but he hadn't taken his other hand away from her mouth. That rancid disgusting hand.

God, please, daddy.

Her vision had become slightly blurred, but she saw him stamp on her iPhone with a boot. She heard her father's voice once more, and in response, the putrid fruit man stamped her phone again, disconnecting the call.

Janeen didn't have enough time to take in what had happened before she was struck once more. This time, she was knocked out.

And she was taken.

PART TWO

FOUR

I could still smell the urinal cake even in the preacher's office. If I worked here, I'd tell the custodian to cut those puppies in half, but I'd wait until after the interview.

Dear Lord, how did the former pastor put up with that? Maybe that's why they were looking for a new one. It smelled clean, but still. Urinal cake wasn't Calvin Klein's fragrance of the year.

In a sense, I was glad the lady Elaina that lined up my interview told me to just come in. I didn't feel like wasting social energy on pleasantries when I was already wigged out about this conversation.

The chairs were as comfortable as a prostate exam, at least from what I'd been told. I wasn't at the age yet to require one. I had seven more years before that became a conversation starter between me and my PCP. I looked up at the lights. Two eyeball floods beamed down on the massive desk, and three were pointed directly at me, but lucky for me, those lights were burned out. So the desk had an odd stage-like quality.

The books on the shelves looked like they were from the

fifties and sixties. They were leather-bound tomes and just at a brief glance at the sheer size of them I felt illiterate, though I loved reading more than most things.

There were three particular ones at the top of shelf almost on display. The spines facing out made it look as though they were not even in English. Cool. I'd never understand the books. But cool.

The office was large, but because the windows were closed up and dark maroon metal blinds were drawn, I felt like I was in a space just a little bigger than a phone booth. The desk was the size of a coffin—a little wider—but I still felt like the office was definitely tight as a tomb because of how dark it was in there.

If this place was gonna be mine, I would have to really do what I could to get a little of Maui in there. I mean, for crying out loud, it's paradise and I felt like I was in Dracula's freaking library! Metal maroon mini blinds?

I get nervous when things are on the line, and right now, there were a lot of things on the line. First, I had this job interview, which was putting me on edge.

Second, there was the business of the jet-black Audi I had seen parked in the lot.

I only glanced in its direction when coming into the church, but the tint on it wasn't regulation. I only glanced because I didn't want the driver to think I was curious, even though I couldn't see him.

You never wanna be curious.

So instead, I pretended like I was oblivious.

You always pretend to be oblivious.

But none of it felt right.

I looked down at the floor. It looked new. Designer and beachy. Distressed light brown tongue-in groove flooring. It was about the only part of this office that was updated. Far as I could see, the computer was as old as Moses's jock strap. I'd replace that, too.

Sitting on the floor was my duffel. It was larger than it should have been, but it was all I could find. Dear Lord, I needed to find somewhere to put that oversized thing. Or I needed to consolidate the contents.

I was sick of making up lies about what was in it.

How long was Hargrove going to drag this out? I almost wish he had been like some of the other churches on Maui and told me, "No thanks, move along."

But they called me, and told me to come this evening.

Elaina, the office administrator, didn't know that I was talking to them on a phone that I had bought at the airport on the way in.

I also hadn't yet procured a place to stay.

That was the least of my worries. I'd get a hotel room someplace, and probably have to cut off one of my arms to do so, but it's not as though this plan was thought out.

I really needed, no, I really wanted this job. I could wait tables. I could do some website work, but in reality, I knew that I wanted to do this. I wanted to do the opposite of what I had been doing in Pittsburgh. And I don't care how tomb-like the office was. If Hargrove gave me even the slightest bit of hope, I'd take the job.

On cue, the solid oak door behind me opened and a man stepped forward. I stood up.

"Ray Hargrove," he said, extending out a hand to me that I shook.

Hargrove was stick thin, bald, and he was dressed in a light brown sport jacket over top of a conservatively pattered Hawaiian shirt. Untucked with dark jeans. He was dressing the part of a Hawaiian somebody, for sure, though he was as Caucasian as the driven snow.

I was sporting a black suit that I'd bought from the mall on Maui. It was one of those tailor-free jobs. I had lost some weight in the last couple months—muscle, not belly fat unfortunately—and the coat was loose in the shoulders. I felt a little like I was wearing daddy's outfit or something.

But I was definitely overdressed.

"Take a seat, Pastor, he said, motioning to the chair with a smile. "Running a little behind because I dropped my daughter off for a formal. Ex-wife is on the mainland. She wouldn't have helped anyway, you know?"

That was the first time that any human being had ever called me *Pastor*. But I "at eased" at his command.

My adrenaline started pumping as he sat down, but my mind couldn't quite let go of that ultra-tinted Audi in the church lot.

FIVE

Stu Gentry was taking a break to do a little shopping. He always found himself when he was at the grocery store—Times, as his route would have it tonight—wandering about the aisles. He stared at the shelves of cheese in the center cluster just inside the main entrance. He loved different cheeses. He also loved that there were so many options.

That's the other reason he liked inventing things. He liked options. His retirement had options. Where he lived had options. His church job had options.

Since it was dusk, the inside of the store seemed ultrabright, alive with the dings of cash registers and chatter of workers. There were a decent amount of people shopping, giving the Times a hurried feel. Felt more like NYC and less like Maui. And Stu had spent time in both.

Stu always liked the grocery store because it was filled with people who had just come in for vacation. And they were doing their shopping for the coming week. He loved watching that.

Families wandered the aisles acting as though each product on Maui was something otherworldly. The price was, for sure. But they acted like they'd reached the top of Mt. Everest if they found a good pancake mix.

A family of four stood over by the deli section doing exactly that. They were ribbing each other about what types of lunch meat they were going to enjoy at the beach that week. The mom was a tall, thin, already-tanned, dark-haired lady. She had wide eyes and giggled as her husband, wearing his Maui Brewing Company baseball cap and a sleeveless t-shirt, suggested they just get turkey and make it work.

Stu remembered feeling that way when he'd first come to Maui and he told himself early on that the feeling would leave.

But thank God, it hadn't.

He'd come to the grocery store to take a break from his tinkering in the garage, but "break" was a liberal term. He didn't consider any of the inventions or anything that he toyed with in his garage "work."

Sure, there were some parts Stu enjoyed more than others, but at the end of it, fun kept him moving like the wind to a sail. Choosing to retire to Maui was a dream that he made happen. He'd paid his price on the mainland, and now he was set to live out the rest of his life wherever everyone dreams to go once in in a lifetime.

Always fun.

He smiled at the family of four who had been arguing over cold cuts and looked down at the cheese. Stu would end up over in the automotive aisle where he always browsed for little things that he might want for his garage, though he didn't really need anything.

A text hit his phone. He felt the vibration in his pocket. With gym shorts, there wasn't much to keep that disturbance from coming through.

It was Miss Elaina. She asked him to stop at the church. Apparently, there was an interview with a preacher going on, and she didn't think Hargrove had keys to lock up. Almost seventy percent of his custodial duties had to do with locking and unlocking.

As luck might have it, he was close to the church. So this was an easy errand. He also had the option to tell Miss Elaina to pound salt and that he wasn't nearby. Having the money he had and freedom he did, left him needing nothing. He loved that he had that option.

But, he liked Miss Elaina. He didn't like the idea of her having to drive that pathetic decades-old Honda across Maui to lock the front door. Even if he were at home tinkering, he still most likely would have come out and run the errand.

He liked errands. More than anything, Stu liked options.

He thought of that as he made his selection on a good-looking block of Swiss. Then off to the register, watching some more elated families stocking up on food for the week.

Then, the road to Resurrection Church.

SIX

The hardest part of the job setup had been securing the two cars. And even that was easier than anything Billy had done on the mainland.

Billy Robertson stood just inside the door of his empty house. His family, including the dog, had gone for a ride to pick up drive-through food. He'd explained to Ellen that this Saturday was a pretty big night for the role that he had just taken at his job.

And nothing he said was untrue.

He stared at the boxes that seemed to stretch on for miles inside a living room that looked the size of a matchbox. How had they accumulated so much stuff? How did toddlers travel so heavily?

Ellen had purged a lot their stuff from Chicago, but this was still an inhuman amount of garbage. That's what he considered it, too. He knew it meant a lot to the kids. A four-year-old's stuffed animal collection. A three-year-old's favorite Nerf gun. But all the garbage only was good for a little bit of time and play.

As Billy had aged, he found the same to be true of every

material thing in life. This is what made him so good at his job. He didn't care about the money, though he made truck-loads of it. He didn't care about driving nice stuff. He had a minivan for his wife and a used Buick LeSabre that he liked because it rode nice on the highway.

The poorest men and women he knew looked at the things they pursued as greater than his son's Nerf gun, but Billy just couldn't do that.

It was all the same.

What Billy did value, was being able to manage people. Manage their behavior, really. Two-man operation tonight. He spoke. They listened. And it was. No fuss.

No nonsense.

This may have been the last big job he'd have to do, and he'd be home free. Paradise everywhere.

He looked out the curtain-free open window to the neighborhood they'd just moved to. All the houses looked similar, and that was okay. He didn't have a nicer house than those around him, and that was okay. But he was fairly certain that he was one of the only ones on the street that paid for the deal with cash.

No big deal. A house, a car, a Nerf gun.

But hearing one of his hired men in a panic because they were upset at the possibility of disappointing him, well, there simply wasn't enough money in the world to buy that.

Only two cars on this crew. An Audi, a little flashier than he liked. Too much tint, and not enough modesty. And a Chevy. That was more the speed of this deal.

And two men, both of whom were terrified of him. Because Billy had a reputation. Not just in the continental forty-eight, but on Maui, as well.

That's the stuff money couldn't buy. That's better than a nerf gun.

His minivan pulled up to the driveway. He heard the blaring noise of the sound system, blaring some sort of tune that the kids were gleefully screaming out. He loved that.

He loved hearing that freedom and joy—

Almost as much as hearing that fear of his disappointment.

He'd heard from Bob. The Malibu had the cargo.

He just had to hear from Riggins and the Audi at the church. That was the easy part. Bob had to do the heavy lifting on this one by going to the school. Riggins was going to the church on a Saturday night.

Easy money. Just had to touch base with Riggins and be off to a free night. The rest of this deal was going to go on autopilot. Easy easy money.

Maybe he could take the kids for some shaved ice while blaring some more of those obnoxious tunes after touching base with Riggins.

Yeah, he liked that almost as good.

Almost.

SEVEN

"How many kids you have, sir," I asked as he grabbed a file from the corner of the otherwise clear coffin desk.

Sir?

Might have been laying it on too thick.

"Just the one, she's the limited edition. They keep things interesting as they get older. You?"

Hargrove had a commanding voice. No accent that I could tell.

"None to my knowledge."

Wow, great job, Pastor. You made the first sex joke of this church interview. Good job comin' out swinging.

He ignored my stupidity and opened the file on the preacher's desk. Hargrove wasn't the preacher, but the head of the pulpit search committee. He didn't look uncomfortable behind the desk, though, as I knew I would. The secretary Elaina had told me that he was chairman on some sort of utilities board as well. I couldn't really remember. I was too shocked that she called me to interview.

Uncomfortable was the only thing I was feeling

watching him peruse the manila folder of documents that I had fabricated on my laptop on the plane.

Well, some of it was true.

While watching the spotlights beaming off his bald head as he read, my mind bounced back to that black Audi with the ultra-dark tint. I didn't think it was the janitor's.

Let's deal with the first issue.

Hargrove looked up from my file with a grin.

This is all lies. That's what he would say. I knew it.

"So, your military background is pretty impressive."

That was true.

"Thanks for saying that."

"And your ministry stuff, whew, you've been working at the same church for a long time."

Total lies.

"Volunteering, yeah. But I've not actually been paid. They were planning on taking me on as the pastor with a salary and all that and it fell through because the church caught on fire and they didn't have the funds to proceed."

Wasn't too heavy on details, but totally believable. And if he googled the church, he'd find that it burned down.

"So, all the way from Pittsburgh. I wish Elaina had told you that we needed to check out your references here before you made a trek all this way for an interview."

The interview wouldn't have happened at that point.

"Yeah, well, I'm interviewing with a bunch of churches (lies), second and third interviews (double lies) out here and I figured I was in the area—"

An iPhone rang from Hargrove's pocket and he shot me a brief look of embarrassment.

"I'm so sorry," he said. "Thought for sure I'd shut that off."

Second ring.

Hargrove took the phone out and looked at a pretty blonde girl holding a golden retriever as though they were dancing. Had to be his daughter. He furrowed his brow at the phone.

"Take it, sir. Honestly."

"Eh," he said as it rang for a third time. "Tell you what, how about a little baptism by fire? I don't have anyone to preach at our mid-week prayer service on Wednesday. Why don't I let you kick the tires a little."

Ummmm, what?

Fourth ring.

Hargrove went on. "Yeah, I'll tell congregation you're a guest speaker. Hold on a minute I should grab this."

He answered the phone and I thought about preaching, to live people, something I'd never done.

Black Audi still dug into my mind. Something was shady out there.

"Babydoll, what's up, I'm meeting Pastor Grant about the church job, is everything good?"

Pastor again. Baptism—

The look on his face pulled me away from my thoughts. And combined with the noise I heard on the other end. It sounded a little like a screech, followed by a smack—phone hitting the ground. It must have slid on pavement. I knew that sound. I'd wasted my share of gadgets.

Hargrove pulled the iPhone from his ear like it was made out of anthrax.

"Janeen, I can't hear you, babe—"

The next sound was so loud that I jumped out of my seat a little. Sounded almost like an explosion. Hargrove jerked his head away and dropped the phone onto the preacher's desk.

Then the familiar sound of the disconnected iPhone.

Three consecutive beeps and the apologetic, *Call Was Lost* screen came up, with the hopeful inviting green button asking if you'd like to try to reconnect.

I looked at Hargrove. He tried to play it off, but no dice. I saw a little bit of sweat beading up on his dome.

"Must be in a bad reception area."

"I'd call her back, sir."

He didn't respond to me. He dialed the phone right back.

No ring. Straight to voicemail. His volume was turned up loud enough that I caught, "Hey, you got 'Neen, you know what to do."

Hargrove didn't wait for the tone. He hung up.

He tried one more time and almost immediately hung up.

The beads were more pronounced on his head. The spotlights almost refracted a prism from them.

"Sir, we can do this at another time."

His eyes were distant, but he stood up, and so did I.

As Hargrove approached the door he said, "Yeah, I'm sorry, Pastor, let's have you take that test drive this Wednesday, I better head over to the school. Elaina will get you up to speed. You wanna come over tomorrow and get a lay of the land, check out the service? Moani Wong is preaching. He's pretty good. A deacon."

"Yes, sir. Thank you, and I—" Lord, what would a preacher do right now?

"I'm praying for your daughter."

Another shot.

"Do you want me to tag along?"

He didn't respond to that, looked ahead and out into the dimly lit welcome area as I myself came out of the office behind him, my obnoxious duffel in hand that somehow had gone unnoticed during the lightning interview.

"Yeah, Pastor. Maybe. I know that might be odd."

"Not at all, we can talk on the way."

He shook his head. I couldn't see his sweat as much as I did in the office. I knew it was there. "Would you mind just following? It's Lahaina Intermediate. It's about ten minutes away. If everything is okay, I don't want to embarrass her by bringing you along."

"Sure, no problem." I said and I waved him off.

He was out the door without a glance backward. "Could you pull the door shut?"

"Done!" I called out as I stepped back and let that heavy oak slam, as if its loudness would give some sort of testimony to my ability to do good work.

I was there in the silence of the entrance, along with the tension of whatever was going on with Hargrove's kid and I couldn't help myself.

I said out loud, "What. A. Moron."

Typically, a person could only follow another person when they actually possessed a vehicle to do so.

Lord, I missed the part of the interview where I'd made the sex joke.

I ripped open my burner phone to the Uber app I'd installed earlier that morning.

I didn't even get to enter in "Lahaina Intermediate" before I heard something shatter inside the preacher's office.

EIGHT

The first thing I noticed when I walked through the door was the broken window and bent up metal shades. It wasn't really a terrible look compared to the shades intact.

The second thing I noticed was a punch to my jaw.

I staggered back without even realizing that the intruder was closer to the door than the window. I didn't lose my balance, but I almost did.

Exactly as anyone might expect. Black on black on black with a black ski mask. Dude was ready to remain anonymous.

"I see your outfit goes with your Audi's tint, jagoff."

He started to advance on me and that was his first mistake. I head butted him. Right in the schnoz. No one ever expects that and it hurts like a mother. I broke his nose because I heard the snap and his groan to give me validation.

He only took two steps back, then we were at it again. He kicked me in my stomach, and my breath was gone. I staggered back once more and I wouldn't have lost my balance except for the duffel. It tripped me like a mischievous middle schooler. I fell backward and smacked my head off the door.

I saw stars but I didn't pass out. I shuffled and tried to get my footing to stand.

The wannabe ninja moved a little faster than me, but he made his second mistake. He got too close to my legs.

As soon as he bent down, I caught him in the side of his head with my newly purchased Clarks. I'd opted for ones with more sole and I prayed this scumbag felt the extra.

That put him flat on his back and he shifted his weight left and right on the ground.

By the time he started getting up, I was already on my feet.

"Listen," I said. "I don't wanna kill you, so I'm going to call the police instead. Go rob a bank, not—"

I stopped cold when he pulled the pistol out. My instincts kicked in and I collapsed and rolled on the floor. Just in time before the shot went off. I heard the bullet cut through the air and enter one of the books on the bookshelf.

Wish I had a couple of those theology volumes strapped to me right about now.

He shot again high and it went just over my body and through the window. Glass rained down around me. I lifted on my legs and dove on the other side of the desk.

The odd smell of gunpowder, urinal cake, and Maui breeze hit me all at once.

I was cornered, unarmed.

And screwed.

I managed quickly to get my legs under me using the desk to stabilize my weight but remained crouched.

As soon as he came across to the other side of the desk, I shot up against him like whack-a-mole, using my body as a rocket. He fired another shot that had no chance of hitting.

And then he dropped his gun as he stumbled against the wall nearest the window.

He clumsily bent to retrieve the weapon when I threw my knee up into his ribcage.

It wasn't as gratifying as the head butt. But he was hurting.

Worst job interview ever.

He reached up to the preacher's shelf and took one of the heavy volumes.

"Yeah, you think you could hurt me with that. It hurts more that I probably can't understand what the book—"

Three distinct shots fired into the air. Once again, I hit the ground behind the desk attempting to preserve my vitals.

There was another shooter in the office. And I was cornered for good this time.

NINE

While it wasn't a job that Detective Kyle Kekoa would typically handle, when he had heard Ray Hargrove's voice on the other end of the line, he had to jump to it. He was on the tail of some scumbags, but it was all slow burn stuff. Nothing big. Nothing that would rattle anyone's cage.

Kyle drove in his black Explorer, a little outdated, but well maintained. He had one tire-pressure sensor blinking at him from the heads-up display, but he knew it was just a computer thing. Kyle Kekoa knew the details. He knew his car. He knew this island.

And he knew when to worry about someone's kid. The way Ray had described the call coming in. The smashing noise.

He had met Ray on Oahu near the time of Kyle's wife's funeral. Ray was vacationing there and Kyle was at the height of his bereavement. He remembered going to a fundraiser for the police and there was Ray. Willing to be there to show his support to the police department.

Since then, they'd always kept in touch.

Kyle knew how bitter the battle had been for custody

over Janeen. Ray and his ex-wife had ended up with a pretty liberal agreement. But every time Ray talked to Kyle, there was a tone of frustration toward his ex-wife.

Rightfully so, Kyle supposed.

Kyle was hoping when he got to the school, he'd only find a broken phone, and not a dead mutilated girl. As the thought crossed his mind, he pushed down on the gas, causing the ocean on his left to blur even more as the Explorer pushed through the warm Maui air.

Kyle's car smelled lived in. And what that meant is that it didn't smell like-new car. That was something that had developed in him after his wife had been murdered. Kyle hated when things became familiar.

He liked the Explorer because it was beefy and he paid cash for it. He gave up his wife's Suburban because it smelled like her. The perfume. All of it. He didn't want to have those smells ambush him every time he went on a case. He didn't want to think about how they'd often driven around Maui looking through those windows.

The Explorer's windows only really had visited police sites and of course, the gym.

Ray's voice. That broken phone. Kyle didn't want to see a dead girl in a formal dress. Ray was a good dad and a good member of the community. For crying out loud, he was in the middle of interviewing a pastor to work at his church. On a weekend! If that's not the definition of charitable, Kyle didn't know what was.

But tonight was proving that being a church goer didn't help as much as people might think.

TEN

The tomb-like office was now hazy with gun smoke. There were splinters of dark wood on the light beachy-looking floor. My head, jaw and gut felt like they had been tossed into a rickety old washing machine.

And a couple feet out of my reach, the intruder's gun.

He was standing over me. He had the high ground. As soon as his partner came to the desk, I was gonna be lit up.

I was going to die, so I had no choice, I had to go for the gun.

In microseconds that felt like eternity, I dove for the gun, while at the same time the assailant dove out the window, pulling the metal blinds down behind him.

It was an unexpected benefit to this tussle.

Why did he dive out—

I didn't allow myself time to process, I jumped at the gun again, grabbed it, and prepared to spring up blazing.

"Rev! Stop, it's safe. We good."

First time I was ever called *Reverend*. Didn't like it as much as *Pastor*, to be honest.

My head was throbbing and for a moment I thought

maybe I was dead and this was some sort of weird transition into Heaven. The confidence I had in the afterlife wasn't quite enough to get me to drop tinted Audi's pistol.

"Who are you?" I yelled, crouched and ready.

"Don't go killin' me now, son. I just saved you. Seriously, I work for the church. It's okay, Rev."

I allowed a quick raise of my head to peer beyond the desk. Standing by the door was an older black man dressed in blue gym shorts and a pink-flowered Hawaiian shirt—revolver in hand. He was not heavy, but he wasn't trim.

This church was getting weirder by the moment.

He held up his hands, shoulder-height, revolver resting weakly against his fingers. "It's all right, Rev. But if I was you I would get out the corner. Not sure if this guy had a buddy."

Good advice. I came to the other side of the desk.

There was something about him that I instantly liked. I couldn't put my finger on it if I tried. He had a face that made you want to spill your guts. I met a couple people like him when I was serving overseas. They were few and far between. Just that face.

He had a little bit of white goatee on his chin. His crow's feet showed that he had both wisdom and a sense of humor.

"Call me Stu. I'm the janitor."

"Janitor? Geez, who's the treasurer? Chuck Norris?"

He relaxed both of his hands and held out the gunless one for me to shake. I put the pistol on the desk and shook without hesitation. I did offer myself a bit of a glance at his gun, though.

"Sawyer Grant."

Stu noticed my nervous eyes and said, "Oh, don't worry about this Rev, it's just a capper."

"Capper?"

"Cap gun, slightly modified for loudness. I tend to tinker with devices and such." He had a bit of a proud smirk at that.

"You came in to a gun fight with a freaking cap gun?" When I raised my voice my jaw hurt and I tasted a little copper. I hoped that cheap shot didn't leave any bloody marks on my face, but could tell by the taste that it was probably just a cut on the inside of my mouth.

"Before you ask me anything else, did you die?"

He smiled.

First time I saw him smile. I knew this guy was awesome. I don't care how heavy-handed he was with the urinal cakes. This was a guy you wanted to have at your party. This was a guy you wanted to have on a car trip. This was a guy that you wanted to burst in with a cap gun while you were on the verge of being executed during a job interview.

"I got the upper hand back, okay, I would have handled that dude."

Stu raised his eyebrows and shook his head.

I inhaled deeply and pulled in some of that air. Equal parts Maui, gun smoke, and urinal cake. My stomach hurt more because of that, but also because I just had a boot in it.

"Any clue who the visitor was, Stu?" I picked up my duffel and prayed for the same invisibility it had during the interview.

"No clue Rev, but he was serious about puttin' a hole in you. I heard the ruckus from the parking lot. You oughtta write Miss Elaina a thank you note and tell her that she saved your skin. Got a text from her askin' if I'd mind locking up after your interview. Lucky for you I was passin' by early. Or else I'd be mopping up white-boy blood from these new floors we installed last year."

Everything he said was true. I did have to thank Elaina.

The discussion of a phone call reminded me of Hargrove and the situation at Lahaina Intermediate.

Hey, you got 'Neen, you know what to do.

"Hey, I know it's a lot to ask on account of you just helped me and all that—"

"You mean *saved your hide?*" Eyebrows up again.

"Tomato, tomatto. Listen, could I trouble you for a lift over to Lahaina Intermediate?"

He tilted his head slightly and squinted his eyes. This guy couldn't hide a thing on his face even if he wanted to.

"I think Hargrove's daughter might be in some sort of trouble. He asked me to follow him over there. Only problem is I don't have a ride. But you look like the kind of person that doesn't mind a little bit of trouble."

He laughed, a belly laugh, "Man, the Lord gave you discernment, I will say Rev. I'll take you and drop you off. Someone gotta meet the police and tell them what's up."

Hadn't even thought of that.

"Good call. If I was the pastor, I'd give you a raise."

Another belly laugh out of Stu as he exited through the door.

I followed behind him, grabbed the duffel and looked back at the gun on the desk. I picked it up as well and threw it into my bag.

Somehow, I felt like the intruder in the preacher's office wasn't the most complicated thing that was gonna happen to me tonight.

ELEVEN

Detective Ani Iona didn't want to break it off, but she had no choice. Lulani's promotion to detective came through. And that meant playtime was over.

She sat at a table adjacent to the glassed wall showcasing the different brewing equipment and beer. It was more for show than anything. As many times as they'd come here together, nothing ever happened behind that window except for people cleaning the glass.

She ran her hands through her thick dark hair. It was so infrequent that she wore it down, the feeling in her fingers was almost foreign to her. Lulani liked it when she wore it down, but, well, that wasn't really going to matter much.

They'd gotten together earlier at her place, fooled around, showered, had sex again, and decided to come for a quick bite at the Maui Brewing Company in Napili.

This might be their last Saturday. It was almost like Lulani knew Ani would be pulling the trigger.

He'd gotten up from the table, and it didn't much matter. Neither of them were speaking much. And Ani knew that they'd been lost in the mess of things when both of them had forgotten their phones in Lulani's car.

There he came, looking perfect. He had a gray muscle shirt on underneath a black-button shirt that he left completely open. He let his hair down, too. Long wild curly locks.

Ani still had that hollow feeling in her stomach when she saw him.

Lulani came to the table, his and her phones in one hand, his other in his pocket. He was shaped like a department store mannequin.

How was she going to do this?

He took a seat at the table. Loud chatter clamored around them, but somehow the bar was too quiet.

"Order yet?"

She'd forgotten. She'd been tasked with one job.

"Ummm, no, waiter didn't come back."

Lulani shrugged. "No hurries, no worries, eh?"

She smiled. "Always rhyming, are you?"

"If I said I tried, you'd know I lied."

She giggled. "Alright, Shakespeare. Thanks for the phone by the way."

Neither of them had said it, but they were nervous that Detective Kyle Kekoa was going to call. They were both on call for the weekend, but it was a dead weekend. There might be a drunk situation here and there, but the patrol people could shoulder that.

But Detective Kekoa went nuts when people didn't answer his calls. She supposed she had a little PTSD over missing a couple of his calls.

"So, when we are doing it?" Lulani asked.

"I don't—"

"Nah, you ain't doing that, gorgeous. Unless you

thought my police skills were substandard, this night was written in the stars, wasn't it?" He smiled at her but his eyes were sad.

All at once, the smell of the delicious bar food made Ani want to wretch. They were heading to the moment.

And Ani actually did think Lulani's detective skills were substandard. And she was terrified that Detective Kekoa was going to eat him alive. Kekoa was a ball buster, and Lulani tended not to take things so seriously. Lulani was on point when he needed to be, but he also had a tendency for distraction.

But his integrity was perfect, and that's why he would succeed. At least, in Ani's eyes.

"I don't believe anything is written in the stars," Ani said. She picked up a chip that the waiter had brought for them to sample. But she didn't bite it. Though she was biologically hungry from their previous activities, her appetite was AWOL. The thought of food was making her a little nauseous and her mouth was dry.

He reached over and put his hand on hers.

She couldn't do this. She couldn't do this here. They'd only been together for six months. But it was six good months. Unlike her previous relationships.

"It was written that you'd be smitten."

I just don't think I can do this.

She didn't laugh at that one. Instead, she reached for her phone and realized she had four missed calls.

She swore and Lulani grabbed his phone too. They both had the same amount of missed calls.

They looked up at each other as the gregarious waiter came to the table. "Aloha, special occasion tonight?"

Both were holding their phones, and Ani was about to click send on hers to connect with Detective Kekoa.

"Yes, as a matter of fact," Lulani said, "I just was promoted to detective, and we were gonna celebrate but it looks like the job is already calling us away."

Ani giggled a little and the waiter raised his eyebrows and said he'd give them more time if they needed it.

Lulani reached back over to her and said, "If we survive Kekoa's fury, we can finish the story."

But for now, it was on pause.

TWELVE

Wow, Stu's Benz was awesome. I don't think I'd seen a ride like this. Everything looked as though it had just been purchased. The leather felt like a showroom couch from a furniture place. I had wondered if any other passenger had ever sat in it.

The woodgrain finish of the dash was so shiny that the interior lights reflected off of it when we opened the doors. No check engine lights. I wasn't accustomed to that from the cars I typically drove back in Pittsburgh.

Even the engine was quiet.

I was surprised at how dark it was around Maui. They didn't feature this on any of the postcards. In the pictures I'd seen, even online, the sun seemed never to set. But driving out of the lit perimeter of the church's lot to the open road of night in Stu's Benz made me feel almost like I had entered a very long dimly lit tunnel.

After we'd talked about what just happened, and about what may be happening with Hargrove's daughter, Stu shut the radio off. I almost knew where it was going. I had never longed for more of Stevie Nicks singing about landslides than I did at that moment.

"So, before I let you loose on this other scene, how about you tell me your story. Not where you was born or anything, but talk to me about what you runnin' from."

As Stu spoke, his eyes never left the road. The occasional passing car on the other side almost made his little patch of facial hair glow.

"I'm not—"

"Nah, Rev. We don't wanna do that. Moment I saw you, I got a sense that we were gonna be good friends. Don't clash with that first impression. Remember, I'm from the mainland, too." This time he did steal a glance in my direction. "We all got a lot of running under our belt."

I didn't think at all that I'd be asked about Pittsburgh so quickly. Therefore, I hadn't had time to sufficiently flesh out my backstory. But, might as well give it a go with the janitor, right?

"I was supposed to do something, and I didn't. I was supposed to—I had a plan to do some work for some people and it all kinda went sideways."

Silence.

"Wow," Stu said. "That was some of the most profound detail I've ever heard. You could fill stadiums telling that story. Hope your sermons are as engaging."

He let go one of those huge belly laughs again.

Come on, man.

"Nah, Rev. Something a little more."

I couldn't think.

"Alright alright, how about this, I'll ask you some questions. You answer them. Just yay or nay. Sound good?"

I took in a deep breath, and exhaled. The car smelled like new car. Or the high end Armor All. But it was enough.

I agreed and I felt the throbbing in my head from the fight seemed to increase twofold.

"Wanted for questioning from any authorities?"

"No."

"Anybody in general coming this way to look for ya?"

"No, not that—no." That was a tougher one. I really didn't know.

"Okay, okay," Stu said, adjusting his grip on the steering wheel. "Anybody you care about know you're here?"

"No."

"Alright."

He was silent for a moment. I thought he was done.

"Did you hurt someone?"

I was also silent for a moment. But I didn't know how to lie.

"Yes," I said. My palms were sweating. And all of a sudden, I felt very claustrophobic in this well-restored Mercedes. A bit of a sour taste rose up in my mouth.

"Good folks or bad folks?"

Longer pause still. I had just met Stu moments before. But, he'd also saved my tail.

I cleared my throat. "Bad folks I thought were good folks. But does it even matter?"

Stu responded quickest on that one. "Yes, Rev, it do. It really do matter."

What could I say to that? I was dealing with the black version of Judge Judy over here asking these questions. And I somehow knew that if I lied, he'd know. And it would sever the newly formed connection between us.

"So, you thinking coming across the ocean and getting in good with some charitable work would wipe that slate of yours clean?" Stu said.

Then, I remembered the meeting with the pastor before

I left for basic training. I remembered how I'd felt leaving his office. I remembered what I knew to be true about my life when I got back.

And how all of it was a lie.

"I'm sure you know your theology. Only Jesus can wipe slates clean." I paused, and added, "But I just wanted to go somewhere that there was less chalk for me to work with, if you get my meaning."

Stu raised his eyebrows and shook his head slowly up and down. "Absolutely do, Rev. That's absolutely right. And after this little chat, I think you and I have more in common than we could identify in one night."

He started to slow as he pulled to what appeared to be an entrance to a private road. I looked down into a valley and noticed a lit-up school with a lot of police cars outside of it. Destination was on the right, apparently.

I thanked Stu for the ride and he waved it off like he was swatting a gnat. But he did choose to add one final thing to this odd yet intimate talk as I got out into the dark Maui night.

"Hey Rev," he called.

"Yeah," I said, leaning down and staring into the door that I'd just shut.

"One piece of advice: Wherever you go, there you are."

THIRTEEN

The tires of the Malibu skidded as Bob arrived at the lookout on Honoapiilani Highway. It wasn't terribly late, but the sun had just about given all of its dominance over to the night. He didn't think paradise would have such an absence of light. The stars salted the black sky with marginal brightness, but it was dark.

Really dark.

Bob got out and walked near the trunk, listening to see that Janeen was still in la la land after the little cocktail he'd given her. He knew how to keep people at rest for a while. But he wasn't as worried about Janeen as he was about meeting Robertson. There were two other cars in the parking lot just as planned. Robertson's unassuming silver Buick, and Riggins's tinted black Audi.

Stupid thing looked like a black crayon sitting in the lot.

His mouth was craving that nicotine taste but Robertson hated cigarettes. Bob thought about saying something came up with the girl and he needed an extra couple minutes just to grab a couple puffs, but he thought better of it.

He was on the job.

Luckily, Janice or Jenny or whoever was being quiet as a church mouse—but that was the only part of luck in this operation so far, from what he understood. That was also the reason for the meeting.

The lights on the highway did nothing to illuminate the ocean, save for casting some vague shadows in the direction. And there he stood on a cliff.

Bob hated that Robertson wanted to meet here. Hated it. Not even tourists liked to be up here. This was a step down from where Robertson originally wanted to meet on the Road to Hana.

Death everywhere.

The state had installed a weak aluminum rail a little above waist height to deter tourists from stepping too close to the edge. Bob would have loved not to climb over it, but he did. He used the flashlight from his phone to give himself more confidence moving into the unknown. The grass felt virgin under his boots, and for a moment, panic rose up as he thought of slipping and falling forty feet down, breaking his back on his way to the ocean.

Robertson selected the scariest places for meet ups.

This was only the fourth time they'd met to discuss the business, and there was always a little bit of fear associated with the meeting places. He didn't like dealing with Robertson, but someone from a previous job that Bob had done made the connection, and well, the money helped to ease the interpersonal tensions, as they say.

He walked a handful of paces to the natural overhang where Robertson stood with Riggins. Bob slowed his pace, checking each footstep in relation to the edge of the flat part of the walk.

Robertson never dressed down. He was wearing a tan

suit, with a striped dress shirt under it. The break of his suit flapped in the breeze from the ocean as Robertson looked out. He appeared mesmerized by the blackness.

Riggins wasn't enjoying anything. He was jacked up. Even in the shadows, his face looked like a swollen beehive. He was shifting his gaze everywhere, except into the blackness of the ocean. Sounded like his breathing was pretty uneven, too.

He was also clinging to, what looked like, a big Bible. Or a textbook of some kind. He had ripped the back cover off of it.

Must not have liked the content.

But Robertson simply looked ahead.

"Can't even see anything, bossman. We could have met at a gas station or something. We don't have to wax so dramatic."

Robertson turned toward Bob and the iPhone illuminated Robertson's features. All Bob could think of was Patrick Bateman from *American Psycho*. He didn't have a wrinkle. Perfectly clean-cut, shaven, his hair was on the long side, but perfectly styled.

The only odd thing about Robertson's otherwise perfect appearance was that he always had that cocktail stirrer in his mouth. The nice ones that they had in the fancy bars, not some of the dives that Bob had chosen to frequent.

Robertson smiled while taking the stirrer out of his mouth. "If you stare at something long enough, Bob, even when you can't see it, you know exactly where everything is."

Riggins sniffled and Robertson's head motioned with slight distraction.

Enough of this.

"Okay, so what's the deal? Where are we on this thing and what do I need to do?"

Bob wanted to get the kid out of the Malibu and he wanted a cigarette. And he didn't want to stand on the edge of this cliff.

Riggins was swearing and muttering to himself. "Preacher. Idiot preacher."

Bob had already spoken briefly to Robertson on the phone about this preacher. Ironic that a pastor did that to his face.

Blessed be the peacemakers, not nose breakers.

Robertson moved closer to Riggins. He said, "So, while we attained what we needed from the school, thanks to Bob, the one from the church still remains. Both are vital. And we now have an additional loose end."

Riggins didn't say anything, just looked down at the ground and sniffled as he did it.

"Now, Riggins. Might I ask if you know the preacher's name and where he is? And also, a little more importantly, did he see you? Your face I mean."

Riggins shook his head.

"Nothing identifiable about you?

Riggins shook his head once more.

"But you couldn't beat a preacher in a wrestling match? And he did that to your face? And he took your gun?"

"He wasn't, like, a normal preacher. And he had help."

Robertson put the stick back in his mouth. "Oh, that's right. Some mystery person came in and shot at you. So Bob kidnapped a girl from a school full of students and faculty but you couldn't get anything from the empty church on a Saturday night?"

Riggins shook his head. Seemed to be his signature move.

Robertson chuckled while smiling, revealing perfect teeth. "Haven't been to church in a while, myself. Didn't plan on going either?" He raised his eyebrows to Bob. His face was expressive, but his tone was cool and unmoved.

"Bob, do you remember the next phase of the plan?"

Bob nodded. The icky parts were coming up, but sure.

"Good, we have to redouble and get what we need from the church. Let's worry about that tomorrow. As Jesus said, sufficient is the day's evil." He paused for a moment and smirked. "Heck, I haven't been much of a church goer. Maybe this is a sign that I could use a little religion."

Bob nodded again, about to say he'd move to Phase 2 tomorrow night. But he couldn't care less about Robertson's church habits.

In one motion, Robertson grabbed Riggins by back of the neck, and effortlessly pulled him, forcing him to stumble and eventually lose his balance, falling to the rocks forty feet below. Bob winced at the sound of Riggins's scream, but more the sound of the impact of his body against the jagged ocean-kissed edges of the rocks.

Icky parts. Yuck. Bob thought about the Malibu with the young girl in the trunk and compared it to Riggins's tricked-out Audi.

Looks like Bob was going to be getting an upgrade on his ride—and a promotion.

FOURTEEN

Stu did as he said he would.

I was standing on the main road staring down the driveway to Lahaina Intermediate. I couldn't hurry. I was still a little jazzed from the Audi intruder at the church, but the moment I'd gotten out of Stu's vintage Mercedes (very slick), I was breathless in the Maui air.

I was also breathless because a dude had just kicked me in the stomach. I was also worried that I was going to have a pretty visible bruise on my forehead. The headache was a pretty good indication.

The air smelled unpolluted by this world. Even with slight exhaust from cars passing, this was the closest I could ever imagine Heaven being like. I felt both blasphemous and elated at the thought of my experiencing it.

Palms rustled above and around and every which way in the absence of many buildings. The sky above was exceptionally dark because of the lack of buildings on the other side of the road. I wondered if the stars shined as bright in Pittsburgh, and I just couldn't see because of the competition of the city lights.

Walking down the road toward the school was a little more than eerie. Because of how far away I was from home and because of how dark things were, I felt like when bad things happened in paradise, they were really bad.

Regardless, I had to stay here. I just had to. This was the opposite of where I was in Pittsburgh.

As I approached, I realized a single guy in his mid-thirties heading to a high school formal in a slightly disheveled black suit wasn't creepy at all. It was fine. It was all fine.

Hargrove was staring at the ground. I saw the outline of his head and I noticed he was standing oddly. His legs were spread apart a little and he appeared to be examining something on the ground.

It had to be Janeen's phone.

The bass from the school was pumping. Those kids were moving and grooving, as they say.

But unfortunately, Janeen Hargrove wasn't part of that. I was almost sure of it. I was pretty perceptive about bad situations, and that phone call was enough. If Hargrove hadn't ended my interview, I would have forced his hand. Something was up with the girl.

As I approached, I realized Hargrove wasn't alone. There was another man standing with him, on the phone. Well, he wasn't on the phone, but angrily waiting for someone to answer his call. I could see it in his grimace.

Guy was just north of six feet and he was standing every inch of it. Hawaiian as the day was long, he possessed all of the look but none of the relaxation. He was wearing a pair of dress slacks with a tucked-in black polo shirt. He had a v-frame and if he constricted his muscles any more as he was waiting for the phone to be answered, he would have busted out of that shirt. He was as ripped as a preschooler's coloring book.

I stopped at Hargrove who looked up at me once with an impassive face, and back down at the object.

The phone.

No surprise.

"Hey, Mr. Hargrove. I—"

I stared at the phone. It was smashed. Really smashed. This phone wasn't just dropped.

"I thought you were right behind me, Pastor?" His tone was empty.

Whew, where did I begin with this?

"Something came up at the church. I'll tell you about it, but I feel like you have a lot on your mind right here, sir."

He didn't look up. Just stared down.

From feet away, a voice ripped through the conversation. "Call, now, it's urgent!" Tall shredded guy would have thrown his phone on the ground if he could have. He was mad. He came over to us and as he looked at Hargrove, his expression softened.

He glanced at me, but for a fraction of an instant.

"Ray, I tried calling my other detectives. No luck. It's a Saturday night and we typically don't have things like this come up. I'll get on it with them as soon as I get some traction."

His accent was awesome. Hawaiian with a flare of mainland urgency.

Hargrove didn't stop looking. He stared down at the shattered front of the iPhone screen.

"Who are you?" Muscle-y Hawaiian asked.

I looked at Hargrove, hoping he'd respond and introduce me. But he didn't.

"I'm Sawyer... Grant." Smooth as a bag full of Legos. "Pastoral candidate for Resurrection Church," I added, looking at Hargrove and hoping for some validation.

"Church doesn't start until tomorrow, Pastor. And this isn't a church, it's a school."

This guy was a real charmer. I thought of reaching out my hand to shake his but I'd probably pull back a stump.

"Kyle, I asked him to come. I was interviewing him when Janeen called me." Hargrove still was staring down at the phone.

I had seen people in shock before, and if he wasn't, he was close.

Kyle didn't seem to care that I was invited. He just glared at me.

"Wanting a Hawaiian job instead of staying on the mainland. Of course. Sure there wasn't a church you could have worked for there?"

"This one was the only one that could accommodate my sleep schedule, with the time change and all."

Shut up, dude.

Kyle chuckled a little, but it was bitter. "You got family on Maui?"

"No."

"Where's your family from?"

"Pennsylvania," I said.

"Big state. What area? Philly?"

"Pittsburgh."

I felt a little sweaty all of a sudden. This was the first police officer I'd spoken to about where I was really from.

"Yinzer, eh." Kyle gave a little grin. "Love the Steelers?"

"Pittsburgh governmental requirement, sir."

I actually didn't follow the Steelers regularly, but I didn't dislike them. My family worshipped them though.

"What's in the duffel?"

My heart skipped. It was the first time it had been

noticed. And the extra second I took to answer his question caused his brow to furrow a little bit.

"Clothes and stuff. Just came in today."

"Didn't you have a chance to—"

Kyle's phone rang, severing the interrogation and causing me to thank Jesus for hitting the call button. He grabbed the device from his belt holster (of course he had a holster for it, along with a gun) and answered by asking, "Is your phone broke?"

Blue and red flashing lights turned down off the road. All three of us looked up at them, and Kyle motioned his free hand toward us.

All the pieces were on the board. I was now smack in the middle of a kidnapping investigation.

Anything going wrong with kids bothered him. And on a night like this, it bothered him even more. That music blaring from the Lahaina Intermediate. He hated it—it was too loud, but he hated more that they all felt safe.

The weather, the atmosphere, the sheer existence of Maui made people feel safe.

Kyle Kekoa had lived on Maui for twenty-five years, but he was actually born on Oahu. He wanted to go back to Oahu after his wife had been murdered three years ago, but he couldn't part from the memories.

Although he felt every time he enjoyed a part of Maui's atmosphere, he was being injected with a slow-acting poison.

But he couldn't bear to leave the life they lived. Even if that life had ended.

The kids marched almost single file out of the school, administrators trying to remain smiling as the anxiety of the students rose. Some of the parents had started to trickle down, cars filling the lot.

Kekoa had his team organizing the newcomers to one part of the parking lot, while the admins, teachers, and students that drove kept their cars on the other side.

Nice and orderly.

Kyle believed every investigation ought to be orderly. If the leader got sloppy, the perp got away.

Bottom line.

It took two minutes for the rumor mill to start, and it took even less time for the glammed and glitzed students to realize that it was Janeen Hargrove that had gone missing.

The doors entering the school were pretty much a joke. They wouldn't be able to keep out a persistent sea turtle. Security on Maui everywhere was pretty much a joke. Lahaina Intermediate was no exception. To be fair, though, crime was low on Maui. Nothing like Oahu. And nothing like the mainland.

Typically, mainlanders brought the problems.

He didn't even have to do any investigating to know this. Between the sound of Ray's voice, the call she'd made to Ray, and the finding of the smashed phone, this was pretty much all textbook.

But as far as mainlanders went, that preacher.

He asked Kyle's permission to walk around away from the crowd and just to be a support if Ray wanted prayer or something.

But Kyle felt uneasy. He tried to keep his eyes on Sawyer Grant most of the time, but he also wanted to see if any of these kids knew anything. And there was something else.

In the course of the trauma at the school, one of the local officers called and let Kyle know that there was some sort of vandalism that had taken place at the Resurrection

Church. Stu the custodian had reported it. The preacher was there and was apparently attacked. That would have been a good conversation starter.

Why did Grant come here? Hargrove had only just met him. And why did Hargrove want to bring this guy to his daughter's potential kidnapping site?

Kyle touched base with two of this three detectives, Ani Iona and Lulani Aukai.

Both of them were dedicated. But Kyle was still a little annoyed at how long it took for them to respond. Of course, living on Maui made everything seem slower. But if they wanted to be a part of this kind of action, shutting the phone off wasn't really an option.

Kyle also had some patrolmen helping. But everything was pretty much a nonstarter with leads. All the kids were organized in groups with the parents. School admins walked around as well. Everyone from the dance with the exception of Janeen was accounted for.

Orderly. Nice and easy.

The preacher stood away from the crowd.

He didn't look like a preacher. He was dressed way too nice for a Hawaii minister. And he didn't have the pastoral garb, the long robe and all that. No white collar. But what he did have was a whole lot of nervousness, and enough muscle to make Kyle nervous.

The pastor stood by the corner of the building, away from all the people. With that stupid white dress shirt, that innocent look, occasionally pulling his phone out—a nervous look—

And that duffel. Grant about soiled his drawers when Kyle had asked about the duffel.

Mainlanders.

The preacher had jet black hair and was shaved with a little bit of stubble. His hair seemed on the long side, but hey, it was 2015. He was tall, but not as tall as Kyle.

The preacher was carrying that duffel like it was his child.

After doing one more round of checks on the interviews, and a quick visit to the top of the parking lot where Ray Hargrove sat on his phone, talking to his ex-wife and son, Kyle went over near where the preacher stood.

"Our conversation was interrupted before. Sorry about that."

Let him feel disarmed.

"You might wanna ice that head. I can see the swelling already, Pastor."

The preacher rubbed his head with surprise. "Yeah, bumped it on one of those overhead compartments on the plane. Like air travel isn't awkward enough without embarrassing yourself in front of strangers."

Lies.

"Thought maybe you might have gotten it from your tussle with the church thief."

"Oh, that, well, no, it was the plane, but yeah, I was going to tell you about the break in, thing. But I didn't think it was a good time."

Kyle shook his head and smiled. "When would it have been better, Pastor? Over a candle lit dinner?"

Grant didn't stutter on this one. "No, I thought maybe when you weren't looking at trying to find a missing girl."

"Do I look like a person that can't multitask?" Kyle felt himself getting angry, but knew that he was in danger of causing drama. The preacher didn't lend himself well to playing nice.

"Not at all, but I don't wanna get you wrapped up in new trouble when you are dealing with other trouble."

Kyle shook his head and pursed his lips. "Information never troubles me, Pastor. You'll learn that real quick. Speaking of which, the only common connection to both of these instances of trouble is you."

He didn't respond.

Good for you, Pastor.

"So," Kyle went on, "we were talking about your bag. I figure since you left an active crime scene to come to another potentially active crime scene, it wouldn't be out of the question for me to take a look in there."

Silence again.

You're learning, Pastor.

The truth always came out, as long as things are done orderly.

Kyle wished the detectives looking for his wife's murderer would have been orderly, but that's why as long as she'd been dead the killer had been free. No leads. No hunches.

No order.

"Well, you gonna let me open it?" Kyle knelt his large but amble frame down to the duffel. "Just to make sure that thief didn't grab anything of yours."

The pastor glared down and met Kyle's gaze. This was the first time Kyle had noticed anything but nervousness and stupid jokes from the man. There was something heavy and dark behind those eyes.

"Detective, you can do whatever you insist to do. But just know you're giving me a very poor welcome. I don't think there's anything there that would interest you at all."

Kyle said, "Sorry I gave you the impression that I was in

charge of making you feel welcome. But I *do* appreciate your concern for what does or doesn't interest me."

Detective Kyle kept his gaze with Sawyer as he felt for the zipper on the oversized duffel.

After the look the preacher just gave him, Kyle's hands simply couldn't move fast enough.

SIXTEEN

While Lulani and Detective Kekoa walked around questioning students, Ani was walking around looking at other things. Less obvious things.

Ani had a bit of a sixth sense when something was amiss. Her mother told her that the spirits of the islands gave her extra insight. She insisted that she'd gone through too many bad relationships for that to be the case.

Until she'd met Lulani, anyway.

Nope, this was just plain observation.

Ani was glad to be busy with work. She was also glad to have dodged anger from Kekoa for not answering the phone right away. She'd hoped that it didn't arouse a conversation about the relationship she'd had with Lulani.

Both of them had chosen not to disclose that to anyone because until Lulani made detective, it wasn't relevant. But unfortunately, now it was.

So, she found herself examining parents. Most of whom had the same sorrowful yet thankful looks about them.

So sorry for this little girl. So thankful it wasn't mine. That's what those looks said.

And Hargrove. She thought of him too. He was there on the phone with his ex-wife. Kekoa had told them that they were in the middle of a nasty divorce and that she didn't live on Maui. Ani thought about the missing girl and her missing family.

Ani got it. She understood. Not from experience. She'd seen enough homicide and kidnapping scenes to be on permanent birth control. She didn't care if she was dating a Greek God with a PhD. She wasn't bringing life into this world so filled with garbage.

Garbage. Something caught her out of the corner of her eye. Ani walked toward the green commercial dumpster. She stopped short when she heard footfalls from the other side of it.

She almost grabbed her gun, almost, but instead chose to hang back and watch.

Emerging from the other side of the garbage dumpster was the pastoral candidate from Resurrection Church.

He was looking around every which way. Like the guiltiest suspect Ani had ever seen.

SEVENTEEN

Sherbet, Physics, and Jimmy Stewart.

Elaina Hale's night was set. Really.

She sat on the couch that she'd purchased from Craigslist. On Maui, Craigslist was even an arm and a leg.

She'd Febrezed it, scrubbed it, Febrezed it again, but it still smelled slightly like dog. Or maybe it was her imagination. But tomorrow after church she'd give it another shot. It had a nice floral pattern to it, different colors. It was the only type of vegetation view she had living in the apartment she was in.

Her TV was from a neighbor in her apartment complex. They had sold it to her when they were high on Maui Wowie and she got a pretty good deal. It was a little scratched, because they also dropped it against the wall when they were high on said Maui Wowie.

Only one of the two bulbs in her seashell lamp on the end table next to her worked. The other was burned out. She was good with one. She had her MacBook open and she was going over some assignments. Triple checking, though unnecessary.

The landlord wanted to put an overhead light in her apartment, but she hated those. Elaina hated having to turn a switch on in the wall. She liked being able to set the lamp wherever she wanted to light whatever she wanted. She had started that through habit in grad school. Now, while working on her PhD, it was a must.

Jimmy Stewart in that hat. Ugh. Was there ever a sexier guy? He was so perfect. Tall, lanky, awkward, and even a little bit of a temper in some movies. In *The Philadelphia Story*, Stewart, Cary Grant, and Katharine Hepburn gave the performances of their careers.

In Elaina's opinion.

She loved the taste of the strawberry sherbet. It was a little treat. She didn't wanna allow herself many more treats, especially working at The Cheesecake Factory. She'd be too big to fit into her apartment. This of course, was an exaggeration, because everyone that knew her said she could stand to put on some pounds. Even the petite pink sweatpants and Princeton t-shirt she was wearing made her look like she was swimming.

What would the extra fat do to her cognitive abilities, though? That was always her thought.

Papers covered Elaina's cheap area rug. Time to shift gears and move to church work.

Elaina did that in-between bouts of studying. And lusting after Jimmy Stewart.

In a four-inch pile were the applicants for the senior pastor position. Resurrection Church was ready for an overhaul. The youngest regular attendee aside from her was fifty-five, and she had them beat by over two decades! That was bad. The age of the congregation didn't bother her as much as the dwindling attendance since the old pastor moved to Oahu.

Her phone rang and ripped her from the pile of applicants. It was Stu.

Golly, this had to be something urgent. She wondered if Moani had gotten sick or something. Instantly, she started trying to think of who would fill the pulpit in the morning.

"What's up, Stu?" No nonsense.

"Hey pretty lady. Don't mean to wake—"

"Never go to bed this early. What's the matter?" Elaina had a problem with small talk.

"Well, two problems, love. One, some moron broke into the church tonight?"

"Broke in? What did they steal, communion crackers?"

Honestly, what would someone want with the church. They had next to no money and the only updated room was the preacher's office—courtesy of Moani Wong's mom—who thought that would be her son's office.

"Ha, didn't get nothin,' except a whopping. That mainlander you had Holgrove meet tonight tweaked that boy up."

Sawyer Grant.

She hadn't selected him because of how qualified he was. Everyone knew that Moani Wong was the most qualified. Maui born. Lots of Bible School. Filled the pulpit.

But Sawyer Grant was an outlier. And even though next to her, Moani Wong had the youngest member slot— fifty-five—he was as arrogant as a lion.

"Grant?" She feverishly ripped through the applicant's files. And they were legion.

He was heavy on experience but not much ministry experience. It was thin. But he had a military background. Vague language describing it. But there needed to be structure in the Resurrection Church leadership.

"Yep. Guy is down to earth. Funny as all get out but I

wouldn't mess with him. Dude took gunfire tonight so we might have to call Moani Wong's momma and ask her for more funds to get that office fixed up."

She laughed. It was funny. Only in ministry can you laugh amidst tragedy. She'd learned in the two years interning there that there was always a funeral, a death, a hospital, a divorce, but if you didn't take a break to laugh, you'd be done.

"Called the police. Filed a report. Said it was probably a kid, but I don't know. Kids packing heat. Something odd about it. But there's something worse."

"Okay, shoot." Elaina stared at her empty sherbet bowl and had a quick mental deliberation about whether to refill it. She wasn't hungry, just anxious.

"Hargrove's daughter, looks like someone took her."

The desire for sherbet left. The desire for Physics was gone. And somehow the slapstick comedy coming from Jimmy Stewart on the screen felt intrusive.

"Janeen?"

"Yeah, not good. I'll fill you in on the details, but you might wanna get ready to have some conversations tomorrow with people that might be curious. It's still a fresh situation. Hargrove got a call when he was with the Rev and ended up over the school."

Elaina couldn't fathom it. She had just been talking to Janeen not too long ago. Janeen had a problem fitting in. Felt out of place. Elaina knew the feeling, not because she wasn't Hawaiian, but because of her brain and drive.

"You still there, Miss Elaina?" Stu's voice was genuine.

"Yeah, sorry. I—wow. I don't know what to say." Maui was statistically known for its low crime. These two pieces of information didn't compute.

"By the way, on the plus side because what else can we look at, Hargrove seemed to like your guy."

"What do you mean?" Elaina couldn't draw the connection.

"Well, apparently in addition to being a bad dude, the Rev must have made an impact. Because Hargrove wanted him at the school tonight. And the Rev is taking a shot at the pulpit this Wednesday for our midweek service."

Elaina stood up with Sawyer Grant's file in her hand. She thought about Janeen, the break in, all a lot to take in.

But at the center, was the outlier.

Sawyer Grant.

EIGHTEEN

Police were pretty aggressive on this one.

Stu thought about how this was probably the first time they'd ever been in the pastor's office at Resurrection Church. In a sense, he was glad that they were there, but there was also something intrusive about seeing them go through the office and look for something missing.

They also had a battery of questions for Stu. He expected nothing less, but still felt a little defensive when they'd asked about his role at the church.

"Yeah, I came to lock up because Mr. Hargrove said he was interviewing a preacher."

The main officer, a patrolman, was trying to assert himself. Stu wasn't used to run-ins with the law in Maui. This officer had a crewcut, and looked like he was a few days past graduating from the academy.

Most of those cats just bided their time on patrol until they could move on to detective or something sexier. This was what Stu understood about the police department there on Maui. This officer's name tag was so long, but his hair and his patience were short.

"What made you bring a cap gun to church?"

Stu smiled. "Didn't know it was illegal to have one. I kinda tinker with inventions and stuff."

"Tinker," Crew-Cut-Long-Name asked.

"Yeah, old habits from my former life. Before I moved over here to paradise."

"So you're an inventor?"

"You could say that?"

"Any patent work? My brother is a patent attorney."

Stu let out a belly laugh. It filled the room and made the other patrolman pause from his inspection of the drawers of the desk and bullet holes.

"Something funny," Crew Cut snapped.

"Nah, your brother chose a very boring line of work. Bet he rich, though."

"He does all right, but what would you know about?"

Take it easy, Stu.

"I was a patent attorney in a previous life. Sick of paying them for their services on the inventions I had so I decided might as well just get my own license."

"So, you're a patent attorney, inventor, and a janitor?"

"Sure."

"Retirement not work out?" Crew Cut was now more amused than he was offended.

"Oh, it worked out fine, but I like to keep myself busy in the Lord's work. I don't need the cash flow. Matter of fact, I never met God, but I'd wager that we both made a killing in the same mutual funds. I don't think I have more money than him, but it would be close, for sure."

Crew Cut shook his head. "Mr. Gentry, you're a character."

No news there.

Crew Cut shifted gears. "So, you said the assailant

tussled with this preacher—we still have to get a statement from him—and what, you shot a cap gun and he dove out the window."

"Best way I could put it." Stu breathed in some of the air that still smelled like gun powder. Another foreign entity to the preacher's office.

"Where's the gun?"

Stu went to motion to the desk where he'd remembered Sawyer Grant leaving it. The desktop was empty, save a little bit of handprints from the scuffle and the dust.

He looked over at the bookshelf to see if perhaps Grant had left it there.

Then he looked back at Crew Cut, who had resumed his concerned stare.

"Guess the perp grabbed it, officer."

Crew Cut pulled open his notebook, looked it up and down several times, and looked back at Stu, who was hoping the sweat didn't start to seep.

"According to your statement, you said he left it in the building and you'd seen it. You sure you aren't mistaken? You didn't happen to—pick it up, did you?"

Stu looked down and looked up at the lights that he'd forgotten to change since the pastor left to take a job at a church in Oahu.

"Nope. Must have been mistaken. Can't you see why I gave up inventing and lawyering? Mind don't work as much as it used to."

Nothing could be further from the truth, in Stu's opinion.

Crew Cut seemed moderately satisfied, but Stu was certain the guy would check every nook and cranny of Resurrection. And that was fine.

But Sawyer Grant, on the other hand.
What was he getting up to?

NINETEEN

My heart was pounding like a bass drum. If Kekoa had been standing closer to me, he would have heard it, I was sure. My throat was as dry as a Baptist's liquor cabinet.

This guy. What a hard case! I mean, okay, I had shown up at a potential kidnapping scene and lied to him about being assaulted by a would-be church robber, but geez, who was he to judge so harshly.

Kekoa ripped through my bag with such swiftness as though someone had set an imaginary timer. His large, veiny hands plunged into my stuff, most of which was purchased hours before on the way in.

I was hoping for another one of those interrupting moments. Maybe one of the students would say something, or maybe one of his A-Team members would come over and interrupt him with a clue. I'm sure those folks needed all the bonus points they could get with G.I. Joe in charge of their professional morale.

After what seemed like an eternity of him shuffling through my limited supply of clothing, toiletries, some Bible books, and an embarrassingly large bottle of baby powder (Walmart was out of the travel size), he stared up at me.

He was even angrier than before.

"Looking for something in particular of interest? If you wanna take a whiff of my fabric softener it's amazing."

He stood up so quickly that I don't think I even saw it, eyeing me like the last piece of pie.

"You're not funny. I do have an interest in you. And I don't like that coincidentally on the same night you land a kid goes missing and a church gets vandalized."

I didn't know what to say so I shrugged. No more snark. This guy was a quick pun away from breaking my head.

He turned back to the groups of kids who were standing with their parents. He put on a different face in front of the kids.

There was something kind about him, but the salt outweighed the sugar with this guy. Especially with regard to our newly formed relationship.

Hargrove was talking to another detective up near Janeen's phone. That man was going through hell right now. His look had remained steady and I hadn't seen him cry. But he was in hell, for sure.

My own experience with family was a little complex. I didn't have kids, but I understood about loss. That's also why I didn't like talking to an overachieving detective about what brought me to Maui.

I pulled out my burner phone, rubbed my bruised head which had a steady dull ache, and shot a text to Stu. He told me to let him know when I was done and that he'd come back and take me to my hotel.

A hotel I had yet to book.

I walked over by the tennis courts and watched some of the kids talking to their parents and one another. Kekoa had it organized, that was for sure. Some of them were laughing. I wasn't entirely against the sound.

A lot of them had overdone on the perfume and cologne, though. It was invading that perfect Maui air.

I actually felt yak wanting to come up at that point. I hadn't eaten much today, save a handful of million-dollar airport snacks. My mouth was getting that sour taste to it.

If I puked, the detective would love that. Add contaminating a crime scene to my list of offenses.

My burner buzzed with Stu's response and it was a little unnerving.

Been with the police got to talk about the gun Rev. I don't like surprises. You're covered but gotta chat.

Crap. I probably should have told him I threw that in my duffel. I replied back, *better to have one and not need it.*

Unlike the detective, maybe he'd still think I was funny.

He didn't respond to my quip, but just let me know he'd be leaving in ten minutes.

That was more than fine. I had something else I needed to take care of.

I checked in with Hargrove. He was a little less far-eyed than he was before, but he was exhausted. I told him not to worry about anything and I'd catch a ride home with Stu. Then, I checked to see if he had my number, but I honestly didn't think that he even processed much of the exchange.

Overdressed kids had started clearing out, accompanied by underdressed adults. Several of the detectives had already left after canvassing the school.

My shoes were killing me because my feet simply weren't ready for dress shoes all day. And a gun fight. And a kidnapping.

I scanned the crowd, specifically looking for Detective Kekoa, who was talking to Hargrove again and looking at a yellow legal tablet that he'd most likely filled with all the deets that anyone had said about Janeen's interactions at the dance.

The timing was perfect. I started back down toward the school.

Past the entrance, on the other side stood my salvation in the shape of a huge commercial dumpster.

I softly walked over—these shoes were as loud as they were uncomfortable—to where I'd hidden the remaining contents of my duffel. I grimaced as I caught a breeze of garbage smell—Hawaiian garbage smelled just like Pittsburgh garbage.

On to the important stuff I'd hidden just under the dumpster, including my newest acquisition, the boosted gun from the church robbery. Glock 19 no less. I threw it all into the duffel and stood, annoyed with the weight of everything.

Then I heard footsteps that weren't mine. A pair, as a matter of fact.

Why not? Probably Detective Do Right and a buddy to kill me and dump me in this dumpster. I crouched down just behind the can.

Stopping just shy of my spot stood a girl and what appeared to be her father. My angle gave me a clear line of sight without being noticed.

She was wearing the brightest red dress that I'd ever seen. It had to be a Hawaii thing that all colors looked more vibrant.

The father looked a mess. Wrinkled gray V-neck, stained khaki shorts (maybe grease), and a pair of beat-up Birkenstock sandals. He was Hawaiian, with a curly mop of hair on top. He was also sweating.

His daughter had been crying. What was left of her makeup had streaked down her face.

I thought for a moment maybe he brought her here to console her, but I only heard bits and pieces.

"—not a word Malia—get it together!" Very forceful.

Nice going, dad.

She sobbed a little more.

I wished I could hear more clearly.

"Not one word—it doesn't matter—you have no idea what would—"

Then the girl ran back toward the exiting students. Dad followed suit, attempting to keep pace. This sat as right with me as a Saint Bernard in a fish bowl. Something was up with that kid.

Something even bigger was up with her daddy.

TWENTY

The smell. She snapped into focus. The smell. It was rotten. Like rancid chemicals or something.

She shot up and wretched, but didn't throw up.

Janeen tried to get her senses about her, but everything was dark.

But the smell. The smell.

Her eyes came into focus and her head pounded. The daze of unconsciousness began to wear off as she remembered what had happened.

Janice

She remembered being hit, maybe explained her pounding headache.

And now, she had no idea where she was.

The room was dark, with four lights, one on each wall—the kind you put batteries in and stick on the wall. She remembered seeing an ad for them on YouTube a couple weeks ago when she was doing research (watching music videos). No wiring. No fuss. Perfect for closets.

And rooms for kidnapped sophomores.

She was lying on a twin bed. The sheets were blue and

felt like sandpaper. There was a loud pink patterned blanket on top.

She could barely see much more than what was in front of her. The lights created an odd, submarine-type feel. Each light was halfway up the wall, except for the one directly across from the bed, where the door was. That was just left of the door.

Her dress, the long dress she had on, was a little ripped. At the foot of the bed, by her feet was a pile of clothes. It looked like a bunch of sweatpants and t-shirts.

In the corner of the room was a small refrigerator. It was the size of a normal refrigerator, but it wasn't as wide. It looked like something in a really tiny apartment.

Was she in a tiny apartment?

There were no windows whatsoever in this room, but there seemed to be foam insulation attached to the ceiling and walls. The foam insulation looked like mini mountains jutting out from the wall.

Then Janeen realized she'd also seen a YouTube ad for that on her computer. It was soundproofing—the kind that recording engineers used to make a studio. This is how they can have a drummer twenty feet from an audiobook narrator and still have productivity.

It was to keep her noise level down. To hide her screams.

Her throat was dry and raw. She felt like she'd been running a marathon but at the same time felt like she was just waking up from an unintentionally long nap.

Janeen stood up and felt a cold, almost damp ground. She was in some sort of underground place. The floor wasn't very clean because she felt grains of whatever type of dirt under her feet. Her skin crawled at the thought that it might be insects. The smell and the feeling on her feet made her want to wretch again.

In that moment, she longed for those uncomfortable heels that she had resented earlier. She couldn't see them in the room. But that wasn't saying much.

She was just about to start screaming for help. Then she remembered the soundproofing. The only thing that would do was make her hopeful.

Drummer. Audiobook narrator.

She walked a couple steps and guessed the room was about ten by ten. It was small, but it was large enough to not feel like a closet.

Though as she thought of this, Janeen's breath seemed to leave her.

She walked over and opened the refrigerator. The light from the fridge was as bright as the next-to-useless portable lights around the perimeter of the room. Inside were some staples. Bottles of water. Lunchables. Hershey bars.

In the freezer, there were Uncrustables—frozen peanut-butter-and-jelly sandwiches. Janeen was relieved to find everything individually wrapped because she'd be afraid to eat anything that could have been drugged, like she'd been.

She shut the door to the fridge and noticed that there was a note held by a magnet. The magnet was one of those junky ones you'd pick up at a gas station as a souvenir for someone you didn't care about.

When she saw the note, the reality of her situation seemed to envelope her. She read it as her arm trembled. It was handwritten and it almost looked like the type of writing used for greeting cards—a perfect and quaint scrawl.

Pardon the smell, but you know how expensive it is to find places to stay on Maui. Please understand, this is busi-

ness. If you don't scream, you hang tight, and don't try to do anything stupid, we'll release you and this will all be over.

But if you don't cooperate, the worst thing you could imagine isn't quite far enough for where we will go. You understand that, don't you?

Mahalo.

Janeen looked at the note, rereading it several times.

She felt a wretch coming on, held her arm against her mouth—

And screamed instead.

TWENTY-ONE

There I stood inside the sanctuary of Resurrection Church.

The morning had come too fast.

Mainly, because I hadn't slept. It had nothing to do with where I had stayed. Stu knew someone that worked on the grounds at Aston Kaanapali Shores. To say that it was a nice place was the understatement of the century.

I wanted my thoughts to die down, but they were innumerable.

Gunfight at church.

Bruised head—no ibuprofen.

Only one suit.

Going to church in the morning.

Preaching this Wednesday.

Almost losing my duffel.

Missing kid.

Detective that hated me.

And he really hated me. At the end of the night, I told him about seeing that one dad with the greasy khaki shorts talking to his hysterical daughter, but he was as interested in that as a cow to a Burger King. He did however, snap at me when I'd repeatedly called the girl Bright Red Dress and the guy Greasy Khaki.

So of course, I had to google where this man might live. And of course, I obsessively thought about what it would be like to go there and ask why he was treating his daughter like she had just committed a capital offense for sobbing.

That thought kept me awake most. But the second runner up was the Pittsburgh business.

The fire.

Baptism by fire.

I tried to put the thoughts out of my mind, but couldn't.

And for that reason, when the morning came, the sun greeted me like an ambitious telemarketer. I wanted more of the night but she refused to stay.

Since my only experience with Maui had been a handful of hurried Ubers from Walmart, Resurrection Church, Times Grocery and finally to Aston Kaanapali at the end of the night, seeing Maui on the way to Resurrection in the light of day was like the unveiling of a beautiful new sports car previously concealed under a cover.

Stu picked me up and brought me to the church for service. And standing in the sanctuary, I thought I either was really late or really early.

The room was overwhelming. Larger than the downstairs entryway for sure, but urinal cake was still vaguely hanging in the air. There were about thirteen rows of old, sandy-brown oak pews with the ugliest green cushions I'd ever seen. It was like if the M&M's got together and had a deformed M&M green baby. Dividing the M&M pews was an aisle down the center leading to a raised platform that was larger than it should have been. And on that platform sat a massive wooden pulpit. It was as ornate as it was outdated.

Maybe it was made out of the same wood Noah used to make the ark?

It didn't appear that Resurrection needed to concern themselves with having more seating. There were maybe three dozen folks there, all quiet and solemn. Most of them looked like they were a day or two late from their meeting with the coroner.

I could only identify one guy, by himself toward the front. He had to be a visitor, because he didn't look like he was wearing a suit that had been wrapped in moth balls up until that morning. I only saw him from behind. Frankly, I didn't have the energy to go to the front to meet him.

Or anyone, for that matter.

I'm not trying to be mean with having these thoughts. I was sure these people were wonderful people, but I was also sure that they had a lot of opinions on whether or not the U.S. should have gotten involved with the whole Vietnam affair.

They had some rustic mixture of Hawaiian-hybrid-hymnal music playing through the crackly sound system. I had hoped that the conversation of the members would drown it out a little, but I wasn't sure they had the lung capacity to match the volume.

The air was working, thank God, because I was already nervous and Day Two in a suit that survived a fist/gunfight might not have fared smelling so well under extreme temperatures. And—

I was glad that there was a little room in the jacket because Black-Tinted Audi's gun came with me. How could I not bring it? I almost was killed! But it did feel weird packing heat in the Lord's House.

A voice from behind said, "Glad you could make it, Pastor Grant. Especially after last night."

I turned and what I saw didn't line up with what I'd processed. Her voice was familiar but I couldn't place it, nor did I care to in the moment. She may have been the most beautiful lady I'd ever seen. She looked native to Maui, but her eyes made me think she'd come from every dream I ever had.

She stared at me through thick-rimmed glasses. Her jet-black hair was up in a messy bun. She had a beautiful elegant light-blue dress that reminded me of the Maui sky. She looked classy and put together and her voice caught me off guard.

"I'm so—sorry, have we—"

"Elaina Hale." She seemed annoyed.

"Elaina? The church secretary?"

"Office administrator. This isn't the fifties."

I might have to turn my charm up.

"You, yeah, you—Elaina!" I went in for an overly enthusiastic handshake which she returned with the warmth of an Alaskan cinderblock. "Thanks, for, um, passing my resume on."

She smiled at that. "You're an outlier, Pastor Grant. It might be hard for a mainlander to take a church like this over, so I wouldn't get your hopes high. Though Stu told me you were preaching on Wednesday."

I chuckled, "Yeah, but with this crew, I don't even know if they'd be able to see if I was a mainlander or not."

Silence.

More silence.

"Umm—"

"I'm not sure what you're implying, Pastor Grant."

I decided that my charm worked on her as well as it did on the detective.

The organ started playing at the same time that I started my sentence, which I found pretty rude.

Elaina Hale held up her hand and said one final thing. "The service is starting, but Stu has to stay today and repair that broken window. Would it make you uncomfortable if I were to give you a lift back to the hotel? It's on the way for me. Or, we could have the church pay for your Uber."

"The only way I'm taking an Uber is if you come with me in it."

"What?" She said, motioning to her ears because of the loud organ crackling over the outdated PA system.

Thank You, Lord Jesus.

"That would be fine, I'd appreciate the lift," I said raising my voice. Then I thought of that dumpster interaction between Bright Red Dress and Greasy Khaki and I allowed myself one more question to Elaina.

"Would it trouble you if we ran a quick errand on the way?"

TWENTY-TWO

Moani Wong had his manuscript typed out, double-spaced, 13-point font. He was ready. This is what God had placed him here for.

He sat in the front row of Resurrection Church, just waiting for the music to stop, the opening benediction to conclude—

And then it was his time. He looked over at his mom. She was lifting her old hands to heaven, praising God and belting out the *Old Rugged Cross*.

This was a perfect one. The sound system sounded especially clear today. There was that intermittent interference, but it didn't matter. The music never mattered at church. They were here to hear a message.

And Moani was God's messenger.

His mom, who had her beautiful white hair pulled up in a tight bun offered a quick glance while she was singing, and smiled.

It wasn't enough.

He turned to the congregation, while he himself belted out the lyrics. Most of them were singing, some of them were praying, but all of them were there. He had a great message to share today. They were in for a treat. There was even a new face or two.

The lights seemed extra bright and the air of the church seemed extra pure, as though the Holy Spirit was telling him that these next couple weeks would be his last preaching as a volunteer. Pretty soon, he'd be the pastor and this church would be his. Then he could really get to work on making sure that it was run the right way.

And he stopped his look when he caught a glimpse of Elaina in the back. She met his gaze and walked toward him.

"Morning, Moani. Can I have you add something to your opening, thought it might be better coming from you?"

"I don't know. I have a lot to say today, Elaina, but what's so urgent."

Elaina looked down. She couldn't be annoyed, right?

She was dressed a little... inappropriately. Everything was covered, but, eh.

"Something happened to Mr. Hargrove's daughter last night. Apparently, she's missing and—well—I don't know all the details, but could you pray for her return. Also, offer a praise to God that someone tried to break into the church last night. God stopped there from being any real damage, save a couple, um, repairs that are needed and a broken window."

"Wow," Moani said, taking a pen and making a small mark on the top of his manuscript. He didn't want to make too big a mark because he saved all of this manuscripts and gave them to his mom every Mother's Day. She'd re-read them throughout the year and tell him how he needed to write a book.

It was on his list. He would.

He himself wore a light-gray suit with a pastel blue shirt underneath. He loved how it looked. Moani must have checked the mirror a thousand times before leaving this morning. He loved practicing his hand gestures in the mirror, thinking of the jokes he'd tell in his sermon, and the points where he'd become emotional.

As the organ blared, Moani spoke up a little so Elaina could hear. "I will pray for Ray, for sure. Can I ask you something else quickly?"

"Shoot."

"Who is the visitor in the back you were talking to. The tall guy in the black suit. Mainlander."

"Name's Sawyer Grant. He's a pastor from Pittsburgh and he's here candidating. Hargrove was interviewing and since he came all this way, he's going to be speaking at Wednesday's midweek prayer meeting. So you'll get a little bit of a break."

His jaw felt like it wouldn't open. His stomach clenched. All of a sudden, the eight-page manuscript in his hand may have been blank.

"Oh, and you might find this funny," she added, still talking low enough to not overwhelm the music, "Grant stopped that intruder last night."

Moani had known that they'd posted the position, but he didn't know that they were going to let any of the rejects have the pulpit. And this preacher was also a hero!

In Moani's church service, no less. And he had a black suit on with a white shirt, like he owned the place.

Moani felt equal parts of intimidation but also rage. Of course this mainlander would come and sit here and try to distract Moani from the Lord's work. That's how the devil operated, even on Maui.

He looked at his mom, still singing, eyes closed, hands lifted. And back to Elaina who still standing there.

"Thanks for letting me know. Looking forward to meeting him. I'll be sure to announce his guest speaking."

Elaina smiled, then stopped. "Nah, actually let's keep it on the down low. He's incredibly nervous and we'd rather just ease him into it with a smaller group, know what I mean?"

Moani did and smiled. He knew exactly what she meant.

A preacher that was afraid to preach. Why don't they just hire a plumber that's afraid of water, or an electrician that's afraid of getting shocked?

Unreal.

Elaina smiled and returned to her seat in the back close to where Sawyer Grant stood, singing with very little expression.

The Spirit reminded Moani of the Scripture that talked about spiritual warfare, and how believers had to be battle-ready. He took in a couple shallow breaths and realized the battle was on. And he wasn't afraid to use any weapon in his arsenal.

He afforded himself another look at the man in the black suit, singing.

Battle-ready, indeed.

TWENTY-THREE

Dickenson Street was more congested house-wise than I thought it would be. More and more, Maui was surprising me. I hoped to own a piece of property here, but I knew that I'd have to stop just short of selling my soul to afford it.

But the architecture of Dickenson Street was fascinating. There were houses on either side far enough away from the street that they still seemed to have some privacy. According to my phone, it was close to Front Street, which, I guessed was a main tourist hub here. There were a lot of unique shops on Front Street, and of course, the most unbelievable view of the ocean ever.

Which so far had been every view I'd seen on Maui.

On the way, I didn't talk to Elaina about how Moani the guest preacher of Resurrection Church was as full of himself as a frozen turkey, or how cool it was to be driving in a Honda Civic older than both of us. I didn't even talk to her about how the errand I wanted her to run veered dangerously on the edge of meddling in police work.

But I did ask her if she liked dogs. Seriously. I was

preaching in three days and I spoke to the administrator-not-secretary with the inquisitiveness of a kindergartener.

"Dogs, sure, I guess. Don't have them because they're too expensive to maintain, but yeah. Do you have any?"

"No, I don't. But I like them."

Silence. I had watched the wind from the outside move her messy bun in disorganized yet perfect rhythm. She was a cautious driver, but she was comfortable. This was a ton better than Uber. Or even Stu the custodian's classic Benz.

Her car looked like it belonged to someone just about half her age that had received it from their grandpa. It had the modified CD player stereo. Elaina had it tuned to some Hawaiian channel.

I really wanted to learn Hawaiian at some point.

I was filled with the pain again of wanting to stay here. I don't know what the flower was that I kept smelling, but the aroma haunted me. It was perfect. The trees, the sounds of the water, and the brightness of the sun. I prayed that I could replace the Pittsburgh smells in my mind. I'd love it if somehow all of Pittsburgh faded from my memory. I didn't mind serving my country. I didn't mind the action I'd seen. But I needed to wipe out Pittsburgh, for sure.

As we drove, I realized every beautiful road and over-look that we passed was the same last night, except the sun brought it to life. I suppose I didn't realize how dark Maui was going to be at night.

Every view from the window seemed like it was worthy of a postcard. And I was certain that no picture would adequately do it justice. This morning, the sun had revealed everything—and the revelation was glorious.

I had taken the time to pick Elaina's brain about the church structure, the other board members, and also what was expected of me for the Wednesday message. She was gracious to give me answers to all these things. She was logistical through and through. She loved talking facts and figures. I could tell she'd stay away from the deep stuff, like whether or not she liked dogs.

And then she talked about the deal with Moani the interim speaker. He had all but moved his stuff into the preacher's office (but he didn't plan for the bullet holes, I bet). But some of the board members, including Hargrove, weren't fans of his speaking. He tended to have a lot of personal illustrations that dealt with his successes in life.

Ummm, yeah. I'd say that was the biggest understatement I'd heard in my life.

He glared at me when I shook his hand and thanked him for the wonderful message. Didn't have much to add. For a moment I thought I was dealing with the detective again. Apparently, Elaina had told him that I was going to have a shot at the pulpit next week. He said, "Good Luck."

Yeah, as if a Christian needed luck.

I almost said it, praise God I didn't. Because if my reception from the detective was the worst that I'd had on Maui so far, Moani was in a close second.

Save, of course, the gunman that tried to murder me the night before.

I wanted to say his eighty-minute sermon was the longest year of my life.

As we slowed to a stop on Dickenson Street, I peered at the houses and looked at the address I'd put into my phone. It was a little further off the main drag, and she drove the aged Civic slowly as I scoped the scene.

I was going to tell her I'd only be five to ten minutes but she didn't have to wait. I could Uber back to the Aston. I was also going to thank her for the details about the church. Even maybe throw a compliment her way about the messiness of her bun and how great of a navigator she'd been getting me to this address.

But I did none of these things.

Instead I instinctively reached to my back pocket but stopped just shy of pulling my stolen Glock out.

A few doors down from where Malia and her daddy lived, sat the overly tinted black Audi.

TWENTY-FOUR

When Detective Kyle Kekoa got the call from the girl he was sitting in his breakfast nook that he used to share with his wife. She loved that there was a breakfast nook in their kitchen. That was the must when they'd bought the house. She didn't have many things on the list, but being able to eat inside her kitchen was one of them.

Kyle had the kitchen renovated weeks after she died. She'd made everything quaint with signs like "Come as guests, leave as friends," and different pictures of Maui that she'd picked up at thrift stores.

He trashed it all and opted for white walls, no decorations, and stainless-steel everything. He couldn't give up the breakfast nook, but he didn't have to live in torture every day thinking of things that his wife purposefully had added to make the house a home.

He sat at the bench, with a black cup of coffee and an English muffin which he tended to burn over half the time. He took bites as he read the local paper and winced at the charred parts.

How could he not fix this? It's not as hard to cook a bagel or muffin as it is to solve a murder?

The sterile environment of the nook calmed him. The bench was white with a black cushion seat and it was comfortable. At the table there were some chairs that weren't as comfortable but they looked nice. Slate gray with hard backs and hard seats. Kyle preferred the bench.

The lighting was dimmable in the kitchen because at night sometimes he would work on cases with the documents and paperwork splayed out all over the nook table. He didn't need them during the day, hardly. The sun poured in from the massive window on the other side of the breakfast nook. He could see the gentle hills outside and a touch of the ocean.

Even though it was a larger space and way more accessible, he couldn't bring himself to work at the dining room table. When she was alive, they'd hardly used it.

He always found himself at the nook.

Turned out it had come to be the hit of the home. When friends and relatives would come, they always would find themselves parked at the breakfast nook, chatting over coffee, drinks, late night snacks. Kyle's house had been known to always have plenty of everything.

Not so much recently. Now, he had enough milk in the fridge for the day. A bottle of wine in case he was entertaining a lady—unfortunately, he had bought the wine two years ago. And either English muffins, bagels, or apples. Most of his eating he did on the go, and he would typically just eat healthier things.

Because aside from the nook, Kyle was partial to the gym.

When his wife had been murdered, he wanted to sell the house. The insurance money that had paid out would have gotten him a nice place on Oahu. Probably twice as big as the place in Wailuku. But he couldn't leave. It meant something.

He had a Dell laptop next to his breakfast plate and was scrolling down through the public records database. He'd spent the better part of the morning exploring derivatives of Sawyer Grant. And Pennsylvania. He'd found squat.

Preacher at a gunfight. Preacher at a kidnapping. Mainlander moving to Maui. Must have some money.

Random thoughts, and he had no connections, but he hated that Ray liked this guy. Kyle was especially worried that perhaps he'd get the church job. If memory served him, the preacher was entitled to a parsonage home. Rent free in Maui was worth the work of just about any job.

He was about to start back on some local Pittsburgh sites when his cell began vibrating on the table. The number was local but that didn't mean anything. Kyle had given his phone number and card to just about everyone at the dance last night.

Something in his burned-toast-eating gut instantly drew a connection.

"This is Kekoa," he said.

"Please," a sobbing voice. A kid's voice.

Janeen. Was it Janeen?

"Janeen Hargrove, is this you?"

"No, please, it's Malia. Please, he's in my house, please come quick. Please."

He stood up pushing the table out. The coffee cup slid and fell, shattering on the ground.

"Address, sweetie, your address, quick."

"Dickenson Street, please".

The call was disconnected.

He stood there for a span of a second and felt helpless. That little girl. The one the preacher had worried about.

The preacher. Sawyer Grant.

He opened the phone again, trying to reconnect to Malia—no dice.

The next call he made was to the station. He did so as he was on his way to his car, checking his gun as he did. Leaving the breakfast nook, and shattered cup of coffee there for his future self to deal with. Right then, he was on the job.

He dispatched all units to Dickenson Street. He was right behind, but he was about twenty minutes away from Dickenson Street even with the lights flashing. Thirty if he was driving like a civilian.

But Kyle was confident he'd get there in fifteen.

TWENTY-FIVE

Something in Sawyer Grant's face changed.

His small talk and questions about the church took place from a different person.

And dogs? Really?

Something was wrong.

"What's up, Pastor Grant?" Elaina said to him. She liked calling him *Pastor Grant* because it reminded her of Cary Grant. Sawyer Grant wasn't Cary Grant but he certainly wasn't difficult to look at. He was athletic looking, and aside from the slight bruise on his forehead, his face was pretty close to perfect. His hair was a little long, but it had a wave to it that the sun seemed to exaggerate, in a good way.

She'd enjoyed the conversation, because Elaina loved the church work. But his humor was corny, his observations were awkward, and he was lost. But he was also charming. She kept wondering what he'd be like behind the pulpit preaching with gravitas.

And she caught a glimpse of it when they'd pulled up in front of the house on Dickenson Street. It was the first time she'd genuinely seen him act serious.

"Listen, Elaina. I appreciate the ride, but I need you to let me off here and I will Uber back to the hotel."

His voice was uneven. Hurried. And Elaina started to feel a little nervous, as though she were about to be in some sort of trouble. And he reached for his back pocket. But she knew his cell phone was in the front pocket of his suit. Then, he stopped.

"I'd feel bad, Pastor Grant," she said, "Stu told me to make sure I got you home and honestly, if you're a little while longer, Sundays tend to be my easy—"

Frantically now. "Look, are you my handler? Pretty sure I got to the church from the airport without you. Now, please, go home."

Wow. This guy was really a jerk. She wanted to think that and only that. But the part of her that found him likable was arguing for its first impression.

"Okay, you don't have to be rude, but okay."

He didn't even look at her. He couldn't take his eyes off the house, then up the street, then back to the house. Sweat seemed to develop instantly on his bruised head. It was hot, but he hadn't been sweating thus far, even though her car didn't quite have the best air conditioning.

"Thank you, forgive me, and I'll call you tomorrow to plan for the office time." He kept moving his head back and forth between the house and the street.

Drugs? That would make his sermons interesting, for sure.

"Okay, Pastor Grant."

But Elaina had no intention of leaving. Nope. She was native. She was in charge of passing his resume. And she'd sit here, and read some articles on her phone or something until he finished talking to whoever it was that he had to talk to—he hadn't really been forthright about that.

That was one of Elaina's qualities—persistence and hard-headedness. It's what got her through school. It's what enabled her to move on when she dated losers to pass the time. It's what led her to take a job at a church when she could be working in a lab somewhere and making good internship money.

She did her own thing.

The preacher got out, waved, and walked quickly away from the house, which Elaina found very odd.

He said he just had to talk to this couple.

It didn't make sense, but she pretended not to notice and drove to the top of the block of Dickenson Street. Lots of cars on either side parked all around, like always, but she found a spot up the street and paralleled in.

She turned the Civic off and sat there. It took approximately two seconds for Elaina to feel overheated so she stepped out and took a look at homes around the street. They all looked different, each of them having their own type of vegetation. Some more private than others.

Sawyer Grant was nowhere in sight and Elaina walked a little back toward where she'd dropped him. She didn't want to get too close, disrespecting his orders, but she also felt this unease about the way he'd exited her car.

She didn't know him, but it simply didn't seem like him.

And what was like him? What did that even mean?

She pulled her cracked iPhone out and started looking at Pittsburgh news articles. She remembered him telling her about the church burning down, and he had to get something soon because he didn't want to give up his ministry experience.

The pictures of the church were hard to see because of her phone being cracked and the sun above, making the picture look more like a shadowy mess.

He could have gone to Oahu and found an easier church job and made more money. If he had any doubt about being able to afford living on Maui, once the board offered Sawyer Grant a salary, he'd be on the next plane back to Steeler Country, or he'd be looking for side work immediately.

Elaina thumbed through the different articles. All said the same thing. Electrical fire. Faulty wiring. Old building. Perfect storm for damage and destruction. And though she'd never been to Pittsburgh, she knew that there were a lot of bars there. The church happened to be by this little dive bar called the *Phone Booth.*

Did it even matter what people called bars?

She started to look up some details about the Phone Booth when she heard the explosion. Maybe it was an explosion, or it was a gunshot. It was a gunshot, not an explosion.

She jumped so hard that her phone dropped to the ground. It might have cracked a little more, but that was the least of Elaina's worries.

The shot came from where she'd dropped Grant off.

And it was only the first of them.

TWENTY-SIX

I left Elaina's Civic feeling a familiar danger that I was beginning to associate with paradise.

The first thing I did was go over to the Audi. I approached it carefully from the passenger side, but it was empty. I peered into the tinted window and saw nothing worth mentioning, simply a regular dash and a driver and passenger seat.

I was certain this was the car from the church, however. It was tinted like a crayon.

That meant that maybe this clown was canvassing the street. Or, God forbid, he was inside the house already.

Malia's house had a little courtyard with a garden in front of it. Lots of color—purples, yellows, and pink flowers surrounded the perimeter of the garden. It was clear that this was a home that was taken care of. Everything was in order.

It made me feel a little disorganized.

As soon as I heard Elaina's less-than-subtle muffler grow quieter as she drove away, I had the Glock out. I didn't know how many rounds I had left in the clip. I was not planning on using the gun at all, but that was optimism. And unfortunately, I didn't have Stu with his muscled-up cap gun behind me today.

I was alone.

The door was closed. It was one of those thick wooden doors with an arch to it. It looked like a custom job. It was painted dark red and was formed by tongue-in-groove wooden slats. I always thought those kinds of doors were a little over the top. I mean, come on, it's a house, it's not Narnia. Just get a steel door and be done.

I approached it and my heart felt like it was going to pump out of my throat.

Should I knock?

No.

Yeah, of course I should knock. I couldn't just go into someone's house without an invitation.

Unless there was a dangerous man parked up the street on his way in or already in.

Well, here goes.

I pushed on the decorative door opener as quietly as I could. The door opened easily without a bit of resistance.

My suit felt like it weighed a thousand pounds. My tongue felt swollen in my mouth.

The contrast of the darkness inside compared to the brightness outside was jarring. All the shades were drawn.

Who would do that in Hawaii on a day like this?

I didn't have my bearings but I saw a set of steps directly ahead, and to the left it looked like a parlor or a living room. To the right was a large kitchen. Dark. Really Dark.

I couldn't bring myself to speak. I didn't want to blow my cover, but I didn't know if I needed it.

There was a couch and a loveseat outlined, by uneven bursts of sun coming through the slats on the blinds of the living room. I advanced in that direction, the Glock at my side, pointed down.

I felt for the impression of a light switch on the wall and clicked it. And I saw what I'd already predicted.

On the loveseat, sat Greasy Khakis.

He was wearing Khaki shorts again, but these ones were stained with the gore of his own open throat. He was slumped against the arm of the love seat, but his face was still visible. He looked hopeless, his mouth hanging halfway open, his throat rent from ear to ear.

How long had it taken him to die? Did he even grab his throat, or did his soul exit at the same time all the blood soaked into the cloth of the loveseat cushions.

I stepped back, Glock raised, heart pounding. I felt a chill run over me while I was sweating at the same time.

On the couch was Mrs. Greasy Khakis. Her death wasn't as graceful as her husband's (or boyfriend's). She was balled up on the couch, but I could see a cluster of wounds open on her chest around her heart. She had a t-shirt on, but I couldn't make out the print. It was stained with blood. Her eyes were open and frozen in a permanent image of horror.

He killed the husband first in front of the wife, and she gave a bit of a fight. Not much, but she didn't make it easy.

Heart pounding, my stomach churned. I didn't want to wretch.

There was still the girl that lived here. And she was alone.

Maybe she was hiding. I did a quick assessment recognizing that the blood was still very wet. Though the couch and loveseat cushions had sponged up most of it, this had just happened.

And Tinted Audi was in the house.

I didn't know where to go. This was my first experience with coming in on a home-invasion type of murder. I wished I could say that this was my only experience with murder, but it hadn't been.

I started toward the steps first. The girl had to be upstairs.

I could have gone through the living room into the back hall, but I had a feeling the killer was upstairs.

I walked with the Glock ahead of me. It was still so dark, but I knew that the murderer might be aware of my presence. Each of my footsteps sounded like a marching band. That happens when you're trying to be quiet.

I got to the top of the steps to find one door closed and another open down a hallway. There appeared to be a bath-room ahead.

I was most interested in the open door. Each step I took made the house creak even more. Might as well have attached a boom box to my back. I breathed in fresh flowery air freshener that had either been sprayed or distributed in the air by one of those plug things. The tropical, sterile smell somehow made the horror of what was taking place seem even more unnerving.

I advanced along the carpet toward the open door. I was praying that the girl was alright. The little red dress girl. Malia.

I peered into the door and saw a messy unmade bed, with posters of Hawaii musicians decorating the walls. Books on a neatly lined bookcase, but no kid. I stood there, afraid to move, scanning.

Maybe she was gone.

Then I heard, the faintest sound of sniffling. Fearful sniffling.

The girl was in the room, maybe even under the bed. And relief flooded my mind.

And that's also when I felt the stab of a knife going into my back.

TWENTY-SEVEN

Moani loved greeting people at the door. He had read that the best of preachers always stayed until everyone left, shaking each hand. They could have chosen to be anywhere on Sunday, but they'd chosen to come hear him preach.

That was great.

He sat on one of the soft, green-cushioned pews. The sound technician had shut the music down, but forgot to turn the PA completely off. There was a slight hum coming through the monitors mounted to the ceiling. It was annoying to him. Moani would have this place updated and overhauled the moment he got the pastorate. He wouldn't do too much to the sanctuary, though. Everything had charm, and character.

The green carpeting, it represented the growth people experienced as a Christian. And also, the green pew cushions. They weren't the most comfortable, but neither was Christian growth.

And also, he'd preached his first sermon in the sanctuary. How could Moani dare disturb the place of God's anointing on his life.

After visiting with some of the older folks in the back of the church—they updated him about their health stuff, family stuff, plans for the day. All so important to them. What was most important though was that they liked the sermon. He always had to ask. Couldn't help himself. And waves of elation washed over Moani when he heard those words that never got old.

God really spoke to me, Deacon Moani.

You're preaching is getting better and better.

Church is blessed to have you, brother.

Sometimes, Moani would remember the compliments and write them down later. Then, when he felt down on himself, or the day was a little dreary, he'd open his book and read the quotes out loud to himself. He never really remembered who to attribute them to, but by that time, he'd considered them affirmations directly from the Lord.

As the last of the flock left, Moani remained inside with his mother.

"Meet the guy preaching on Wednesday, Moani?"

She always knew what was on his mind. Didn't waste a moment.

"I did."

His mother pursed her lips together tightly. She had the lightest shade of lipstick on. She was a woman of class. Lila Wong. Hawaiian as they came. She was tiny, though. Thin and frail in her age. She'd had Moani when she was older. She always made it a point to tell everyone she met that he almost killed her.

Then she'd transition to say that now he almost kills her because of how proud she was of him.

That didn't get old, either.

She looked at Moani's eyes and shook her head up and down. "Seemed a little full of himself, didn't he. Just comes here from the mainland and expects to get a job. Your job."

Moani shrugged.

"Maybe I'll tell Hargrove and the other trustees that my charitable giving is going to start being diversified elsewhere, on account of my fixed income and all."

It wasn't true. Lila Wong was one of the wealthiest women that Moani had ever known. She told him after his father had died that neither she nor Moani would ever have want of anything. Sure, Dad had left a great insurance policy, but Lila Wong was an investment master. The insurance money was the cherry on top of some already thick icing, she'd been known to say.

And there was a lot of icing.

"I wouldn't do that, Ma. God will put me where he wants me."

Lila's eyebrows raised. "You ain't a little nervous?"

From the middle of the church a voice spoke, "I'm so sorry."

Moani jumped out of his skin. He'd thought for sure they were the only ones left in the sanctuary. He would have bet his life on it. But there was the guy that he'd seen. The visitor.

The man stepped out into the aisle.

The man was tall, wearing a navy-blue sport jacket with a white-and-blue pin-striped shirt. Perfectly pressed khakis and the shiniest shoes Moani had ever seen. For a moment, Moani felt underdressed.

"I'm so sorry," the stranger repeated, "I was so lost in prayer time, I guess I didn't realize that everyone had completely cleared out. Forgive me, Pastor."

Moani forgot he was talking to a stranger, and he tingled at the idea of being called *Pastor*.

"No need to apologize, sir. We are glad you can pray here."

Lila didn't speak, just stared at the visitor.

"Well thanks, and hey, thanks for the sermon too. My goodness, I felt like God had a megaphone attached to you aimed directly into my soul."

Moani would certainly write that one down.

"Well, it's all the Lord, but thanks, brother."

"Might I ask, are you the pastor?" The stranger smiled and each one of his teeth seemed whiter than the next.

Lila's turn. "No, sir. But he will be. This is his church as sure as Jesus anointed Peter. I mean you heard his sermon."

"Who could argue?" The stranger lifted his hands with a shrug.

Moani began to blush a little. But this was a great moment.

Lila responded, "Gotta let other people candidate, to see what the church wants. It's only fair. Even though we know who God picked."

"So, forgive me," the stranger said, tilting his head slightly, "there are other preachers interviewing for the job?"

Moani nodded.

"Well, they have pretty big shoes to fill with you, Pastor."

Going in the notebook.

"You even stopped a robbery last night, too. According to what you said in the sermon. God protected the church."

Embarrassment hit Moani like a brick.

"Yes, God protected us, but I wasn't there. Mom and I were at the Cheesecake Factory. It's a tradition that we go the night before I preach."

"Oh, I'm sorry. Wow, so who was there last night?

Because according to your sermon, it sounded like a dangerous situation."

Moani looked up at the oversized stage and couldn't quite recall sharing this much detail about the break in. But he might have. He didn't like to have too much distract him before preaching.

"I'm not sure who was all there. Some other preacher, Sawyer Grant. He was there. I think the janitor was there. But I didn't really get the whole story yet. It's hard to keep a sermon straight in your head."

The man's eyes narrowed as he smiled with that shining smile again. "I couldn't possibly imagine doing what you do, wow."

The visitor looked down and back up at Moani, then at his mother. Moani liked this man. He was kind and free with his compliments.

"Can you permit me, Pastor, one final indulgence. Since this is my first time and you've already told me so much of what God had done to protect you from the vandalism that could have happened to such a wonderful building. Could I possibly see that office that you mentioned?"

Moani felt a little uneasy. The office would eventually be his, but it wasn't yet.

"Sure," Lila piped in, crashing the silence. "I paid for it. I can show it to you."

"Wonderful, ma'am. God's grace is in this place." He smiled so wide and put his hand in his pocket, pulling out something small in his hand.

Moani was still uneasy, but this guy really appreciated how great the church was. Plus, it was just a quick tour.

And besides, how much harm could a man dressed so well do to the church. Even though it was a little weird that he was chewing on a black beverage stirrer.

TWENTY-EIGHT

I turned around and popped a shot off as I tried to reconcile what had happened to me. I knew I hadn't died because heaven doesn't look like a jerk-face wearing a ski mask.

The second thing I realized was that this wasn't the dude I'd tangoed with at Resurrection.

He swiped at me with the knife again and didn't connect. This time I kicked him right in his balls.

No rule against that.

He grunted but didn't drop the blade. Instead of collapsing backwards he fell toward me. The Glock flew from my hands like rice at a wedding. I heard it softly thud on the carpet and knew I was in trouble.

My shoulder and back throbbed as I tried to brace myself. We fell onto the floor of the young girl's bedroom. He was bigger than the other guy from Resurrection. Wider and more solid.

God, don't let me pass out or I'm dead.

He was on top of me and raised the knife above his head. I punched him as hard as I could in the throat. It wasn't hard at all due to my angle. But it was enough to get him off target with that blade. He brought it down just inches away from my head.

I threw my weight to the left, and rolled him. No one was straddling me without permission. When he fell over, the knife came free from his hand. We were both on our sides like awkward lovers. He grabbed at my throat and suddenly I couldn't breathe.

God, don't let me pass out or I'm dead—Part Two.

As he attempted to strangle me, I poked him as hard as I could in the eye with my thumb. He cried out like a little girl. He pulled back but not all the way. It was enough for me. I took the bottom part of my palm and drove it into his nose with as much force as I could manage.

Like his partner's, his nose cracked like a Thanksgiving wishbone. He had to be seeing stars. He groaned and swore.

Breaking someone's nose is a good way to get them to stop trying to strangle you. The moments of disorientation allow for opportunities.

What I saw in that moment was the Glock. I rolled the other way as the masked murderer was trying to put his nose back together. As I finally got the weapon back in hand, I heard sirens faintly increasing in volume.

The calvary was coming. *I might actually get through this.*

Thank God the little girl called the cops.

I stood up with the Glock in hand and pointed it at him.

"It's over, bro. You better start—"

He charged me and knocked me onto Malia's bed.

I was almost certain she was hiding under there.

We both were struggling for control of the gun. I kept pulling it away from him while at the same time, trying not to do something foolish like shoot myself.

In the tussle two rounds went off and through the

window. Glass shattered. The girl screamed. And sirens closed in louder now than ever with the broken window.

God, please let her be safe. Please let this little orphan girl be safe.

The intruder wasn't interested in fighting me anymore. He was trying to get out of there. Trying to get free himself from the sirens. I still had the Glock.

He bolted toward the door, clumsily reaching for the handle.

"Stop, I'm—" I couldn't get the words out. I shot a round right into his calf. I didn't know if the bullet went in or just grazed. But he groaned and collapsed onto one knee like he was proposing to the doorknob. He got to his feet and opened the door.

I was behind him as he bolted down the steps. I felt really tipsy, and was worried I would lose consciousness.

The guy ran out the open door, past Malia's parents' corpses and veered left. I saw him do it.

Toward the Audi.

When I got to the bottom of the steps, I thought I would pass out. I still had the Glock. But my shoulder pounded through my suit.

I hoped nothing major was hit, but I thought it was blood loss or shock.

I finally got myself enough adrenaline to surge through the door. As I bore left, a body was on top of me, knocking the Glock out of my hands—

And me unconscious.

TWENTY-NINE

The police were on their way, but they weren't coming fast enough.

That's why Elaina moved her Civic closer to where she'd dropped off Sawyer Grant.

The houses on Dickenson Sptreet were a little too close together for Elaina's taste.

Didn't you live in a shoebox? But if you were paying that much money to own a house, you'd at least want a yard.

She also, didn't like how the landscaping was different for all the houses. There was no uniformity to the street. She liked uniformity. She liked when everything lined up.

But none of that mattered. What did matter was that Elaina glimpsed a man in some sort of mask limping out of the house and into a jet black sporty-looking car.

What could possibly be happening?

The windows were so dark that she couldn't see, but the guy started the car and threw it into gear almost immediately, peeling out and right past her up Dickenson Street, the hot sun bouncing off the shiny surface of the car. Probably an import.

Either Sawyer Grant was dead—a mathematical possibility because of the gunshots, or he was okay—just like he was from last night's fight at the church office. He looked like he could handle himself.

Either way, the police would be there any moment, but that masked guy was on his way to freedom. And there was no way anyone would know what happened to him.

She didn't quite think it through when she pulled her own car into drive. While she didn't match the black car's urgency, she pushed it pretty quickly. The muffler sounded way faster than the Civic went. But she floored it up Dickenson Street and pulled right onto Highway 30.

Elaina kept the pedal to the floor but it didn't much matter. The smell of exhaust invaded the cabin. She felt short of breath but hadn't moved. Panic.

She kept the pedal pushed to the floor, until the black car appeared ahead of her. He had to have been slowing up, which was exactly what Elaina figured he would eventually have done. Speed brings suspicion.

In her relief at realizing she hadn't lost him, Elaina noticed an ache in her fingers from the grip she had on the ragged old Honda steering wheel.

Elaina maintained speed along Highway 30, and closed the gap between her and the black car. She let up off the gas, read the license plate out loud several times, and dictated it into her phone. She almost couldn't hear herself because of the muffler on the Civic.

Now that she had the plate she called Sawyer Grant's cell phone.

Her mouth was dry. She looked down in the cupholder and wanted a piece of gum, but couldn't allow herself another free moment without clutching her phone or the steering wheel.

No response.

Had she left the preacher there inured? Dead?

Those gunshots.

The police were there, Elaina. They were tending to him right now.

She knew the value she was bringing to this situation was in seeing where this guy was going. Even though she really had no idea why Grant had asked Elaina to take him to Dickenson Street to begin with.

Miles up the road—the mountainous uneven wall on her left, the ocean and cliff on her right—and the sports car began to slow.

Elaina hit her brakes and glanced in the rearview. She was still going faster than the other traffic, but she was afraid of being rear-ended.

She came upon a scenic overlook, and Elaina was rather shocked as the black car pulled into a lot filled with other cars. There were several visitors parked there and Elaina passed right by as the black car came to a stop in a stall. Right in front of three people, dressed in logo t-shirts most likely purchased at a souvenir stand. Selfie stick in hand, making memories.

She was frustrated at not being able to pull in, but she didn't know what else to do without blowing her cover with this stranger. Another moment of *what were you thinking* washed over her.

She dialed Grant's number again as she kept on the highway, looking for the closest place to turn around without killing herself in a U-turn.

No response.

She pulled onto to Maalaea Bay Place road to get herself turned around. But she couldn't go confront this stranger. What was she going to say? Dust rose up round her car as she stopped, waiting to pull back onto the highway.

As she merged, Elaina only had one thought:

Sawyer Grant still wasn't answering his phone.

THIRTY

There I was, in Pittsburgh. In Lawrenceville, right at the corner of the Bloomfield Bridge and Liberty Avenue.

The sounds of old brakes, passing cars, and horns filled my mind. Something didn't smell right about the corner. I'd been on this corner a million times. It was probably one of the first places I'd walked on my own. Right outside the Phone Booth.

The neon letters of the sign attached to the top of the two-story frame building had been burned out for ages. My uncle had neither the allocated capital nor the desire to repair it. And he chose instead to just put up a cheap white vinyl banner sign below the neon. In black all caps, it read: PHONE BOOTH.

I was dressed differently. I was wearing a Hawaiian shirt. Blue with the flowers. To my knowledge, I'd never sported one of these things in my life. It was super baggy on me. But the jeans I was wearing felt okay. In my one hand, I had a copy of the newspaper dated from the last day I was in Pittsburgh. In my other hand, I held a Sig Sauer pistol.

I had no clue of the time, but the sky made it look like it was just after 8 pm.

I had an appointment to keep. Well, only one of us knew about the appointment. The poor guy that would be waiting at the bar didn't know about the appointment. He just knew that he was drinking and watching that old rickety tube TV they'd suspended above the bar.

I had told my uncle one bad thunderclap and that TV was gonna come down on the bartender's head.

The guy inside would be under the impression he was there to get paid. Ready to get his cut from that week's take. A modest stipend off of all of it. The poker machines, the women, the coke. Pay day. Some complimentary suds. And a MASH rerun blaring from the accident-waiting-to-happen television over the bar.

I opened the splintered wooden door that anyone could practically see through. Charlie the bartender wasn't there. No one was. He was supposed to be. Then when I came in with my heat, he'd make an excuse to hit the stock room.

Oddest thing. No one was in there. Bar, smelling musty and mildewy as always. Alan Alda doing his schtick in a show that lasted longer than the war.

And no one waiting to be paid.

This is a dream, moron.

And where was that flowery smell coming from? The only smell I was used to from Liberty Avenue was exhaust, sewage, and the waft of an occasional cigarette.

I stepped back out of the bar and glanced left at the church next door. One of those big ornate churches. Our Sacred Peace Church. The white stone building, stained glass, the bright red double doors.

I thought about my meeting with Pastor Clint before I went into the service. That meeting that someday I'd tell someone about. I thought about the chaplain I'd met overseas.

I even thought about Jesus.

Something seemed inviting about the church.

For the first time, the church was more inviting than the bar, even though I'd built that bar, in a sense. The work I did paid the bills.

So I stepped out of the Phone Booth and into the church.

It was empty. But not just empty. It felt barren. I inhaled the smells and to be honest, it smelled like the bar. That mildewy bar smell. The smell of soaked-in alcohol that had dried in crevices that the bartender couldn't see and didn't care to find.

That's how the church felt to me. It felt barren and polluted.

The pews looked like a picture from a church magazine. It's as though no one had ever sat in them. Heavy, wooden and useless.

It was hard for me to imagine people being in there. I wondered how many people would stop in here and pray for strength to withstand the temptation of their addictions. Drugs, sex, and booze. And only find themselves right next door at the Phone Booth, realizing that those prayers were not answered.

So I walked through the church. There was the pastor, or priest or whatever. He was shocked to see me. He smiled. I smiled back. But then I looked down.

I felt embarrassed because I was dressed in a Hawaiian shirt. He had his priestly garb on. The white collar, long robe with the emblems on it. Whole nine yards.

The smell of the flowers started to grow stronger, as the pastor saw the Sig in my hand. I'd felt as embarrassed about it as a freshman feels about being caught with a *Playboy*. But there it was.

There I was. Seen by him.

The look on his face. Shock, horror. I didn't really focus much on it. Instead I raised the Sig, aimed it at the preacher's shocked face, and fired off a shot. It went dead center into his head.

And that's when the flames erupted—starting at the altar. The candles all seemed to grow in intensity until all of the wood, the velvet table coverings, the ornate cups for communion—all of it was under hell.

The flames swallowed the priest's collapsing body, consuming his flowing robe and traveling up to what was left of his head.

I felt the heat and the flowers grow intensely. The smell. *Baptism by fire.*

How much of this was real?

How much of this was a dream?

How much of this was a memory?

I had no idea.

THIRTY-ONE

Dickenson Street was Detective Lulani Aukai's first assignment in homicide. Well, his first real assignment. He didn't consider the questioning of the kids at Lahaina Intermediate the night before.

He also didn't want to think about the night before, because that would mean he'd have to face the reality that he probably wouldn't be a part of Ani's life anymore.

They were detectives on the same team. And it opened up a whole new complicated door for them. With his luck, Lulani'd be shipped to Oahu like a case of coffee. Ani had seniority. She had the brains.

Ani had it all.

Lulani and Detective Kekoa were standing at the ambulance, waiting for the preacher to regain consciousness. Some other patrolmen kept the onlookers at bay. Everyone knew what had happened, or at least they had their suspicions. It was going to be hard to conceal two bodies coming out of a crime scene.

It was also hard to keep people from staring on Dickenson Street. The houses were pretty close together. And

Lulani imagined people using that as an excuse to be lookie-loos.

Lulani was glad he had been the one to tackle Sawyer Grant, but he also didn't feel quite like Grant was the guy.

Detective Kekoa wasn't so objective.

Even if the preacher didn't cause the bloodbath inside the Dickenson Street house, he was involved somehow. Trouble didn't just follow people the way it was following this guy.

Hargrove's kid.

The church break-in.

Now this. Double homicide on a Sunday.

No work on the Sabbath, Pastor.

The streets were lined with three medical vehicles, including the one holding the preacher. Everything else looked as picturesque and perfect as it would during any other day in paradise. Beautiful breeze. Plumeria in abundance. Lots of Aloha.

Ani's unmarked pulled up to the scene behind the ambulance with the little girl who had survived.

Ani.

Was this their first day *not* together. He had told her that they were pausing it, but Ani wasn't one for leaving things hanging.

He walked up to the unmarked Ford and saw the restraint in her face.

This was going to be harder than he expected.

She had her hair down, the way he liked. He was surprised.

Ani must have noticed that Lulani noticed, because while still in the car, she pulled it back into a tight ponytail. She got out.

She was wearing a white blouse and a dark black skirt.

She looked all business, but she couldn't hide beautiful even if she wanted to.

"Didn't know you'd be here, thought you were covering the kidnapping," Ani said.

Was she trying to sound cold?

"Well, this is connected, right? Kid from same school. Questioned last night. Preacher—"

"Preacher?"

"Yeah, that pastor from last night. He apparently had an altercation with the perp. Took a knife to the shoulder and he's passed out in the ambulance. I tackled him coming out."

"Why would you tackle him?"

Lulani felt like he was being interrogated. So far as he could remember, she'd never talked to him like this. And he wasn't a fan.

"Because, I was around the back of the house, I heard some crashing and breaking inside, I came to the front and Grant was making a break for it."

"Well, where was the perp?"

Now, he was getting irritated. "I don't know, Ani. Kekoa thinks that the preacher might have something to do with all this. You know how it go. Sometimes easy, sometimes sleazy."

She didn't even respond. They both walked to the ambulance were Grant was.

After last night, they'd parted ways at the crime scene. He had texted her earlier to see what she was up to but he'd only received one-word responses.

She was really trying to bring this adventure to an end.

After staring at Grant for a moment, Ani turned back to Lulani. "How about the girl?"

"Untouched as far as we could see. Social worker and

patrolmen are over there with her," Lulani said as he motioned to the ambulance. "According to the kid, Grant neutralized the killer. Said she didn't see anything because she was hiding, but the bedroom looks like a war zone. Seems legit. Detective Kekoa thinks it's a little too tidy."

"Tidy? The pastor looked like he lost eight gallons of blood!"

"Yeah yeah, he does, but he's also been at the sight of three different crimes. Something fishy there."

He was getting tired of it. She knew that he wouldn't just listen to Detective Kekoa. Lulani had a problem with the preacher, too. Why was he even here? If he didn't have some sort of involvement, why was he always in the center of the nonsense. Especially him saying he tweaked up the church burglar.

Kekoa's Explorer pulled up and he got out with a slam of the door. He came over immediately to Lulani and Ani.

"Nice of you both to respond today."

Lulani wasn't ready for this fight.

Kekoa softened his gaze, "No, honestly, thanks. This whole thing, the preacher, Hargrove's daughter, now this. I'm a little rattled. Did you already check out the scene?"

"Yeah," Lulani said. "M.E. is on the way, but it's pretty clear what happened in there."

Kekoa shook his head and walked toward the house without saying more.

Ani glared at Lulani. "You doing all the talking, now?"

Lulani grabbed her by the arm and she let out a shocked gasp. He wasn't pulling her hard or hurting her, but he was being forceful. She followed up the block of Dickenson Street until they were separated from the fold.

"What's with you?" he asked. He let go of her arm.

She was filled with vinegar. "Nothing, you just have been on the job two day—"

"Don't do this, you know it's not the job."

"I—"

"Ani, don't."

For the first time that day, he caught a glimpse of the eyes he was used to seeing. Lulani grabbed his badge off of his belt.

He had eagerly dressed like a detective today. First opportunity out of the blues. But he also wanted that shield prominently displayed on his belt. He loved being plain clothes.

"I'm going to let you decide."

He put the badge in Ani's hand. She gave it right back.

"What are you doing?"

"Here it is, if we can't be civil, I don't want this role. In fact—"

He looked down. He didn't want to see her face when he said what he was about to say.

"Lulani, you are being a little dramatic."

"No, here it is. This is all I wanted forever. This. Being called first."

He wasn't telling her anything he hadn't already told her since they started their thing.

"And you got—"

"Until I wanted something else more."

She didn't say anything else as he pressed the badge into her hand. He squeezed as he did it and moved in close to her, giving his best smile.

"If you think there's a shot, I'll give what I got."

THIRTY-TWO

They'd made a mess. The preacher, the intruder. This wasn't something Stu was glad he'd put off, but it was what it was.

The bullet holes pierced some of the books.

Those books were expensive. The previous pastor didn't seem to read them much, Stu had noticed.

Stu planned to get to those burned-out lights above the preacher's desk, too. Might as well do it all. He had brought up some steel bars that he wanted to install outside of the windows. If someone wanted to come in, they were gonna have to get violent to do so. He'd also changed the lock on the preacher's door. One thing he knew, if there was some sort of break in, security had to get beefed up and fast.

It was a little inconvenient because he had his church clothes on—gray polo shirt and jeans. Let the Hawaiian garb take a holiday. Sunday was for church clothes. He hadn't planned on getting too messy fixing up this office.

Stu was about to head out to the janitor's closet to grab a rag for the dust when he was stopped at the doorway by Moani, his mama, and a guy that looked like he just stepped out of a Men's Wearhouse catalog. He recognized him from church, but church was over.

"Stu," Moani said. He had that holy tone he used with outsiders. Stu knew the other side of Moani. The one that wasn't afraid to cuss out Miss Lila.

People never pay attention to the cleaner.

Lila motioned with a grand gesture at the office. "This is the preacher's study." She sent a soft glance to Moani who cracked the slightest of smiles.

Stu focused back on the newcomer. "Didn't catch your name, sir?"

The visitor was checking out the office as though he were sizing up a yacht.

"Sure," he said. "William Robertson."

He extended out a hand that looked like it was a day removed from a fresh manicure.

"Stuart Gentry,' he said, shaking. The visitor's hands were like ice.

William returned to his wonder-struck perusal of the office. "This would make a fine study." He looked at Moani who was as proud as a cat with a mouse in its jaws. "Gonna be yours, huh?"

Moani laughed. "Just about. But they just had to post the job online for the sake of making it fair."

"Waste of time," Lila said, running her hand along the wooden molding of the wall. "I paid to have this office redone 'cause I knew my baby would be writing sermons in here."

William raised his eyebrows and looked at Stu. "Sounds like she's got it all planned, huh, Mr. Gentry?"

Stu nodded, "Yeah, but you know what the Scripture teach, 'Man makes the plans but God's driving the car.'"

They all laughed except Stu. This new guy was making

him a little uneasy. Most visitors wanna talk to the pastor. Some wanna know where the closest restaurant is that's not going to be too crowded.

But none of them wanted to see the preacher's office.

"God certainly drives the car," William said as he moved over to the desk, the same place where an intruder's smoking gun sat less than twenty-four hours before. "So, I heard there was a bit of a problem here last night with another preacher."

He was staring at Stu when he posed the question. Stu said nothing.

Something wasn't sitting right.

"If ya ask me it's a sign. Some mainland—sorry Mr. Robertson—preacher comes in, trying to pastor in paradise and our beautiful office gets ransacked."

William clicked his tongue. *Tsk Tsk.* Stu wasn't responding.

Silence seemed to expand in the office. Awkward.

Moani broke it. "Yeah, and on top of the problems last night, the guy is speaking this Wednesday at our midweek prayer meeting. I guess Hargrove wants to give the appearance of giving others a chance."

"Wow!" That delightful eyebrow raise came back on William's face. Expressive as all get out. "So, he'll be at the service this week? It would be interesting to meet another mainlander that wants to relocate. Solidarity, you might say."

He walked toward the door of the office. Stu stayed by the broken window, watching. Moani and Lila followed behind. Stu heard his phone begin to ring, and could have sworn he saw the visitor pick up some speed in his pace.

William Robertson paused and looked at Moani with a

smile, then back to Stu. "Looks like you all sold me on a second visit to Resurrection!"

THIRTY-THREE

The heat.

The crashing.

The gunfire.

I couldn't get myself out fast enough. The flames were consuming me.

Baptism by fire.

Preacher's desk.

Glock 19.

You didn't do what you were supposed to.

My duffel.

My eyes flew open and closed again. My back felt like it was torched with kerosene. I didn't know where I was. Darkness.

Was this Hell?

Darkness.

But I recognized the sound of machines and knew I wasn't in hell. Voices. Hell doesn't have machines. But Hell probably has voices.

Pastor.

Paradise Preacher.

Grant.

Grant.

I was starting to come to.

Smelled that flowery Hawaii air. I made it here. I was free.

"Grant, you're fine." The voice.

I opened up my eyes and force them to remain. And there was the muscle head that hated me. Detective freaking Kyle Kekoa.

If he rescued me from Hell, I should've been grateful. But the look in his eyes told me that he would just have saved me to send me back again.

We were in an ambulance. It wasn't quite as dark as I thought. I was on a stretcher, my suit jacket was off, and my white shirt was covered in blood. It had started to dry, so it had this odd starchy quality.

I tried to reach my hand up to see how much damage was done but couldn't. My arms were handcuffed to the bed.

I pulled and at the same time, looked up at Detective Kyle.

Jesus, help me, this guy is on the verge of smiling.

"Sorry, Grant. I can't take any chances."

I was dumbfounded. "What are you—"

Couldn't even finish the sentence.

He shook his head. I felt like he was going to take those beefy arms and crush my skull with them. "I need to know exactly what happened and how you showed up at a house with two murdered people."

I felt flush. That red feeling I get behind my ears. It's the red feeling. I got it at the Phone Booth a lot. I had to stay cool, though, because I had just invaded a crime scene on a hunch. But this guy was too far up my butt to see clearly.

"I had a feeling about that—the guy, the dad and his kid. I told you—"

"Another reason we are here," Kyle said, motioning with both hands.

I felt worse. Angrier.

"Listen, Muscle Milk. I'm sorry I figured out that something was going south before you did. And I'm also sorry that the kid—"

I lost my breath.

"The kid. Is she—"

"Fine." Kyle said. "But that doesn't change that you were in there. I need to know what you saw, know your involvement, know if there's something you maybe wanna tell me."

Red.

"Hey Kyle, I'll tell you. First, I told you that something was up with the Greasy Khaki guy and his kid. You waved me off like a fly at a picnic. I then figured because I talked to a detective that already thinks I'm a criminal—"

"Do you blame me?" He gritted his teeth as he spoke.

"—that it would be a good idea if I came here, killed the parents, and then stabbed myself in the back. That sound like a good plan?"

"Do you use that kind of language in the pulpit?"

Ugh, great. I still wasn't used to this title yet. And the potty talk came as natural to me as measuring macros did with Detective Kyle Kekoa. I'd do better in the future, but these circumstances allowed for it.

Plus, Jesus forgave me.

I took a deep breath. "Look, there was a car in the lot at the church. That car was here, but I shot—"

"I know, that's the other thing. How were you on Maui

for two minutes and already have access to a Glock 19? Did you buy it at the airport? Or did you boost it off this guy?"

In the "Choose Your Own Adventure" books, this was the feeling I used to get when I picked a path and saw I was heading to certain death. Then, I would immediately backtrack to take the other choice.

Only this time, instead of certain demise, it was probably jail time on Maui.

"Pastor Grant." Elaina's voice came through ambulance from the street. She sounded both anxious and accusatory. Good combo. This was going to be fun.

I instinctively tried to pull my hands up again but—handcuffs. "I'm good, Elaina. Where were you on the back up?"

Kyle looked toward her. Elaina was standing on Dickenson Street next to some of the medics who had stepped out when Kyle was interrogating me.

"Ma'am, we have to work through some stuff with the pastor—"

"Officer, please. I know where the guy is that you are really looking for."

Third time I tried to raise my hands with the handcuffs.

"Detective, can we do away with this? I didn't kill anyone, I'm trying to help."

He looked down at me. "You're not going anywhere." He then turned toward Elaina, "Ma'am, who are you?"

She was awkward but cute about it. "I work for the church, the one that Pastor Grant is interviewing with."

Kyle shot back at me as he motioned for another officer who was outside to come in and undo my cuffs. I could see the readiness in his face as he prepared to hit the road after Tinted Audi.

He stopped and turned back to me. "You brought the church secretary to a murder scene?"

"I didn't know it was a murder scene, Lou Ferrigno, and she's the administrator." I looked at Elaina, who was still just as panicked. "It's not the fifties."

Kyle grabbed the other detective that had tackled me and said they had to get on the road. I looked at them and saw a striking woman. She looked like one of the detectives from the previous night at the school but I didn't quite remember her.

She threw a badge to the tackler. The guy looked down at the badge, back at her for a really long time, then clipped the badge on to his belt.

There was something up there.

THIRTY-FOUR

Billy hadn't even gotten twenty feet through the door before the kids were at his legs. Both of them. And the dog, KiKi the Bichon. Her little paws clacked excitedly on the gray tile in the entranceway of their new apartment.

Ellen must have been baking, because the whole house smelled like banana bread. His four-year-old, Trista, wanted up on his shoulders. Billy took his jacket off and hung it on the door handle behind him, then in one effortless motion, his dark, curly-haired daughter was on his shoulders, screaming to touch the ceiling of the new apartment they were renting.

Billy was pleased to see more kids' toys out in the living room, and less in the packing boxes that had made their home look more like a warehouse than an abode. Daniel Tiger was blaring from the flatscreen on the wall. Daniel was talking about what to do when you get mad.

His feet hurt a lot, but Billy had been through a rough day so far. Working Sunday wasn't out of the question, especially at this point in their relocation. He was glad

Ellen could stay home with the kids while he figured out how to get them settled into Maui.

This was the dream. He was only a few great business moves away from setting them up permanently. Then, paradise would become normal. And Maui would be home.

Ellen came in, dish towel over her shoulder, dark hair in a ponytail and a frustrated look on her face.

"What's up," Billy asked. His tone was kind and somewhat humorous.

Ellen pursed her pink lips. She never needed a bit of lipstick. They were always the perfect shade. The light bounced off her eyes as she looked at Billy. He never grew tired of her. Two kids. Fourteen years.

All the good things.

"Bit of a lunch malfunction," Ellen said. "I was hoping you'd have grabbed something on the way home from your meeting. Thought Sunday afternoon meetings should at least give you some food."

Billy smiled and looked down. "Oh, hun, I'm sorry. I would have, honestly. It's just been the worst day. I wish you had texted. And the meeting ended early. Believe it or not, I actually stopped at a local church service after the meeting."

She gave him a puzzled look, but dismissed it. "I didn't want you to think I was throwing the towel in on getting lunch ready," she said.

As she spoke, the kids were demanding to change the channel, put a different collar on the dog, and eat dinner immediately. Communication in their home had turned into *who can shout over the kids the loudest.*

"Ha, no, your hands are as full as they could be. What did you—"

His cell vibrated in the jacket that he'd taken off and hung on the doorknob. His eyes narrowed.

He gave the family the *give me a minute* look as he headed over to the phone. When he looked at the caller id, he realized it would be more than a minute.

Billy stepped outside the door and answered.

"Problems with the preacher again," the voice on the other line said.

Billy sucked in the plumeria-scented air. The sun beat down on him as he stood in his driveway. He caught a glimpse of a kid with a baseball cap on, shirtless, riding his bike. No cares. No worries.

"You there or what?" The voice demanded.

"Elaborate," Billy said. "I'm a little tied up."

"This phase didn't go well. And I got hurt—a lot. Not going to hospital. But if this guy's a pastor then I'm the Pope. I gotta get myself fixed up."

Billy tightened his grip on the phone. Watched again as the careless kid on the bike made his rounds across the serene street.

Kids.

"Let me get to a better place to discuss this and think about it. It's unfortunate that Riggins also had a run-in with the preacher. And you know what happened to him."

"Yeah," Bob said. "Preacher tweaked him up. I know the feeling now."

"Yes," Billy said, "and it ended up killing him."

No response.

"We'll get a plan together because we are just about done, but I need time."

Billy hung up his phone as he looked from his driveway to the front door. The kids were still there, waiting for him. He loved them.

He had to finish this for them. There was so much at stake, but unfortunately, some more people were going to have to die.

Did he want them to die? No. But people died every day. People died every day for meaningless reasons. Reasons that never benefited anyone. And whether Billy believed that there was a God or not, God pretty much let the strong run the show on this planet if he existed.

He opened the door again. The kids were at him. Dog at his feet. He grabbed his jacket.

"Ellen, I might be some more hours, but why don't you guys get some take out. Anything you'd like. As long as you save me some of whatever it is you have baking."

Ellen resurfaced from the kitchen, dishtowel now on the other shoulder.

"Huh?"

"It smells heavenly," Billy said.

"Oh!" her eyes widened with recognition. "It's not anything I've baked. It's a candle."

Billy laughed, hugged his kids, patted the dog, and walked toward his silver Buick.

He had to make a plan to kill a preacher.

THIRTY-FIVE

The ambulance took Grant, and Elaina was glad. He had a nasty wound to the shoulder. She planned on asking him later what exactly happened inside that house. Specifically, how did two people die and a preacher survive?

What was this guy about?

She stood on Dickenson Street seemingly unnoticed. Once the detectives left and the ambulance took Pastor Grant, only one medical vehicle still remained.

The one with the girl.

The shrubbery and different landscaping on Dickenson Street should have been more even, in Elaina's opinion. She liked symmetry. She liked when things matched. That's why she was going to school for engineering. She had switched it from Molecular Biology because she liked more math. She loved math. She loved puzzles.

Not as much as classic movies, though.

As Elaina approached the ambulance, she saw the girl sitting with her legs dangling off the tailgate. A well-dressed woman frantically taking calls on her cell phone stayed pretty close, but wasn't really paying attention. Must have been a social worker.

Elaina imagined the social worker trying to find next of kin to finish raising the orphan.

The girl.

The survivor.

Elaina knew that this girl's parents had been murdered. This girl's life was over. Or at least the life she knew.

"Aloha," Elaina said to the young girl.

The girl was a teenager, and Elaina knew that as the girl grew older, she could become a model if she decided to pursue it. She was flawless in beauty.

The orphaned teenager sat there with a cup of some sort of pink-colored juice, still mostly full.

Someone had a blanket near her, but not on her. It wasn't cold, and it was dumb for a paramedic to even think that a blanket would be necessary with the sun beating down as it was.

People do dumb things around those experiencing trauma. Elaina had learned that in ministry and helping to organize funerals. If you wanted to know how dumb human beings could be, watch how they handle interacting with people in the middle of tragedy.

It was way too warm for a blanket.

The girl had a faraway look in her eyes. Elaina wondered if she was traumatized from knowing her parents were dead or from the fact that the killer had almost gotten her too.

Why not both?

Elaina thought back to her own childhood. She thought of her dad leaving her, and her mom depending so much on her. It wasn't until grad school that she'd recognized how unhealthy it was.

But she wasn't an orphan.

The teenager looked up at her but didn't change the expression. She was wearing a long-sleeve t-shirt. Plain white with a pink flowery logo on the right side. Small, modest.

"My name is Elaina."

She was terrible at this stuff and just realized she had cast a judgment too early on the hero that brought the young girl a blanket in eighty-degree weather. She didn't know how to talk to most people, let alone someone who had just experienced a loss like this.

So typically, Elaina would say nothing. But this time, she felt compelled to reach out to this girl. Was it the Holy Spirit? Or was it her insatiable obsession with trying to fit puzzle pieces together.

"Malia," the girl said, after a while. Her voice was crackly. Elaina wanted her to drink a little of the drink they gave her.

"This is terrible and I'm sorry. I'm not going to talk down to you and give you some sort of promise, but I'll tell you that you're gonna be okay."

The girl named Malia stared up at her again after staring down at the drink for a moment. Malia's eyes became glassy. Tiny windows formed over her corneas.

Elaina thought if the girl were to blink that the tears would trail all the way down to the ground. But Malia didn't blink.

"If you talk to some of these people, they might be able to find out who did this."

Elaina's mind flashed to her original love. Puzzles. Things with no answer. Why were Malia's parents slaughtered? What did this have to do with anything? Was the murderer the same person who kidnapped Janeen Hargrove?

Again, the girl looked at Elaina without blinking.

Blink, for God's sake, blink!

"Maybe, I can even help find this bad man. He hurt a friend of mine, the man that was here. He hurt your family."

Malia blinked once and the tears fell. That's when she started talking. It wasn't much, but it was something.

"It was my fault. It was all my fault," she cried. Elaina glanced at the social worker, still on the phone. She was hoping that the conversation wouldn't be broken up.

"No, sweet girl. There's nothing you could have done to stop this man—"

"No, no, no!" Malia cried. Heaving sobs now.

Elaina stared at the social worker that stepped further away. Okay, when this was all said and done, Elaina was going to report her. But right now, she was grateful for the social worker's lack of attention to detail.

"Janeen, I just did what Daddy said. I don't hate her that much. I don't hate her at all."

Floodgates.

"Janeen? Hargrove?" Elaina started getting that sick feeling, accompanied by a brutal sense of a picture being formed.

Malia nodded.

Elaina didn't need to write anything down that she was saying. She was able to focus on every detail, despite all of the chaos of activity on Dickenson Street. The social worker came over and broke it up.

But she saw a piece. Another piece.

Because though she couldn't put the pieces together, Elaina knew a puzzle when she saw one.

And she also knew that she needed to speak to Sawyer Grant again.

THIRTY-SIX

Ani didn't only watch Lulani bolt into the distance with Detective Kekoa, she noticed the young lady that had given them the tip about the black car. Everyone else was doing their own thing, but this girl was worried about Grant.

She looked over at the social worker who was talking with the surviving girl.

God help that poor girl.

Ani pulled her phone out, and allowed herself the indulgence of sending Lulani a text.

I'm sorry. Let's keep the talk on pause. Once we catch some killers and find a missing girl, we'll figure out what to do with that badge.

She couldn't. Couldn't think of it. Couldn't think of asking Lulani to give up what he wanted most at the hope of having a committed relationship with her.

What? Would she stay the detective? He stay the patrolman? Would he resign? Go do another job?

Pause, Ani, pause. You don't have to make the call on your own.

He returned her text almost immediately.

We'll have this talk again, if I survive the drive.

Rhymes.

She felt her eyes warming with tears and looked up, getting back to the scene.

There went Grant's medical transport. He needed to be checked out for sure. If that preacher had anything to do with the killings, it went south for him. There was a chasm carved into his shoulder.

Ani looked on and saw the girl, the one who'd told Detective Kekoa and Lulani about the sports car. She was wandering, almost carelessly, toward the ambulance that had the girl in it.

The girl looked lost, hanging her legs over the tailgate. They gave her a juice or a milk or something that was worthless. What she needed was mom and dad, and they were gone. This was it.

The social worker was feverishly trying to connect on the phone. She probably couldn't get the next of kin immediately. But while the social worker was trying to get someone on the phone, the church girl was making a connection of her own with the survivor.

The detective inside Ani wanted to run and confront the church girl. But the woman in her realized that there was something happening between them that was probably better than the young orphan sitting on the edge of the medical van swinging her feet and thinking of mama.

Ani took a couple steps further. The girl started crying. Rather loudly actually. And she was saying a name. The name—

Janeen.

The missing girl, of course.

At this, the social worker came over, and shooed the secretary away. The secretary didn't seem to care. Ani didn't know it for sure, but she guessed the church girl actually wanted to help.

Elaina wasn't paying attention, and Ani liked that. Ani followed slowly behind, remaining in earshot as Elaina opened her phone and dialed a number, leaving a rather hurried message.

"Stu, please answer. I want to come over. I need your help. Please."

Stu. Stu?

No idea, but Ani had a feeling if she were to look over the case notes, she'd be able to figure out who Stu was.

And at this point, was she searching for a child or searching for a murderer? Detective Kekoa and Lulani were checking a lead, but what about this?

She was overwhelmed and knew anything she obtained from a talk with Elaina or the orphan Malia would be pretty much worthless. Especially because Kekoa seemed to wanna keep the focus on the preacher.

The secretary got into her piece-of-crap car—

How could the church not offer to give her some help with it?

And pulled away.

The preacher definitely had a role, but there was something else here.

Ani knew that Kekoa would get to it. She knew that Detective Kekoa would have her and maybe Lulani overturn some rocks that would lead them there.

But it wasn't his priority, now.

Ani had her own phone out, ready to text Lulani. Bring him into the fold a little. Get his insight.

Then she thought better of it.

This was his time. He was with Kekoa. Lulani was going to make a great name for himself.

Later. Lulani and Ani would talk about their future. Later she'd get to formally interview the girl.

But she'd wait on Kekoa to give her the marching orders.

None of this was going to stop her from thinking of Elaina the church secretary and her talk with the little orphan girl though.

THIRTY-SEVEN

Even in paradise, a hospital room was a hospital room. And I was wearing out my welcome in this one. I was sick and tired of looking at the cotton curtain they'd secluded me behind. I stared at it so much, I swear I started seeing previous stains on it that had somehow withstood the bleach the hospital used to clean it.

And trust me, the bleach was about the only chemical I could detect. I smelled it from the moment they brought me into the room at Maui Medical Center.

It could have been worse, I suppose.

My first visitor was Detective Kyle Kekoa, of course. He pulled back the curtain like he was revealing the final act of a magic show. As though he was going to catch me doing something.

He was so big and frankly, I was sick of making eye contact with him. I stared instead at the little white board mounted to the wall behind him.

Written in Sharpie with a yellow smiley sticker, *Sawyer Grant's goals today: feel better and go home.*

What was home, at this point?

Kyle didn't waste a pleasantry on me. "Spoke to your doctor. Said you'd be up to continue that conversation we started back on Dickenson Street."

He was wearing another polo. This one was dark navy blue, stretched out around his arms and chest. I was beginning to think the only thing this guy did was hate me and lift weights. He had sunglasses on top of his head. I was hoping that meant he wasn't planning on staying long.

I kept looking at the yellow smiley next to my name on the progress board. "Didn't think there was anything more to finish."

The detective wasn't having it. I was a civilian, with the exception of my military background. What would this monster be like with an actual suspect?

Yowza.

I looked at him this time. "Seriously, what else do you want me to say. I told you about the girl and her dad. I told you something hit me about them."

Kyle nodded. "You did. And I told you I will never be upset for you sharing too much information. But there are still some things that remain in the question column with you."

"Such as?" I hit the button that made my hospital bed elevate at the speed of a snail's sabbatical. Honestly, I never felt less intimidating than motorizing myself up in my hospital Johnny to stare down Mr. Freaking Universe.

"The gun? It's dirty, Pastor. Serial numbers are bogus. Only prints on it are yours. Which kinda jives that you said it was from the church thief. But what would possess you to take—"

I interrupted him. I had been thinking through this one. I decided the truth might be in order. "Detective, the guy in the church tried to kill me. I figured it might be better to have a gun on me in case I was almost killed again."

"Good call, huh?"

"Not the worst decision I've made."

"Why didn't you call me when you saw the vehicle on Dickenson Street."

Despite the pain, I straightened up again. "Did you find it? The car. Was it where Elaina—"

"Pastor, you're not running an investigation here. I can't tell you anything about that, and you know it."

I stared at him. "You didn't find it."

He said nothing. He took the sunglasses off the top of his head and hung them off his polo.

"You hate that you lost it, and you're furious."

"Pastor—"

"No, let's just get it out. You had a problem with me being invited to that crime scene. You had a problem with me handling my business at the church and getting that guy to hit the street—"

"According to the report that was Mr. Gentry that got the thief—"

"I was gonna—I had the guy right where I wanted him, okay. But besides that, you have a problem with me and you have been itching to burn me since we met, so let's just open it up."

Kyle stepped back a little and looked at the ground. "I wanna really know what you're doing here."

Something in his tone shifted. This one was more accusatory than the surrounding questions of the incidents.

He didn't let me answer. He went on. "Why did you move from the East Coast with nothing but a duffel bag full of clothes? And at the hopes of getting a job that will pay you less than peanuts. You don't look, talk or act like a pastor—"

Kyle was holding back, and I was okay with that. Because this was a discussion I hadn't expected to have so soon on Maui. I wanted to at least get a tan and do some snorkeling.

"—something else. I checked the area you said you lived. Checked databases of people who served in the military. I have access to that kind of thing. There's no record of a Sawyer Grant from Pittsburgh that served. Nothing."

I felt pretty weightless in that moment. Like all the oxygen, along with the feeling in my hands and feet, along with every bit of confidence I could muster had been sucked out of the room with a vacuum.

My mouth instantly felt like microwaved crackers. Dry, warm, and completely incapable of communicating.

Kyle softened his gaze which meant only one thing. He knew that he had me. The bad cop was turning into a slightly more bearable version of the bad cop, but a victorious cop, nonetheless.

"We don't have to do this now, but you're not coming into our community and lying about everything. While at the same time finding yourself in the middle of some pretty terrible chaos."

I didn't know what else to say. "Well, if you consider the goings on in your community being a double homicide and a high-profile kidnapping, then I'd hope we would agree that you checking the references on my resume should be your lowest priority, Detective."

He chortled, looked down, shook his head, and looked back at me. Bad cop, coming in for the KO punch.

"Yeah, lying about everything to work for a church isn't just an exaggeration on your resume, Pastor. And yeah, your

Pittsburgh stuff is a hundred miles beyond my back burner, but—"

He paused for a long time, then put the sunglasses on as he walked toward the door. "You're still on my fire, Pastor."

"Metaphor's wearing thin there, Detective."

He left without saying goodbye, and it took me a moment to realize I'd been holding my breath.

THIRTY-EIGHT

It was a good call on Robertson's part to stake out the hospitals. Bob knew he'd done the preacher good with that blade. Two minutes longer and the pastor would have been called to glory and Bob would be resting in a job well done.

No such luck though.

Instead, he was sitting outside of Maui Medical Center. Just like when he was staking out Janice or whatever her name was, he brought along that Audi, against Robertson's wishes. He parked it in front of a dumpster around the corner. No one would see it. Bob didn't feel that he was in the mood to go boosting a ride after getting tweaked by that preacher. Plus, if he had gotten picked up grabbing a vehicle with a broken face, and a hole in his leg, it would have been game over.

He had grabbed some ice packs from a market and had taken turns switching them on his broken nose.

He cursed the preacher under his breath.

This guy needed to be taught a lesson. Bob was in the mood to educate tonight. Especially now that he was the one that had the element of surprise. Not like that dumpster fire that was Dickenson Street. That was an unfortunate turn.

Maui Medial Center was lit up like a Christmas tree amidst the otherwise dark area. Bob loved how it looked, its beautiful windows revealing all sorts of activity going on behind them. It looked a jewelry store boutique with the different lights shining out.

But Bob was only concerned with the preacher and where he was heading. This part of the plan was a bit of a Hail Mary, but hey, wasn't his operation. He was just the muscle.

If he hadn't been given the green light to sentence this man of the cloth to the afterlife, Bob planned on taking the liberty after the operation was over. After all, they were still in the USA, the land of the free.

When he had called the hospital to ask for information, he said he was a member of the church and to ask if he'd be able to stop by and see the pastor. Oddly, the nurses were pretty liberal about giving out information about patients when they thought they were talking to a man of God.

He might have to pull this religion angle more often. It was working for the preacher. Because the bullet hole in his leg (which Bob luckily was able to patch up) and his broken face proved that this man was not clergy. He didn't fight like a clergyman. He didn't come past a crime scene with two dead bodies like a clergyman.

This guy was something else.

The clouds looked like a faint afterimage in the sky, and Bob strained to see them. This was boring as all get out and he was hoping that something would happen soon. He had already scarfed a gas station sandwich, but his stomach was still rumbling. In Maui, a gas station sandwich tasted exactly like that. Nothing sexy at all.

After what seemed like a lifetime, he heard a familiar noise that brought pleasure to his pounding head and throbbing leg.

A loud-sounding muffler.

Sounded more like a lawnmower than a Honda. The driver pulled right past his Audi and up to the entrance of the Maui Medical Center. This was easy. He wasn't going to have to measure whether or not Grant was coming out. His girlfriend was going to do that.

It would be ideal if she took him home! Boy, that would make this situation a slam dunk.

He checked through his window to see the troublemaker that tried to tail him.

She was a fine-looking thing, pretty tight jeans and a top that was a little too conservative for Bob's taste. In his line of work, he was able to tell the girls how he wanted them to dress. It was a good arrangement.

The girl was Hawaiian and that made her easy on the eyes all day long. He was starting to like this job a little more, again. And, if Robertson gave him the green light, he might even be able to take this girl as a bit of a perk.

Bob would make her scream louder than the muffler on that Honda.

The Hawaiian Flower walked into Maui Medical center, and Bob opened his phone to give Robertson the good news. But first he had to shake himself out of the reverie.

There was still a chance to redeem this day!

THIRTY-NINE

I just had one final thing to do in the hospital, walk up and down the hall. I had gotten the transfusion, ate and drank, had a bathroom trip, and even managed movement in my shoulder despite the discomfort.

So, there I was, with a nice Hawaiian nurse who was as excited about me walking around the hospital corridor as I was about having to preach a sermon in seventy-two hours that I had not prepared for.

Yeah, I was still thinking about that even after seeing a double homicide and almost dying in the process. That's how freaked out I was that I had to speak. For the first time at Resurrection. It's true what they said. People really do fear public speaking more than death.

As I walked, and the lovely nurse texted feverishly, I suddenly realized that this had only been my second day on Maui. Day One I almost got shot at church. Day Two, stabbed.

Could I survive a week in this place?

Then I thought of the trouble at home. I thought of the duffel. I thought of why I ran.

I turned to head back into my room when my second and final visitor was there. She looked just as beautiful as when I'd met her at the church earlier. The look on Elaina's face was—

Troubled.

I hadn't been very forward with her, and though we'd only shared a couple interactions, I felt I owed her something. From the look on her face, she seemed to agree.

"Figured I should probably speak to you before you come to work on Monday to learn about Resurrection. Or are you taking a sick day?"

"Hear anything from Hargrove?" My mind went to those dead people on Dickenson Street. And I thought about Hargrove's daughter.

Somehow this whole thing was connected to her—it had to be.

The nurse looked up for a moment, but then went right back to her phone. She looked like she was perhaps Crushing some Candy, as the kids were doing these days.

"Not to me. He just texted me and asked if you were okay. I told Stu what had happened with you."

Hargrove had also texted me. Stu had texted me as well, saying something along the lines of trouble following me like sinners followed John the Baptist.

I was starting to feel connected to this big dysfunctional family.

But I saw something in Elaina's eyes. Something concerning. I switched subjects.

"Doctor said guy didn't hit anything I'd need to be a preacher. Good luck day."

"Yes, but apparently the doctor doesn't know the non-preachery type things you've been up to."

Elaina was immune to my charms at this point. She

added, "What is going on? What happened and why are you in the center of it? And the girl from Dickenson Street? We need to talk about her, too."

Ugh, I had just done this with Kyle.

I leaned against the hospital wall. I was exhausted but not from what I'd experienced physically. My shoulder was sore. I think I was due for another pain cocktail. I'd pitch the pain killers and opt for ibuprofen later.

"This is honestly a classic case of 'wrong place, wrong time.'"

Her face was as expressionless as it was beautiful. She had changed out of that church dress and was wearing a pair of blue jeans and a deep purple short-sleeved shirt. Dressier than a t-shirt but she looked relaxed.

"I don't think that's possible. What did you expect to find in that house?"

I didn't want to bring this lady into my thoughts. Plus, the hospital hall, with the bustle of nurses in and out of rooms, elevators dinging, and patients doing their exercises around us, I didn't think it was an appropriate forum to put out a conspiracy theory.

"Look, I don't wanna share any more with you. I apologize for bringing you into this and please, I promise, I'm just here for the church work."

She pushed open my door and motioned with her arm for me to enter. "I'll drive you back to the hotel. You can share as much information as you can in the car ride. And I had a conversation with the girl, the one who's life you saved."

It was nice that she said that. But the appearance looked like I was saving my own skin. Especially to Detective Kyle Kekoa.

What could the girl have said, though?

I stood upright, not leaning, and tried to do my best to be a little more forceful.

"Hey, I said I wasn't going to share anything more. Honestly, I don't want to put you in this situation." I walked in the room ahead of her and to the pile of mangled clothes that had been graciously stuffed in a hospital Ziplock.

"You've already shared more than you wanted, Pastor," Elaina said. "You should have had your nurse tie up your hospital Johnny."

FORTY

Kyle sat at his house, breakfast nook of course. The rest of the house was absurdly dark. Sometimes he wondered what the neighbors thought about when they looked in his house to see it dark most times.

When his wife was alive, his house was a hub of activity. It looked like a museum now. A relic of days gone by.

But in the nook, the uncomfortable bench, the table, there was a bit of a reunion going on. A reconvening with the files from the Hargrove kidnapping and the Dickenson Street homicide spilling over the table.

What was missing?

A file about Sawyer Grant. The mystery mainlander. The Pittsburgh marine with a desire to bring the Gospel to the suffering residents of Maui.

What was that guy up to? Kidnapping scene, homicide scene, and the secretary? Involving the secretary.

That was the other bad part. He pulled the yellow legal pad out. He and Detective Lulani Aukai, the junior detective, had investigated Elaina's lookout. Nothing there but a bunch of tourists more concerned about their Instagram filters than standing too close to the edge of a dangerous cliff.

That's one of the things that made Maui so interesting to Kyle. It was so dangerous. There were so many different parts of it—the highways, how dark it got at night compared to other places, the cliffs, the oceans—but tourists acted like they were immune to these things because of how beautiful it was on Maui.

An orphaned girl from Dickenson Street and a kidnapped girl could attest to just how dangerous it was.

He had just finished a grilled burger and veggies. He was starting to get sleepy, but he also was tired from the events of the last couple days.

That's when his phone rang. He hoped it would be Hargrove with some sort of communication from the kidnapper with a list of demands.

It wasn't.

"This is Kekoa."

His other detective, the one that had been stationed at the hospital, was on the other end. "Yeah, the pastor's on the move."

"Figured as much. He Uber?"

"Nope, secretary again," the detective said. "I'll let you know what's going to happen. Pretty sure they're heading back to the Aston. I'll keep a tail and let you know if anything happens when they get there."

This is exactly what Kyle had wanted. He asked Detective Aukai to babysit the medical center after Kyle concluded the makeshift interrogation with the preacher. Every time Sawyer Grant moved, trouble followed. Detective Aukai was good, ambitious, and hungry.

"Thanks, Lulani. Thanks for hanging out and I'm sure it will be uneventful," Kyle said and immediately hung up the phone.

Kyle really wasn't sure.

FORTY-ONE

Sawyer Grant told Elaina all that she'd asked, and she did believe him. There wasn't anything more that he could say. His timing in all of these situations sucked.

She thought about looking at his file when she passed him for the job.

Outlier.

He also seemed the least presumptuous of the other candidates. But he was smart.

They walked into the lobby of the Aston Kaanapali. She'd never been there. Never had occasion to stay somewhere so nice. As the automatic door opened before her, she felt ashamed thinking about the shared walled apartment she called home on the "poor" side of town.

Which, was there such a thing on Maui?

But who would be indulgent enough to stay there?

Grant looked pale. She knew enough medically to know that he was going to crash like the Hindenburg as soon as his head hit the pillow.

They continued to lightly talk about the various terrible situations he'd been in since coming to Maui. Elaina absently found herself exiting the elevator with him when they arrived to his floor. The outdoor corridor greeted them as the music blared from the courtyard beneath. It was seven floors up, and Elaina could hear every lyric of the songs playing from the little straw hut bar. She was also certain that the hotel was swanky enough to make sure that the rooms, and the doors entering them, were sound proof. As high up as they were, the invading ocean breeze still smelled like heaven.

There was something about her that didn't want that conversation with Sawyer Grant to end. Though she knew she needed to get home, Elaina didn't want to see him off. She was going to ask him how he felt about the classic movies she liked. *Philadelphia Story, Mr. Smith Goes to Washington*—classics.

Elaina had almost told him that he'd reminded her of Jimmy Stewart, as odd as that might sound.

"Look," he said as he steadied himself against the wall. He'd done the same thing in the hospital. "I don't want to give you the impression that I want you to follow me into my room. I'm not that kind of preacher, young lady."

"Well, I'm just trying to make sure you don't get yourself killed anymore today." She was kidding.

But not really.

He laughed and pulled out his key card from his little hospital baggie of destroyed clothes. "Only chance of that is if those sheets are 200-thread count instead of 400, because sleeping in such conditions would positively end me."

Elaina couldn't help it, she laughed out loud. "Are you going take anything seriously, Pastor Grant?"

He looked down at the ground, almost as though he was embarrassed. Elaina hadn't intended to do that, but she wasn't going to apologize either. He'd given her a long day.

"Good night, Elaina. I'm seriously sorry about all this. Two people died today, another girl is left without parents, and one is missing. Humor is what God has gifted me with in addition to good looks and amazing communication skills."

"Light on humility, though, huh?"

He smiled and walked back into his room.

Elaina watched him the whole way.

FORTY-TWO

Bob had gotten a little more pineapple from a fruit stand on the way back in. He figured he owed himself. This job was not at all what was advertised. Hopefully, Robertson would give him a little more than their agreed-upon price.

He cursed the preacher under his breath. Felt like his face had been hit with a waffle iron.

Bob ditched the ski mask. That was worn out. Now, he wore a pair of athletic shorts with a black t-shirt he'd bought at a souvenir stand. He had a baseball cap on that read "Hang Loose" with some neon green pines on the brim. He also had to wear sunglasses, on account of the preacher rearranging his face.

Maybe he'd go to church some time. He'd love to show up and give that guy the sermon illustration of his life. With a bullet to the head.

Thoughts of rage and hate typically didn't last long with Bob, but this was different. First, the preacher stopped the church part of the assignment. Then he botched the Dickenson Street hit. This guy deserved it at this point.

And Bob wasn't especially keen on killing kids for sport,

but with parents like the one the Dickenson Street girl had, she probably would have ended up dead early anyway.

Bob rubbed his hands together rapidly, attempting to rid them of the pineapple residue. He needed his grip. He pulled out the pistol. A .40 caliber.

This would leave little chance of survival.

Robertson better be increasing his price with all this.

Especially since he was now carrying the weight of Riggins along with him.

And now, Bob got to do what he really wanted to do.

He was on the seventh floor, same floor as Sawyer Grant. And he was overlooking the courtyard. It was a pretty brilliant plan.

Bob had watched the girl, the pretty little Hawaiian thing, leave his room and absentmindedly board the elevator.

It was a bonus that Bob saw how Grant was babying his shoulder on the way in. That made him happy.

Next time, it'll be the throat. Next time he'd take a knife right into his throat.

However, despite Bob's bitterness, the new plan would probably do more psychological damage to Grant in the long run than just killing him. And he was glad to be a part of it.

Bob stood up and made his way to the stairs to get into position.

It was time to set this thing in motion.

And in the end, Bob would probably still kill Grant anyway.

FORTY-THREE

Nothing but breaks for Lulani.

He sat there doing literally the most boring job he'd ever done. Waiting for a preacher to make some sort of move. He felt bad because he had tackled the preacher earlier and made him pass out.

Well, Lulani hadn't made him pass out, per se. He had just started doing cross fit, and his ability to move quickly increased with every session. But the preacher had quite a shoulder injury that had most likely caused him to fade into black for a bit.

This was one of his first assignments out of patrol it was pretty, pretty fine.

But then, there was the business with Ani. What of that?

Lulani sat at the large open-air courtyard area of the Kaanapali resort. He was resting on a stool that had been previous occupied by one of those Time Share vampires that always promised you something for a two-hour presentation.

Swanky as could be. The water feature in the courtyard alone most like likely was worth more than what Lulani would make in—well, he didn't want to even measure the years. But it was mucho.

On the subject of catching breaks, Lulani wanted one badly. He wanted to somehow have Ani and his new role as detective. He could never get enough of Ani. He'd thought of how she'd tossed him his badge back.

She couldn't have meant that she didn't want him to choose her.

The thought of the interaction made him want to go to the hut-looking bar that sat in the open courtyard.

In fact, as a patrolman, many times he and some of his buddies found themselves at some awesome after-hours haunts. A day beating the street, responding to domestic calls and pulling over speeding tourists earned him the right to get a little sloppy from time to time.

But Ani showed him that you didn't need booze to be happy.

So there Lulani stood, looking at some patrons that were doing exactly that. Lulani longed to be at the bar, designed to look like a hut with a straw roof. There were some lively people there, talking, laughing.

He could have been one of them.

He was wearing tan khakis and a black button shirt, tucked in. He looked like a cop compared to the tourists, but from what he understood, if he lived on the mainland this would be dressed down for a detective. He may have overdone it a little bit, because he had his gold badge attached to his belt along with his service revolver.

Now that he didn't have to dress like a patrolman, he loved the vibes he'd put out wearing those kinds of clothes with his shield for people to see. It wasn't like he was under-cover. It wasn't like he was hiding that he was watching this shady preacher.

Good vibes.

When the receptionist came over from the front desk, she was gunning for him. For a moment, Lulani thought that she was going to tell him to go somewhere else, almost as if she were reading his thoughts about wanting nothing more to do than party.

But she didn't.

"You're a detective, right," she asked. She had a nicely pressed, dark black uniform on with a white collared shirt underneath. Nothing but swanky at this place.

"Yes, ma'am. Help you with something?"

"No, not actually." She held a sticky note up at eye level to look over a note someone had scrawled. "There is a Sawyer Grant, he's a guest up on the seventh floor, he asked if I could let you know that he'd be coming down in a couple minutes. He said he had some business to discuss with you."

Lulani could hardly speak. What a turn.

"Yes, perfect. I'll be here."

The concierge smiled as she walked back to her place at the front desk.

This was unreal. Absolutely perfect.

He couldn't get to his phone fast enough to text Detective Kekoa.

"Bossman," he said out loud to no one. "After this, you will be giving me the rest of the night off! Yowwwww!" He looked longingly at the Tiki hut bar. But he thought even more about Ani. Maybe they could sort through their business tonight.

Maybe she'd ask him for that badge. And a life with him.

At least he caught a break with the preacher that finally wanted to talk.

Easy work with a good ending. Good vibes.

FORTY-FOUR

Getting back to her car, she recounted to herself everything about that day. From the church service, Dickenson Street, to the black expensive-looking car that she'd tailed going on Route 30.

Once inside her beat-up Civic, she was reminded of how poor she was. Well, poor was a state of mind. Once she finished school, and started working in her career, she would be able to afford to stay in some place as nice as this.

But she wouldn't want to do that. She knew the value of a buck.

She tried calling Stu Gentry again. Elaina needed to talk to someone about all of what happened, but couldn't seem to think of anyone but him. He had always been the person she could talk to. Even when the church went through the chaos of losing the pastor. Stu was steady.

She also wanted to get his take on this preacher. She knew that he'd spent some time with Grant the previous night, and that they were both involved with that break-in, but she still didn't entirely trust Grant.

Stu still wasn't answering. Elaina hoped he was okay.

Elaina drove out onto the road, leading her back to 30. She glanced left at the Times Supermarket lot. There was a concentrated cluster of cars in front of the entrance, but for the most part the lot was pretty empty.

She would have kept going but something caught her eye and made her do a double take, while at the same time laying off the gas of the Civic.

Elaina noticed one random car before pulling out on Route 30. And after that second look, she slammed her brakes and cried out to God.

The jet black sports car was parked in the lot. The same one she'd tailed earlier.

And that meant Grant was in trouble.

FORTY-FIVE

I had just started to get a minute past comfortable in the room when the front desk rang to tell me that there was a detective that wanted to see me.

The room was easily the nicest room I'd ever been in, but with my insomnia from last night, my lack of ability to come to it at all today, and the fact that right now I was going to have to go downstairs and answer questions that I'd already answered, I'd say that Stu could have just hooked me up by giving me a cot in the furnace room of Resurrection Church.

The room had a huge eating area with wicker table and a glass top. There were six seats, five more than I'd need.

There was a breakfast bar in the kitchen with stools and stainless steel appliances that I'd never use. It had two bedrooms and even a laundry room. I thought about using the laundry tomorrow considering the one suit I had was toast, and I only had one rather simple outfit. Blue button-down short sleeve shirt and a pair of blue jeans. Same ones, coincidentally, I was wearing in that dream that also had a lot of memory mixed in.

I left my room, checked the door behind me and prepared to meet the detective. This was getting old. I hadn't slept. My shoulder throbbed. I was hungry. The office administrator saw my bum in the hospital Johnny.

Today had sucked.

I hit the button and turned around to face the open air of the deck. It was dark, but the light from the pool area below and the lights of the individual rooms made the hotel almost seem like a helipad. Any aircraft could land there. I sucked in that air. When would it get old?

But more so, when would trouble give me a break?

I assumed that Detective Kyle Kekoa had people watching me, and I knew that there was more going on, but I had to cooperate. It was my only chance of making it here. Otherwise, I might as well head back to Pittsburgh and dance with the Devil that I knew.

I did find it pretty odd that Kyle would send someone to interview me now after he'd come to the hospital. Watch me, sure. But not ask me more questions. We were coming dangerously close to police harassment. I might have even had enough to file a grievance.

But I had to play it cool. This was it. If I had even the appearance of guilt, Kyle would be on me like a pit bull on a porterhouse. And probably not be as graceful about it, either.

I got off the elevator and I looked into the courtyard. I saw a little cabana-looking bar thing with a bunch of sloppy fools gathered around it. In another life I'd be one of them. But now, I was a man of the cloth.

He was standing there like he was the most brilliant man that ever lived. Maybe he'd found the girl and the police were going to thank me for preventing another girls' kidnapping (or worse) on Dickenson Street.

This guy needed to take lessons from Detective Squats-A-Lot on how to lift, because he was skinny.

My phone vibrated and I opened and answered without checking the Caller ID. I stopped just outside the elevator. The detective still hadn't noticed me.

I heard Elaina's voice and instantly begin turning on the charm.

"Look, if you're asking me if I'll—"

"Grant," she said.

As always, she found me as funny as a paper cut.

"Yeah, Elaina."

"Grant, I don't know what's going on, but you have to—"

"Elaina, I'm just about to meet a detective. He called to ask me some more questions. Can I call—"

"Grant, you have to run. Run. Get out of there."

It sounded almost like she was going to cry. I stood frozen.

"The car, the black one, sporty. It's over in the lot across from the hotel, they must've tracked us or something—"

I had a striking moment of sentimentality that she would call with such worry, but it didn't last. That's when the shot went off.

FORTY-SIX

Moani Wong had been out of the loop with regard to the preacher they were bringing in to preach on Wednesday.

How could they do that? How dare they make him feel this way? He and his mom had been too good to the church. And besides, this guy was incompetent.

Afraid to preach?

Moani was in his office. Well, it was a basement office that he'd repurposed. His mom had called it his study. She was going to remodel it for him, but instead chose to use the funds to remodel the preacher's office at Resurrection Church. Which was fine. Moani would end up there anyway.

The joists in the ceiling had silver canister lights suspended in between them, beaming down onto an old wooden desk. It was made of mahogany, and his mother had always told Moani that the desk would be there even after their home was bulldozed to the ground.

He had an iPad, a blue Gatorade, and a Moleskine notebook on the desk. He was working on the wording for something very special.

"Moani, are you coming up, hun? Dinner is just about done." His mom always made dinner super late on Sunday nights on account of their Cheesecake Factory tradition after church.

Moani had tried to eliminate this habit, as his suit seemed to be tighter and tighter each Sunday, but he was a man of tradition.

Her voice frustrated him that night. This happened to Moani when he was really busy on something. And this was important.

"Mom, I'll be up shortly, I'm working on a church thing, huh."

He was already getting distracted by the cooking—smells of the Huli-Huli chicken she was preparing pulled at his concentration. She made the best Hawaiian cuisine of anyone on the island. The smells were wafting down the steps, but he didn't need much longer.

He heard her voice call down from the top of the steps. "What church thing? Sermon? I thought you were ahead on those."

He wished she would just let his answer be his answer. She always had to follow up everything with another question, as though his answer or opinion didn't matter.

"No, it's something administrative." He paused. "It's something for the new preacher that's coming."

"What?" Her voice changed and she started descending the steps, stopping halfway down.

"No, look, Mom," he said, turning and putting up his hands signifying that she stop. "I'll be up shortly. I'm trying to show I'm a team player. Initiative. God says a lot about envy, you know."

His mom clapped her hands together and smiled. "My baby boy. So virtuous. I'm so proud of you."

He smiled at her, held the gaze and then went back to the iPad.

A preacher afraid of public speaking. What a joke.

Moani had the intention of helping Sawyer Grant to get over his fear of public speaking. The best way is with practice. And with a big audience.

He'd connected to all of the local Maui church groups and designed a really nice ad. Maybe some of the best internet work that he'd ever done.

The ad was simple. It was a picture of the familiar Maui backdrop. It had the mountains and the sun beaming over them with the ocean showcasing the unique topography. But the ad copy was over-the-moon good.

Come this Wednesday night to hear from Sawyer Grant, the Paradise Preacher that boarded a plane all the way to Maui just to share a message on what God wants for your life.

He smiled as he fiddled with the text contrast on the ad. It shaped up way better than he'd thought. And, he thought the way the ad was written it would garner quite a few visits to the church. Maybe even more than they had Sunday.

"Moani," his mother called again. "Your food is going to get cold."

"Coming up, Mom," he said. He stood up still holding the iPad in his hands. He thought about Grant. Thought about stage fright. And couldn't help offering a quick prayer to God that this would be the last time he'd have to deal with someone who wanted to take the job that Moani should have had.

Mom's cooking smelled even better than it did before. He set the iPad back on his desk, after he hit "publish."

FORTY-SEVEN

Lulani was ready to talk to Sawyer Grant, then immediately he'd be at the tiki hut. Maybe a little liquid courage would help to guide his conversation with Ani.

No chance Kyle was going to have him do anything else on a Sunday night. Heck, if this went well with Grant, and depending how it went with Ani, he might even treat himself to a vacation day tomorrow.

The boss's text was a little unappreciative. He said he'd be coming by later to debrief with him.

Maybe Grant had chosen to talk to Lulani because he was a lot easier to get along with.

Win more battles with honey than with salt, bossman.

He saw the beat-up preacher step out into the lobby, looking around for him. Then he took a call.

Popular guy maybe.

The dude had a super frenzied look on his face. Lulani was pretty certain if he'd had the kind of days that preacher boy had, he'd also be feeling strung out.

Yep, Grant was gonna tell Lulani everything. Maybe even confess his involvement. This would be his big break.

He'd shine like a star in Detective Kyle Kekoa's book, he'd get a bonus for catching a mainlander that was causing such a ruckus in Maui, and in the end, Ani might even want to reconcile with him and start this thing up again. Maybe she'd ask Lulani for his badge.

And despite how much he loved being a detective, he'd toss that badge her way again in a heartbeat.

This was all gonna work out just fine.

Lulani was straightening up his shirt. He wanted to have the intimidating persona that Kekoa had. Grant wasn't going to push Lulani around, that was for certain.

Grant moved closer, looking at him with that worn and weary face.

Sermon's over preacher. Now let's get to business.

Even if he had to resign to be with Ani, Lulani daydreamed of what a career-making break he was about to experience here.

And then the bullet went through his head.

FORTY-EIGHT

The detective that had asked the receptionist to page me to come down was still in the courtyard. Well, his body was in the courtyard. It stood in an inanimate state, because the detective's head had been blown apart. The wound in his head looked as big as a silver dollar, but blood and brain decorated his face and the dark tile floor beneath him.

I don't know how long the body stood before it collapsed. Longer than it should have, but not long enough for me to be able to count.

Elaina was ringing my cell. I ignored it. Her words broke into my mind.

Grant, run.

And I was off. I didn't go to the elevator, I went right for the steps. I did so to the sound of screams, and wailing from the scene.

Yet another murder scene.

My shoulder pain was through the roof, but I put it in a completely different compartment. I was basing everything I did on nothing but instincts.

I knew that the elevators were going to clog up. People were trying to get back to their rooms. As I got up to the fifth flight, I heard a frenzy of talking on the other side of the doors. Word was traveling up that there was as shooter in Aston Kaanapali.

As I reached the final set of steps, the wind burning my lungs as it exited and my muscles feeling pushed, I realized that everyone in this hotel was safe. The killer set me up. I was being dealt with because I was causing too much trouble.

I got up to seven, and I smelled the powder.

He had to have done it on my floor. He did it on purpose. If I had longer, I'd look for the shell casing. Probably shot him right from the balcony overlooking that stupid hut.

I took my key out and with shaky hands, opened the door to my room and didn't bother shutting it behind me. I had maybe ten minutes. Fifteen at most. The front desk people would pull it together. They would think I killed this police officer because he wanted to meet with me.

I didn't think the charges would stick, but I'd definitely be tied up for a while. Detecitve Kyle Kekoa would be sniffing like a blood hound.

There was no chance I'd keep my freedom and there was no chance that I could find Janeen.

I grabbed the duffel out of the top of the closet. I threw in the few outfits (all the outfits) I had into it. Then I started grabbing what I had hidden at the dumpster of the Lahaina Intermediate School.

Lord Jesus, I wish I had a gun. I wish I had some sort of a weapon to defend—

No sooner had I thought the prayer that I heard the door creak behind me.

I was dead. Since I was on my knees it would take them two seconds to kill me execution-style.

So I turned to face the killer. And there was Elaina, staring down at me, with my duffel. That panicked look was back again. I had a feeling she'd forever associate that look with my presence.

Elaina wasn't staring at me that way, though. And I understood why, of course.

She was staring at the contents of my duffel, which was, give or take, over $100,000 in cash.

"Grant, did—"

"Come on," I said, standing up as I zipped the bag, throwing it over my good shoulder but feeling exhausted.

"I'm about to be framed for murder. And that makes you an accessory."

FORTY-NINE

Robertson was back in his driveway when the call came in. The kids were still playing outside, and he stepped onto the sidewalk to distance himself from their banter.

It was Bob.

"Tell me better news than earlier, please."

"Contingency complete, bossman. Leaving the hotel about to hop into the car."

Relief flooded over him. Suddenly his children's laughs sounded like heaven. The air smelled purer.

This situation may have even worked out better than he expected. The preacher now was going to be detained, most likely by the same detective that had gone after him at the Dickenson Street scene. And maybe, if they didn't dig too deep, they might pin it all on Grant.

Sometimes it was better to leave someone alive than to kill them. Despite his ability to do so, Billy didn't always like the idea of having to end a person's life. Especially a preacher. Something about that felt challenging, even though the idea of God seemed so foreign to Billy.

But something didn't sit well with the timing of every-thing for Billy.

"You really moved everything into place quickly. How did you boost a ride so fast," Billy asked. "I thought that would take you a lot longer."

Bob didn't respond. Billy had a bad feeling. He didn't double check the details. But Bob's hesitation spoke volumes.

"Bob, where *did* you get the car? We never talked about it."

More silence.

"Bob, are you still there?" As he spoke he took a swizzle stick out of his pocket and popped it into his mouth. It helped him think.

"Yeah, here. Uh, didn't get around to ditching that Audi yet, but I'm going to do that now."

Billy felt exhausted all of a sudden. He felt his face getting flush and it was his turn not to speak.

The idea that Bob would take a car that was implicated in a previous crime with him to commit another crime was beyond infuriating.

"You there, bossman?"

"Yes," Billy said.

"I—didn't wanna lose the time. I figured—I'm on my way to ditch it now. I'll make sure it's gone soon. Trust me. You'll be glad I did the hotel deal because that preacher is toast now."

Billy didn't respond. He took a moment to listen to his kids playing. Sometimes, they would just launch into their own dialects, with intermittent bursts of giggles and sound effects for good measure. Billy didn't understand it. Ellen didn't understand it. But the kids had fun.

"Listen, Bob. This seemingly simple operation has

morphed into something anything but simple. I can't have you disobey what I tell you to do again."

"But I—"

"Listen to me closely, if you can't understand this (he thought of his kids' gibberish), you will be dead inside an hour. Is that clear enough?"

Now, it was Bob's turn to be silent.

"Your silence shows I'm understood, Bob. Remember, you're helping me do this. If I have to keep reinventing the plan based on stupidity, one of us is nonessential."

He thought of Riggins and the dive he had taken off that cliff.

Billy didn't like meeting in conventional places because the people that he typically employed were some of the most unstable in the world.

It was amazing how cheaply you could hire someone to do incredibly unspeakable things. But just like all animals, they needed to be trained.

"What's next, then," Bob asked. His voice sounded more even.

Billy had already made the decision to kill him the moment Bob questioned him. All animals need to be trained.

And sometimes, put down.

FIFTY

The transmission of the Explorer jerked as Kyle flew down the highway.

Kyle was barely able to process what had just taken place. Detective Lulani Aukai was dead.

Dead.

He had just spoken to him. All he was doing was watching the preacher. The fact that Kyle had gotten the preacher so wrong made Kyle sick. Next time, there would be no second chance. This sum bag was going to stay on Maui, alright.

In a cell for a long time. Maybe even get the needle for cop killing.

The tires screeched as he made the bends of Route 30. A couple times, Kyle was a little afraid of running the car off the road. He thought of how his wife had hated his driving. She said he always drove like he was in a hurry for his own funeral.

Lots of irony in that, considering he'd buried her.

But it was an occupational hazard.

His phone rang and he let up off the gas a little. He was still ten minutes away.

"Kekoa," he said. He didn't look at the phone, but kept his eyes glued to the road ahead.

"Detective, this is Sawyer Grant."

At Grant's voice, Kyle almost veered the car into a guardrail. He would have ended up over a cliff in the drink, and that would have made four deaths this pastor was involved in.

"Where are you, Grant?" He tried to sound calm, but his voice came out almost like a growl.

"Listen, Detective, this was a set up. There's—"

"You killed one of my—"

"No, please, you have to listen. I'm going to cooperate—"

"Cooperate?" Kyle slowed down a little more, trying to compensate for his lack of control on the call.

The police siren attached to the dash bounced its familiar troubled lights off the jagged landscape on the right.

"Yes, believe it or not, we want the same exact thing. I wanna catch this guy too, honestly."

"Grant, you are the guy. Don't even tell me you're going to cop a plea of in—"

"Listen, please listen because I know I don't have much time." Grant's voice sounded worn out and worried, as it should.

As soon as Kyle saw him, he was definitely going to work Grant over a little.

"You have to get an APB on that black Audi. The one that Elaina had trailed today."

"Yeah, you mean that black Audi that doesn't exist. The

black Audi that conveniently had been reported stolen. Your unicorn Audi. Why don't you just tell me where you put it. You'll save us all time and money and no one else has to die."

Kyle was getting close to the scene. He thought of Detective Aukai. Rage filled him to the brim. Aukai was so happy to be moved to detective. He was good at it. He was confident.

Now he was dead.

Grant continued, "Listen, please. If you find that car, you'll find the killer. And also, what did the girl—the orphaned girl from Dickenson Street—what did she say—"

Kyle smacked his hand off the wheel. "Do you really think I'm going to share details about anything with a suspect. When I see you—"

"Please detective, I can find out who kidnapped this girl. I might even be able to figure out where she is. But you have to try to trust me. I am giving you all the information that I can, but you can't arrest me. That's what they want. They want me out of the way."

"You're a cop killer and a coward. And when I see you, I'll treat you as such."

Kyle hung the phone up, infuriated that he somehow didn't have a way to trace the call.

The other flashing police cars illuminated the road leading to Aston Kaanapali.

As Kyle waited to turn into where all the police cars had migrated, he sat at the light and waited from the green.

As it turned green, the oncoming traffic going right onto 30 started moving. Kyle had no other car behind him coming into the street leading to Aston. And he slammed his brakes on.

Coming out of the complex was a black Audi, with windows tinted as dark as paint.

In the force, Kyle was known as the most decisive. He knew what he had to do and when to do it. Detectives like Aukai expected him to make the tough calls.

The Audi pulled out onto 30 and Kyle sat in the middle of the street. He couldn't see anything as it turned, and it went the speed limit.

"It might not even be the same car." He said out loud to no one.

Follow this car or go into the Aston and find the murderer that actually killed the detective.

He couldn't make the call. He was paralyzed and he knew his window to track the Audi was closing.

"What grounds would I have for pulling him over? Some preacher said you were really the murderer and imagined your car at a church and on a street with a double homicide."

He could follow and just get the tags and see if it was the stolen one.

He glanced over to outside the Aston, the flashing lights, combined with his flashing lights.

Kyle slowly put his foot down on the accelerator, and advanced toward the Aston.

"I don't let killers call the shots," Kyle said to himself as he prepared to tear the Aston apart looking for Sawyer Grant.

FIFTY-ONE

Somehow, I found myself back in Elaina's car, the exhaust intermittently invading the tight cabin. She was driving, but her mind was a million miles elsewhere.

I brought her into this. This poor church administrator is now chauffeuring the prime suspect in several grisly murders. I rubbed my hair which was damp with sweat. Probably from pain meds wearing off (and boy, were they ever) and the tension. But since seeing that young detective's head exploding, this was the first time I'd felt like resting.

Here, with this stranger.

"What do we do, Grant. You're going to go to jail. They're going to think you killed that guy."

"Yeah, but I had no motive."

"Motive," she said, keeping her hands at ten and two but going just slightly above the speed limit. "He was there to watch you to see if you were doing anything shady. And now he's dead."

"Well, okay, you stated the obvious, but it's going to be—"

"Where did you get all the money? That *cash*?"

Okay, I preferred her stating the obvious, that was better.

We were driving on some back streets near Dickenson. I felt uneasy when I saw the street sign. I was beginning to associate Maui with death.

"Are you a killer?" She was scared to ask.

"That's complicated."

The car swerved a little and Elaina regained control. I was a little nervous we were going to have an accident.

"What does that—it's either yes or no? You're either a drug dealer, a criminal, a killer—why do you have a bag full of money?"

I don't know why, but I honestly didn't want to lie to her. I felt like it was being—I don't know—unfair. She was the reason, after all, that I was here being interviewed. But at the same time, the story that I had was just as unfathomable as being a part of all this chaos and having no part in it.

Both things were true, but harder to swallow than a horse pill.

"The money—is it like—for a contract—or something?"

Elaina was so close to the actual truth of the origin, but to say yes would force me to tell her. And about my dream.

And as she was desperately trying to figure out my story, I couldn't help but find her undeniably attractive. She was so strong. Maybe stronger than any girl I'd met. She came back to help me, but she didn't have to. She could have gotten killed.

To say I liked her was the biggest understatement.

"Yes, it was money for a contract I had."

"You're a preacher, for crying out loud!"

I could tell that she was at the breaking point. Not that

she would do anything like call a detective and turn me in, but that breaking point where she was genuinely trying to determine if I was a bad person.

People did that. They had to cross that threshold. And most people are gracious. They want to give others the benefit of the doubt. But I exceeded my shadiness to Elaina. And to the church, for that matter. The thought that any of these people would want to hire me had now become pure fantasy.

Maui was really starting to suck.

"Okay," I said. First, keeping my tone even in hopes that she wouldn't wreck the little rickety Civic, "Here it is. You know my resume. You know about my military service. Well—could I just say that I was on a bad path until God put me on a different one."

"Umm, no you can't say that."

"You shouldn't swear at a preacher." I mainly said that to try to lighten the mood, but I could see by her face that my humor was having its usual effectiveness here.

"Grant, please. People are getting killed. What's your deal?"

I heard that break-up thing in her voice again. Dear Lord, I didn't want this to happen. I just wanted to get the job, fade into obscurity and enjoy paradise doing something with my life that I thought might actually make a difference.

No dice.

"Okay, here it is. But I need something in return from you?"

Her jaw dropped open and I felt her on the verge of punching me in the face.

"No, Elaina, listen. Just hear me out."

She closed her mouth, and tightened her grip on the wheel. I felt her car seeming less out of control as we drove.

I also felt like I was going to pass out because of the throbbing pain in my shoulder, my head, my stomach. Just a big freaking mess.

"Elaina, the people that are doing all this are very, very bad people. They are gonna kill me. They are gonna kill anyone around me. I made enemies when I messed up the Dickenson Street plan, I know. The church was the tip of the iceberg. There's something all connected here and I know that Hargrove's daughter's at the center of it."

She didn't say anything. Silent. Still breathtakingly beautiful. But quiet.

"So, here's the deal. Help me figure this out because I obviously am up a creek without you, and also because at this point, I need to keep my eye on you. These guys are serious."

She stole a glance in my direction. I couldn't entirely read it, but I felt like it was equal parts understanding and also fear.

"I'm going to tell you as much as I have ever told anyone about me, but in return, help me to burn this operation to the ground."

She didn't say anything. But she did nod.

I felt relief, and as I always do, I was just about to start talking some more when she said quietly, "We're gonna need help."

Okay. Okay. Now, we were in this.

FIFTY-TWO

Stu Gentry had disassembled some of the sound system of his Mercedes. He wanted to have something a little more current in the dash to listen to tunes, but he had been super lazy about doing the work.

Much like when he'd been inventing things, Stu went through frenzied times of working obsessively on a project. Those times would be followed by lulls of nothing. He was never a steady-drip kind of guy. It was all flow or no.

Such was the case with the Benz. He started working hours after he'd gotten home from church and finished supper. His being a bachelor at this point in time made it easy to not have to worry about an agenda.

In his garage, the lighting was fantastic. He had enough fluorescents overhead to light a room three times the size. Stu hated dark spots. He hated losing things on the floor and having to get flashlights to look for those things.

When he designed the garage, he had the contractors make this room as bright as they could. And they didn't disappoint. The house was a modest ranch on Maui. Just enough space for him and an occasional guest, if needed. But that time hadn't really come.

The only part of Stu's place that really looked lived in was the garage. All the tools out in different sections. On one workbench, he had inventions he was tinkering with. On another, he had some things he'd brought from the church that he was messing with. Some automated lighting and things that would help make his job a little easier.

One whole bench was devoted to cap guns and other similar types of toys. Some might say that it was where he worked on "weapons." But Stu figured it this way. Guns, bombs, anything with the appearance of danger only became weapons depending on whose hands they were in.

Under this roof, they were just projects. Things to tinker with.

One thing Stu hated doing was leaving his phone on when he was working on a project in a garage. That's why he didn't notice until he took a break to grab a Pellegrino that he'd missed four calls from Miss Elaina. She'd also sent him a couple texts, which he read. One of them was an urgent invitation to come to Resurrection Church.

He got that rumbling feeling people get in their stomachs when bad things are about to go down.

Stu said out loud to the disassembled car parts on his work bench, "What are you getting us into this late Sunday evening, Rev?"

FIFTY-THREE

Ani felt tingles through her arms as she entered the automatic doors of Aston Kaanapali. All of the sights hit her at once.

The press gathered around the crime scene. Ani took in a moment of relief knowing that they wouldn't ask her questions. She had a pair of jeans on with a dark black t-shirt. She didn't look like a cop, but a guest.

Cameras and recorders restricted by the yellow tape. Medical examiners pulled out a body bag. Aukai's body bag. They were going to put him there, where he would remain until the autopsy, as if that would be necessary.

The Crime Scene Investigators stood around a body near a straw hut bar. The body was devoid of life. On one side, Lulani's curls looked untouched and perfect. Ani thought of the nights where she grabbed onto his hair, how she'd rub it between her fingers as Lulani slept.

She thought of what it felt like between her thighs when they were in the heat of things.

All of a sudden, Ani had to throw up.

She ran out the door and tossed what was left of her

dinner into the greenery along the side of the entrance. Acidic odor rose up to her, almost causing her to repeat. Some hotel guests and some reporters gave her looks of disdain.

To Hell with all of you.

Ani took a piece of chewing gum out of her purse and attempted to purify the rancidness from her mouth as she prepared reentry to the place where her lover lay slain.

Why hadn't she been given this assignment?

Why didn't she cover Sawyer Grant?

Why didn't she keep his badge and say she wanted him? Why did she let him go?

She walked over to the crime scene and there was Detective Kekoa. Ani kept her head eye-level instead of looking down. She had no reason to see what was left of Lulani's head. He was gone. This vessel on the ground was only useful to catch the person who did this.

She thought about how yesterday he had reached across the table and held her hands. Now his hands were incapable of reaching for anything. She thought about Lulani's stupid rhymes. She thought about him not being willing to let her speak to him about ending their relationship.

She thought of his willingness to give it all up. And he would have. Right there on Dickenson Street.

"Detective Ani, thank you for coming." Kekoa looked at her. His eyes showed empathy. Ani wondered if Kekoa knew. She wondered if he knew about their affair, despite how quiet they had kept it.

Ani wanted to scream. What would happen if she did? What difference would it make?

He put his large hand on her shoulder. She'd never seen Kekoa look like this. "I can't imagine what you're going through. I know how close you both were."

"Who did this?" Ani said. Her voice came out stronger than she thought it would have in her mind.

Kekoa shook his head. "Main person of interest for this is Pastor Sawyer Grant. He asked Lulani to meet him down here. Guess Grant realized we were tailin' him. Lulani thought he was gonna confess or something."

"Grant—"

It didn't make sense.

"Yeah, Grant. Front desk confirmed that they received a call from him wanting to know if Lulani would hang out in the courtyard. Attendant relayed messages. Couple people saw Grant in the lobby after Lulani was hit. And him running to the staircase."

"You really think the preacher did this?"

Kekoa started to return to his normal state. "Got someone better in mind? He had motive. Opportunity. We have witnesses—"

"But sir, Grant was the one that told us about the guy talking to his daughter. The guy that ended up dead on Dickenson Street."

Kekoa opened a small notepad. Kekoa always had different notepads. This one was a pocket pad.

"Let's review," he said. "Grant was involved in burglary at church. Grant was involved with whoever was at Dickenson Street that killed that girl's parents. I don't think that he did it, and the doctor said he couldn't have injured his shoulder like that. But who's to say that Grant isn't having some falling out with his bosses or co-workers?"

Ani somehow felt herself going the opposite way.

"Sir, if Grant did this, that would make him the worst criminal in the history of the world. He keeps staying in the center of trouble instead of getting himself out of it."

"Detective," Kekoa said. He was getting angry. "I didn't say he *did* it, I said he is *involved* somehow."

"Okay, let's say we agree there, but if he's only involved, don't you think we should be also looking for someone else who *actually did* do it?"

Kekoa closed the notebook and rubbed his head. "Ani, I know this is a terrible night for you. I'll call you when we get more details. I—"

"What? You're not letting me work this?" Ani felt herself wanting to cry. And also beat the tar out of something. She figured she could take a shot at Kekoa, but he probably wouldn't even notice. He was like a brick wall.

"Detective, we still need to find Hargrove's daughter. As far as I'm concerned, that's its own situation. Sure, they connect, but right now since Detective Aukai—" Kekoa cleared his throat. "We have no one working on Hargrove's daughter at all. That girl could still be alive. I need all your focus on that."

Ani didn't know what to say.

She was going to let Kekoa handle the death of her lover? Really? Like this.

"I think we need to talk to Grant again? I want the number—"

"I already talked to him," Kekoa said.

"What? And you spoke—did he say anything?"

"You're not on this case, Ani. That's it." Kekoa started to turn.

Ani grabbed his shoulder and he spun toward her. She figured if he wanted to, he could flick her away like a fly.

"You can't do this, please. You know—" the tears started coming and she was afraid he was going to see, so she looked away. At the same time she caught a glimpse of the M.E.

checking Lulani's lifeless body on the tiled floor of the outdoor courtyard.

"Detective," Kekoa said, placing his hand on Ani's. That empathy was back.

"Please." That's all she could manage without losing it. All she could do.

"Grant said he was set up. Still spouting off about the black Audi, said the girl—"

"Girl?"

Kekoa sighed. "Church secretary dropped him here and saw the black Audi."

"Did anyone else see it?"

Kekoa hesitated. "Ani, this is a bait and switch. He's literally going to have us all over the island looking for a car. When we really don't even know this guy's story yet."

"But the secretary saw it," Ani said.

"Yes," Kekoa said. "But I haven't had a chance to talk to her yet. It's on my list. But first thing I want is Sawyer Grant in my care."

Secretary. Grant. Black Car.

"I'm going then," she said. She turned back toward the door, where she'd moments ago puked in the greenery.

She had to talk to Sawyer Grant.

Ani also had to figure out what she was going to do without Lulani.

But that would come later. For now, she had a church secretary to find.

FIFTY-FOUR

Next to the steel door of her room, in the corner, sat a bucket, a roll of toilet paper, and hand sanitizer. A large bottle of sanitizer that someone would purchase from a bulk store. It took Janeen several hours before she had to pee in it. The smell of her own pee made her retch. She almost threw up.

Was it the drugs? Why was she so sick?

It could have been the smell that was permeating from the other side of the door. She hadn't quite gotten used to it. Her room was on the other side of something putrid. She wanted desperately to be used to the smell, but it seemed like it was getting stronger.

Her blonde hair felt like it was clinging to her head.

Janeen had no way to measure time, and she was nervous that the cheap lights illuminating her space would burn out. Then she'd be left in total darkness. And even if she knew the layout of the room, the idea of being trapped in a completely dark room was unbearable.

As she thought of unbearable, she heard metal on the other side of the door. She had changed into one of the t-shirts that had been left for her along with some sweatpants, but she felt naked. Completely vulnerable.

She drove onto the bed and covered herself with the sheet.

As if.

As if the bedding would protect her from this nightmare like her sheets protected her from imaginary monsters of her childhood. She missed her dad. She missed her mom. She wanted them badly.

The door opened, and Janeen's eyes were glued to it. She lost her breath at the sight.

A man came through the door wearing a mask like a clown. She'd seen the mask in some sort of scary movie at one point. It had red rosy cheeks, and tufts of hair sticking out of the side. Aside from that, he—she thought it was a *he*—wore a black jumpsuit.

She couldn't move. She couldn't blink.

He entered her room, and as he stared at her he raised his hands. Was he trying to be *calming?*

Janeen almost wet herself, but didn't want to add to the humiliation of being in this room. She was so frightened her teeth began to chatter. But still, she couldn't look away. She knew that if she did, the clown monster would be on her. And who knows what he wanted with her?

"Listen, Janeen," he whispered. She could hardly hear him. She also noticed some sort of machinery-type noise coming from the other side of the door.

She allowed herself a glance behind the clown man and he must have seen it.

He slammed the door behind him, and threw his hands back up in that "I surrender" fashion.

"Janeen," he said. She heard him more clearly now that the door was shut. "I'm only coming in here to check on you. I'm not going to hurt you. I'm not even going to touch you."

His words were measured. Each syllable emphasized. He was clear. And she had no doubt in her mind that he was the one that wrote the note on the fridge.

"You're safe, Janeen," he said. There was nothing reassuring about him. Nothing. But she did feel as though he didn't plan on hurting her.

But in the documentaries she'd watched, don't all psychopaths think they're nice?

Was this guy the exception?

"What do you want?" She spoke and didn't even realize she was speaking. Her voice shook.

"I am not going to hurt you, that's all. I wanted you to know. All I want is out of your control. But I had to do this to be sure that I get what I want."

The whispering voice made Janeen want to scream again. She couldn't handle it. She felt her face flushing with tears and her mouth was dry as cotton. She didn't want to speak again.

"I'll take care of you, Janeen. And this will all be over soon. I promise."

He turned and left his one hand up while opening the door with his free hand.

Then he paused.

Janeen's momentary relief melted into panic once more.

He turned to her as he opened the door a little wide. Again, the sound of some sort of equipment broke into the room.

"I promise I won't hurt you, as long as I get what I need."

And on that, in one swift, frantic motion, he left, slamming the metal door behind him.

FIFTY-FIVE

I could barely keep my eyes open. I wanted to take one of the pain pills that the medical center had prescribed me, but I knew I wouldn't make it.

And I was suddenly annoyed that Stu had fixed the burned-out lightbulbs in the preacher's office. They shined brighter than the third Heaven, and my head was pounding.

Sitting in the uncomfortable chair next to me was Elaina, my new partner in this mess. She also looked exhausted, and somehow I felt worse for her. But, still, she was even prettier as the night had gotten longer.

Stu was sitting in the pastor's seat. The desk didn't seem to bother him. He had his hands folded in front of him on the desk as though he was a judge hearing an important piece of evidence to decide a case.

Hard to believe I had just had a gunfight here twenty-four hours ago. I noticed that Stu had installed some bars over the windows. Guy didn't mess around.

"So, what's the what, Rev," he asked. That little gray patch on his chin made him look legit tough.

Stu had to be irritated for my causing so much grief, but he didn't look at all like I was bothering him. His face was—

Well, it was trusting. And sympathetic maybe.

Or maybe it was the drugs. I was so tired.

"I—okay, I think we should try to find that car. Or at least try to figure out how the car was here last night and showed up at a double murder the next day."

Stu nodded his head. Elaina had a MacBook open and was typing?

"You're not, taking notes, are you?" I asked.

She looked embarrassed, like she had been caught bringing fourteen items to the twelve-items-or-less line. "Yeah, you said we have to make a plan. Plans need written down."

"Not if they become evidence, they don't. You're not working on a documentary here. You're one note away from going to jail for cooperating with a potential cop killer, for crying out loud."

She didn't miss a beat. "It's encrypted, Pastor Grant."

Stu let out another one of those laughs. I chuckled a little too, but I was in too much pain to really let it rip.

"The car—the kid, kidnapper—" My tongue was about a mile and half behind my brain.

"I got the perfect idea," Stu said. He stood up from the desk.

"What's that," Elaina said. She was clacking the keys loudly at the idea of discovery.

"We gotta get the Rev to bed. Nothing gonna happen tonight. Plus, I wanna make sure we are all home when the police start comin'.'"

I loved this idea a lot. Actually, it was the only idea my brain would consider.

Elaina shrugged. "Okay, I guess we can brainstorm tomorrow."

She replaced her laptop in its case and made her move to the door.

I got up last. Stu laughed and said, "Looks like you burned my bridge at the Aston, which means you crashin' at my place tonight."

I didn't know what to say except that if I tried to do anything aside from what he told me, I'd end up in jail.

"It's not like the Aston, but don't worry, I'll make it as accommodating as I can. I got to. Because tomorrow we gotta figure out how to catch some killers."

FIFTY-SIX

Talking to Elaina turned out to be the worst thing that I could have done. Not because it was wrong. Not because I didn't trust her.

But because the dream/memory started again. This time clearer.

I stood at the corner of Liberty Avenue and the Bloomfield Bridge. The air was extra humid, or muggy as we would call it.

I was there early. The instructions indicated that the mark had arrived early. I knew what needed done.

I felt like I was choking on the moisture. Walking a couple blocks in the humidity made me feel like I'd just run a marathon, and even in my runs during boot camp, nothing compared to the stifling heat of a Pittsburgh summer. Relentless, unmerciful.

I stood outside the Phone Booth bar. That dumb sign flapped in the wind. The grommets had come loose from the bottom so half the time the wind obscured the junky looking black lettering on the white banner. But people going in there knew where they were. And they knew what they wanted. To get drunk. To get paid. To hide. To get laid.

There weren't options beyond that.

And occasionally, a patron would wander in under the impression that it was his idea. But it was someone else's. Then someone like me showed up behind them.

That was this deal.

I stood there at the base of the steps looking over at the open door of the church next to the Phone Booth. The door was open which led me to believe that like most of the churches in the city, they'd not invested into air conditioning.

Since I'd only been a church goer myself for a little bit of time, I'd become convinced that the bigger ones were the size they were because they ponied up the money for some cool A/C. It was hard to be moved by the Spirit with swamp crotch.

I had one job to do, but the church being open was odd to me. I'd developed a relationship with the pastor next door. Pastor Larry.

We'd gotten close. He knew my family well. He knew our business well. And needless to say, if he was lacking for an illustration regarding sin, he only needed to glance next door.

But my relationship with him deepened as I'd come back from my overseas tour.

I walked in and looked into the Phone Booth. No Alan Alda. TV was off. That was weird.

I had my heat at my side because there was someone in there that needed dealt with. Someone that was coming to hurt my uncle. Someone that deserved it.

We all deserve it, according to the Bible. I somehow rationalized that this would be my last one.

I somehow told myself that God was going to allow me one more—

—job.

And then I'd leave altogether. But getting up the nerve to look for this guy in the bar was impossible. I was especially unnerved because the church door was open. And what if the pastor would see me doing—

—a job.

I looked in the bar, empty. Bathrooms—empty. It still had that stale smoke smell that I'd always associated with the Phone Booth. Mixture of poorly cleaned surfaces spattered with beer and nicotine.

So I stepped back out onto the steps of the Phone Booth.

The doors to the church were open for me. Calling me. Maybe the mark hadn't gotten there yet. Maybe they misinformed me.

I walked over and through the propped-up open red doors into the vestibule of the church. I smelled the incense, the candles. They were burning. This was the kind of church where you felt you were really at a church. The stained-glass windows going down either side depicted the various stories in the Gospels. The Lord walking on water. The Lord making water into wine. The Lord healing the man with the bad hand.

All the stories brought to colorful life by the sun's rays piercing through them.

The smell of the candles grew stronger as I walked to the front. Pastor Larry was there. He was bent over the front of the altar looking through some sort of box. More candles? Incense? Different accessories for his robe?

I spoke but quietly. I didn't want to startle him. "Pastor

Larry." As I said his name, I realized I still had my gun out, so I tucked it into the back of my blue jeans.

He turned and I had startled him after all. He was flustered.

I think he called my name. Not Sawyer Grant, the real one.

I think he called my name and had the most curious look on his face. Then, I saw his complexion change. He was in his fifties, but I swear he aged ten years when he saw me.

He turned back around to that box, and pulled out a hand cannon. It was silver. Like a Dirty Harry gun. It looked almost fake. In fact, I almost laughed at him. I thought it was a joke.

I didn't think the shot he popped off was, though. That was as serious as a communion shortage on Easter. The shot was so loud that instantly my ears rang. He was wide, and it ricocheted off one of the old wooden pews.

The sound—how deftly it echoed—shocked Pastor Larry. I could tell he wasn't used to this. I could tell it was out of character for him.

I almost sympathized but not for very long.

I pulled out the gun that I'd meant to use at the Phone Booth, and shot the pastor in the throat instead.

PART THREE

FIFTY-SEVEN

Ani stood at the door of Resurrection Church. The parking lot was empty and in need of repair. Large cracks had developed through the asphalt and the lines were faded. Once pure white, now translucent.

This was the first time she'd ever attempted to go to church on a day that wasn't Sunday. And actually, she didn't really ever go on Sunday.

But it seemed—haunted.

Maybe it was because she hadn't slept. Maybe it was the Xanax that she'd popped. Maybe it was how much she'd screamed all night and morning.

She took in a deep breath and her nose was still congested from the sobs. Some from sadness. Some from rage. Despite her congestion, rain was in the air. The clouds overhead didn't seem too dark, so she imagined that the storm would come later.

Who cares about the weather? It's Hawaii.

She was a shell. She looked it, too. Ani's hair was greasy with sweat. What little makeup she had on, she'd applied yesterday. What remained was a streaky and inconsistent mess.

Memories of a girl who cared.

Ani had made sure to spray perfume. But when she thought about taking a shower, she thought of her and Lulani together in her apartment. How they'd showered. And went back to bed. Then went to eat at Maui Brewing Company Restaurant.

Was that only two days ago or was it a lifetime?

And she remembered his head being blown apart. Parts of his skull scattered across the floor of the Aston. A tiled floor where right now guests were checking in and walking around it, prepared to enjoy their trips of a lifetime.

And now, she was at Resurrection Church. Hopefully finding Lulani's murderer.

She didn't believe that Grant was the shooter. It was too easy. But it seemed to fit without any type of scrutiny. Some cops loved those types of cases. Ani thought for sure there was no way after Grant had been involved in a double murder scene earlier that day that he would kill a cop. Especially one that he had openly told witnesses he wanted to meet.

But whether Grant was the shooter or not, he was certainly in the middle of this. And he was missing.

And, if there was even an inkling that he was the shooter, Ani would never arrest him. A bullet would do all the police work for her.

Ani didn't care if she went to jail or not. As far as she was concerned, when she threw Lulani's badge back to him on Dickenson Street her life as a cop had ended.

Because if she had held on to his shield, he'd be alive.

But now, she was standing before the entrance of Resurrection Church.

She pulled the glass entry door to find it locked.

Monday? At 11:00 am? No one is here?

It was presumptuous to think that church staff worked normal banker's hours. How would she know? She hadn't been to church since childhood.

She walked through the run-down parking lot to her unmarked patrol car when another car pulled in. It was a silver Lexus SUV. Off-white. Expensive.

Ani wasn't much of a prayer person, but she shot up a hope that it was Grant himself. She prayed he'd be ready to be questioned. That somehow, he would write down the address to her boyfriend's murderer.

The prayer went unanswered. Raymond Hargrove got out of the car. His face looked like she felt. He was wearing a blue suit with a checkered blue dress shirt under.

For a moment, she forgot about Lulani. Hargrove was missing his daughter. Two days now. There was as much of a mystery surrounding her disappearance as the preacher being in the middle of everything.

"Mr. Hargrove. I'm not sure if you remember—"

"Yes, ma'am," he said, "you were at the school, helping to interview people. You work for Detective Kyle Kekoa."

Ani shook her head. "Forgive my appearance. I was— wanting to talk to—um—" Ani's mind froze on the secretary's name.

"Elaina? Or Stu?"

She felt the wind get knocked out of her. *Stu!* That was the name Elaina said when she was on her phone after the Dickenson Street murder. It was Stu. He worked with her! No case file required.

"Yes, them. I—"

"Detective, forgive me for not saying it right away. I'm so sorry about what happened with your detective friend last night. You all have been so gracious helping me with my Janeen. You've all been more attentive than Janeen's mother. And—I just—there are no words, are there?"

"No," Ani said. She didn't want to get into the emotion of anything with a man tortured by his daughter's disappearance.

And the mom, from what Ani understood, was on her way to Hawaii from the mainland. They had a brutal divorce between them. And as always, the kids are the collateral damage.

Hargrove rubbed his bald head and widened his eyes with an inhale. "Okay. So it appears no one is at the church, correct?"

"No."

He pulled a phone out of his jacket. Ani could tell he was texting. Before she asked he gave her an explanation.

"I suppose Stu and Elaina are staying away from here. Considering the authorities are looking for the preacher. Maybe they thought it would be too dangerous."

"Makes sense."

"Listen," he said. "I'm heading into the church. I need to check the preacher's office to see how much damage was done. Would you like to come in?"

Ani felt relieved. Of course she wanted in there.

"Sir, that would be great. Thank you. And I can even tell you some of the things we were looking into with your daughter since the Dickenson Street incident."

He raised his eyebrows but didn't smile. "I really trust you all. I really appreciate anything."

They walked into the lower entrance of the church. It was exactly as she'd imagined. Outdated. Ugly carpet. It smelled clean, but chemically clean. Not "lived in" clean.

Ani shared some things with him about the case. Most of which didn't surprise him. Not really any leads. She shared a couple of details that Kekoa most likely had already relayed to him.

Hargrove didn't seem to think Grant was involved. But he was agitated that Grant wasn't willing to cooperate with police.

Ani made a mental note that she'd look up Stu and Elaina's addresses as soon as she left. Elaina's especially. The girl had carted the preacher to at least two crime scenes.

Maybe Elaina also took him to his hideaway.

Raymond Hargrove searched through key after key attempting to unlock an office. Must be the preacher's. The door looked heavy. Even sort of new. After several unsuccessful attempts, Hargrove cursed.

"Forgive me," he said.

"No worries. If you're looking for forgiveness I feel like you are in the right place."

He smiled. But it was a worn-out smile. "Aside from maybe spending time in prayer in the sanctuary, this trip was a little pointless. Unless you wanted to look outside and see if you could enter the pastor's office that way."

"Don't think I'm weird," Ani said, "but I actually already thought of that. Someone put bars outside of the windows. Looks like it was done recently."

Hargrove nodded. "Yeah, Stu. He's proactive about a lot of things. The decor in this place, not so much."

Ani laughed, but it was forced. It was time to go. She had other things to do. She'd start at Elaina's place. She had no warrant. She had no authorization. Kekoa had told her to take time off.

But she didn't care about any of those things.

As she left the church, she thought to pray. Maybe pray for Lulani's soul. But she didn't.

She had a feeling she was going to need to return at some point anyway, to ask for her own forgiveness.

FIFTY-EIGHT

Still in the dream, but it was a memory. I hadn't thought at all about the events that brought me to Maui since getting there.

But here I was, and the picture that I'd left had started to develop. I felt like I was shaking a Polaroid and watching the edges of the images sharpen.

The pastor's body was lying on the altar. I didn't have to look to know it was a kill shot, but I did see the dated pinkish colored carpet of the church darken to crimson.

I kept the gun out just in case he had help. Also, I had a feeling that someone was going to be coming by to get my body.

What should have been my body.

I moved over to the altar and looked in the big duffel bag. It was filled with cash. Cash for the hit on me. It looked like a lot. I would say that it was at least a hundred thousand. Maybe more. I was a hard target, as they say. It's not like the fifty thousand I'd get for whacking someone in the Phone Booth.

This was more.

And now it was mine.

The thought crossed my mind that someone's hands had put that money in the bag for the pastor. Someone who knew me.

Someone who wanted me dead at the Phone Booth.

My phone vibrated in my pocket. I took it out. There was sand on it. I hadn't been to the beach recently, so I was a little alarmed. But there, was the text.

It was my uncle.

"Hey, are you heading over to the Booth soon? Need to make the move."

Of course, he was waiting to get confirmation from the pastor but hadn't heard from him. It's because I was early that he was concerned. He didn't know that I had been really early. He didn't know that I destroyed this operation.

He'd know when he saw the dead pastor.

And that's when it hit me.

I took a deep breath. Gunsmoke, church candles, a little bit of musty carpeting.

If I left, I'd have to play the game and pretend I didn't know I was on his list.

If I left, it would only be a matter of time before they would be after me.

But time is what I needed. Maybe that's all I needed.

I glanced up at the candles, small occasional eruptions of smoke coming from the flames.

The church.

The bar.

I needed time.

I looked back at the bag. Next to the bag was the preacher's phone. He didn't keep a passcode on it. It didn't matter. I only had to say a handful of things.

Opening to his texts, I saw the messages. The top one

was the only one I needed. I had seen that message too many times from my uncle.

Let me know if you were finally able to log on.

That was the code. That was a layer of cover. Every crime family had some sort of code. This was primitive. But it worked.

I replied.

Logged in.

That meant the target was dead.

I looked down at the preacher's body, his throat expelling less blood than before onto that outdated carpet.

The target was down. Absolutely it was.

Then, the next line I sent.

Shutting Machine Down Now.

That meant body disposal. That meant clean up. It meant a lot of things. But it meant essential that as far as the order was concerned, the situation was white-glove done. No more worries. No more loose ends.

That wasn't entirely true.

There was a loose end. The fact that the preacher was dead and this church was now a crime scene.

But I had an idea how to remedy that as well.

I looked at the candles and allowed a smile to cross my face. Then I glanced to the right. The Phone Booth Bar and the Church were almost sharing walls.

Uncle wouldn't send anyone until later so they could have deniability. It was plenty of time.

Couldn't take my eyes off those candles. Couldn't quit thinking about that empty bar.

And I had only one regret in that moment.

That I wouldn't be here to watch these buildings burn.

FIFTY-NINE

Billy Robertson pulled into his office lot at the Maui sewage treatment center. He pulled closest to the building because he knew he'd be leaving soon. He just had to check on Janeen. Wanted to be sure she was still handling being down there.

He felt completely free of the burden of any investigation, considering Sawyer Grant was Public Enemy Number One. Bob did good. Billy thought about maybe forgiving him and not forcing him to take a dive into the drink, but Billy wasn't fully committed to the idea yet.

The Audi.

He got out of the car. Thought he'd take in a little Maui air before heading inside. It was a little cloudy today. Rain on the horizon. Which for Maui, that meant a drizzle here and there. Nothing torrential.

It took Billy no time at all to be out of his car and feel overheated. He'd chosen a dark blue suit for today, even though he wouldn't be seeing anyone. He had the suit on thinking the business was almost over. And pretty soon, Maui would be his retirement spot.

As he started into the building he paused and noticed a small Honda Civic that looked like it had been through a war. It was dented in and the paint was mismatched. The tires looked maybe ten years old if they were a month. Billy thought maybe someone had left it here in hopes of having one of the office administrators tow it, until he saw a young lady get out.

Neither she nor her car looked like they belonged in the sewage treatment center. She was wearing a dress under a jacket.

There wasn't supposed to be anyone there at all. His first appointment with the pipeline division wasn't until later afternoon.

She looked a little awkward but beautiful. Billy could tell that she was there to do something uncomfortable. His first thought was that she was a salesperson, and this was maybe her first cold call. She would attempt to cajole him into buying janitorial supplies that are more eco-friendly or something.

Then he'd have to let her down gently, because he had a lot to do in order to bring this complicated business to an end.

"Aloha, can I help you, miss?" Billy said.

"I am not sure. I'm hoping so. You had two employees here, husband and wife in different departments. They were just murdered yesterday."

Was she a reporter? She wasn't a police officer.

"Yes, we have heard that. It's a tragedy. From what I understand, the company is going to be helping with funeral expenses, luncheon, that sort of thing."

He paused.

"Forgive me for being indelicate, miss, but could you tell me how you're connected to the family."

She looked flustered at that. She was so awkward, but she was also stunning. Then all of a sudden it clicked for him.

Bob had told him about this girl. Yes, the attractive lady that was very attached to Sawyer Grant. And yet, here she was.

And yet here, another loose end.

"Sure, I don't mind. I'm a friend of the girl, the—she survived the attack."

Loose end, loose end.

Billy took one of his black plastic swizzle sticks out of his blazer pocket and placed it into his mouth. His teeth made that familiar clicking noise against the plastic—he loved that.

The girl was puzzled.

"What is that, if you don't mind my asking."

The girl was forward. It was annoying to him.

"I gave up smoking years ago. My wife told me the best way to do it was to switch to something similar that wasn't killing me. And this kinda stuck. I don't do it very often."

She stared at Billy. "Do you do it when you're nervous?"

Suddenly, the thought occurred to Billy that the parking lot was empty. And he already had one girl tied up in the basement of it. It wouldn't bother him at all to snap this stranger's neck and put her in the high school girl's room as a bit of a warning.

But he didn't know who knew she was here.

Loose end. Loose end. Loose end.

"What did you say your name was?"

"I didn't," she said. "Elaina." She did not extend her hand and Billy wasn't surprised.

"Bill Robertson."

He looked at her Honda and thought of what Bob had

told him when he mentioned her. He also thought how Bob wanted her as a conciliation benefit for how difficult the mission was.

Once this job was over, Billy had his own idea of what should be done to her. But before that, it probably wouldn't matter what Bob did with her.

"Look, Elaina. I never really knew the deceased, unfortunately. I am not a formal employee of the company. I am, what you might call, a contractor. I have to oversee a particular tricky part of their business, and then most likely my family and I will be moving on to other pastures."

She stared, but didn't respond.

"So, I'm afraid my ability to help you is limited. I could get you in contact with the managers that worked directly with the family. But I'm afraid they all tend to keep to themselves."

The strange girl once again didn't respond. Billy was getting the impression that she was evaluating each of his answers.

The thought of snapping her neck once again crossed his mind. The idea seemed like a viable one. Who cares who knew? In days, this would be all over. And he'd be free of the details. So, why not?

"Come to think of it, young lady, maybe I could help you. I think their personnel files are still in the building." He smiled and motioned to the door of the building opening his hand in gesture of invitation.

This will be the last time anyone is ever civil to you, you little meddler.

Her cell phone chirped, causing her to break her stare from Billy. He watched as she pulled it out of her jean-jacket pocket. She looked at it, then replaced it.

"Maybe another time, Mr. Robertson. I was really

hoping to speak to someone who knew the victims. I appreciate your willingness to let me in there."

Billy was doing a little analysis of his own. Calculating who knew she was here, what she had to do with Grant, and finally, who it was that sent her a message. Were they checking on her? Were they asking if she confirmed any suspicions?

Too many loose ends.

"Too bad, Elaina. Perhaps another time, then."

She nodded, thanked him again, and boarded the ratty Civic.

As the sound of her car ripped through the silence in the lot, Billy kept his hand on the door of the plant, and as soon as the sound of her exhaust seemed to diminish enough that Billy knew there was some distance, he walked quickly to his own car.

He didn't have to hurry. Her car's exhaust was as effective as a GPS tracker. There'd be virtually no space between them on the road, and he'd make sure he stayed far back.

Janeen would have to wait a little. He had another young lady that he needed to check on.

SIXTY

Stu had a large eat-in kitchen with tons of cabinets. It was immaculate. The gray tile floor looked like it had just been installed. There wasn't much in the way of decoration, but there were two wide French doors that opened up to a spacious deck outside. Despite how much my head hurt, I managed to look out at the Maui sky. It was a little darker than it had been the previous day.

Stu had allowed me to crash in a guest room, where apparently he had woken me up. I was so out of it, that I felt like forming a sentence was like trying to take an admissions test to become an engineer at NASA.

We sat at a large table with four flowery placemats at the table settings. The table would easily seat double that. My head was pounding and I wanted nothing more than to go to bed. But I was also hungry like a hostage and twice as thirsty.

Stu had gotten me some ice water and a peanut butter sandwich. He apologized for being out of jelly, but that sandwich tasted like a freaking filet mignon from Gordon Ramsay.

He also had gotten me some Motrin and a fresh bandage for the shoulder job. I felt like I was staying at some sort of an outlaw's bed and breakfast or something.

"Miss Elaina is on her way over. Think we should probably make a plan for the day. Things are getting a little tense."

"Yeah, I'll bet," I said, mouth full of God's peanut butter sandwich. I drank water to try to clear it quicker because I felt like I was on the verge of embarrassing myself.

"She's managing stuff at the church office. Apparently everyone is looking for you, Rev. Including Hargrove."

Yeah, of course they're looking for me. Allegedly, I murdered a police officer, maybe a set of parents on Dickenson Street, and I also was able to break into a church in my spare time.

Church. I thought about my speaking this Wednesday.

"Guess you better cancel my speaking engagement for Wednesday night."

"Ha, Rev, things have gotten a little more complicated on that front, too. But Miss Elaina can fill you in on that deal."

I gulped what was left of the ice water. "See, the thing is, if we could catch this murderer today, I could get myself into the clear and still have time to prepare the message. I'd only need a day. It would be good."

Stu looked down at the table, as if he was holding back bad news from me. He had a cup of black coffee in a stained white mug. Steam rose from it, but he hadn't really touched it.

"Day's gone, Rev. It's almost four."

I couldn't compute.

Stu went on. "You see, you were so messed up, that you

slept the whole day. I tried to wake you, but you weren't moving."

"So, I slept this whole day?"

Stu shook his head. "You needed the rest, Rev. You got cut up bad. And on top of that, you got a little beat up."

"Look, I had that guy under control if he hadn't stabbed me. But—a whole day?"

"Yes, sir."

The door opening startled me and I instinctively wanted to run like I'd been at the hotel all over again. Stu waved me off, like he was trying to comfort a kid that had just spilled a little bit of water on the porch.

I turned and there she was. I was sick of the fact that every time I'd seen Elaina she looked better than she had the time before. She was wearing a yellow dress with a jean jacket over the top. Her long black hair was pulled in a tight ponytail, but she was stunning.

I instantly felt naked in the pair of gym shorts that I was wearing that were about a mile and a half too short. On top of that, I was wearing a white t-shirt that just said Aloha in black letters across it.

"Welcome to the Resurrection Church meetin' Miss Elaina," Stu said. Game-show-host tone perfect. "Come take a seat at the table and see what your prize is."

Elaina came over and took a seat right near me. Her perfume or body wash smelled as if Giorgio Armani and Calvin Klein had a love child. That's how pretty she smelled. I probably smelled like Stu's pantry, because I'm pretty sure he had gotten my Aloha shirt from the pantry, which led me to believe this is what he used to clean with.

Stu had poured all three of us coffee that looked like it was out of a Starbucks commercial. Despite the steam coming from the cup, I gulped three swigs instantly. I was hoping it would make my headache go away a little. God knew it tasted terrific.

"Little bit of a development, but not much," Elaina said. "I went over to the Sewage Authority."

I couldn't believe what I was hearing. "Wait, you're doing police work now?"

Elaina looked at me. I got that cold look from her again. "Well, it's not like I can stop trying to figure this out. We are all a part of it now, Pastor Grant."

She was right. And I was guilty. I thought about the dream I had of the Phone Booth. I thought about my own guilt getting on a plane and coming to start anew. And I thought about the fact that the identity that I'd chosen had already been wrapped up in at least three murders and a kidnapping.

We were all in it.

"Alright, Miss Elaina. Don't keep us in suspense, what should we know."

"Nothing much that I could see," she said. She took a cautious sip of her coffee and opened her iPhone. "Place was empty, but there was a man—"

The door rattled with three distinct pounds. All of us stopped and we were all of one mind.

The calm that Stu displayed when Elaina was at the door was not what he did after we heard that knock. "Rev," he said, and pointed down the hall to the spare room that I'd slept in.

He didn't have to tell me twice. I was up and moving in that direction before I heard three more insistent knocks.

Whoever was on the other side of that door wasn't here for a courtesy call.

SIXTY-ONE

Robertson drove far enough behind Elaina to keep her from seeing. His silver Buick was in good shape, but it was inconspicuous enough to keep him from arousing any type of interest. He especially loved the classy feel of the interior. It was worn, but whoever owned it before him must have taken care of it. The leather still smelled like leather.

But it was a blender car. Didn't turn someone's eyes. That was key.

Not like that Audi which had been such a source of irritation for him. And it was *going* to become a source of conversation for Bob when they finished the end of this mission.

All in time.

The Hawaiian girl called Elaina continued heading west. Billy didn't know as much about Hawaii real estate as he wanted to, but judging by her car, he was surprised. The homes in the area looked pretty nice and way out of this meddling woman's price range. At least if her car was any measure of her income.

Surprisingly, she turned down a nice, quaint street. The

trip seemed faster than expected, but Billy knew that it was probably because of how on-edge he was.

The plan still had a lot of snags. And with the involvement of yet another person connected to Resurrection Church, it was more complicated still. As Billy kept his distance from the nasty, rust-bucket Honda, he thought of his own family. He thought of the hero's welcome he received every time he came home.

He also thought it unfortunate that he was probably going to have to kill more people than he'd intended before he could get home and finally be able to put the final part of this plan in motion.

This was his swan song. His retirement party.

Billy could collect seashells or do whatever those people do that he so often saw die. What was the dream? What was the end?

All he knew is that he had just gotten a house on Maui. And Maui was just about the best place to retire. No debt. No loose ends.

No problem.

Elaina pulled into the driveway of a modest ranch home. The outside looked pretty outdated, but it seemed solid. The grass was cut. The porch light was on.

There was no way this young lady owned this place. She had to be sharing space or renting a bedroom or something. He stayed about a block away, having pulled over before she stopped completely.

A part of him wanted to throw caution to the wind and just kill everyone in that house. Sure, it was the sort of thing that he paid Bob to do, but he was better at it. Billy had more experience. On top of that, there might even be a chance that he could pin the murders on the preacher. He was already wanted for killing a rookie detective.

He took a black stirrer out of his pocket and placed it into his mouth, clacking on it with his teeth. If he focused hard enough, he imagined biting down on one of the previous grooves.

He also reached into his glove box and took out a Smith & Wesson M&P 9mm handgun. From underneath his seat, he pulled out the silencer and screwed it to the barrel as he chewed the swizzle stick.

Yeah, let's tie up this loose end tonight. They'll pin it on the preacher because she works at the church.

Billy sat for a moment more thinking, chewing, and flexing his fingers on the grip of the Smith & Wesson.

He drove a little closer to the house, and that's when he realized the plan was shot.

A car parked a couple houses down reminded him of the Audi. Not in how it looked, but because of what it was associated with. It was an unmarked police car. He was certain of it. He'd seen them enough. He also had dealt enough with police who were not afraid to play for the other guys, so to speak.

This can't be.

Fury overtook him. The complexity of this plan. Now, instead of looking at the well-manicured outdated home, he was staring at the car. He couldn't quite see if there was someone in it, but all of his doubt vanished when the door opened, and the detective stepped out.

She was definitely a detective. Not by how she dressed. No. She was wearing a black t-shirt and jeans. But the fact that she was carrying a sidearm toward the house like she was moving in for a raid. That's why Billy knew she was a cop.

She moved slowly toward the house as Billy disassembled his gun, replacing it back in the glovebox and the silencer under his seat.

He didn't replace the swizzle stick, though. No. As he reversed his car he bit down hard on it and it snapped. Billy hated when that happened, but this time he barely noticed.

In a moment, that cop was going to be talking to the girl. The girl was going to be telling her where she'd been. Who she'd spoken with at the sewage plant.

And the fact that Billy had to kill a whole lot more people didn't bother him as much anymore.

SIXTY-TWO

Stu had been on the other end of trouble too many times to remember. So a door rattling with a bad person on the other side didn't do much for him. But what bothered him about this situation was Miss Elaina and Rev Grant.

He could handle his own business. But things always got sticky when you involved other people.

Grant ran down the hall, and Stu almost laughed. Preacher looking like he just robbed a Hawaiian souvenir shop running away.

"Who is it?"

"Detective Ani Iona. I have some questions."

Stu looked at Elaina who was still at the table, but motionless. He was worried she was going to pass out there. He didn't know what her tolerance for this sort of business was.

"Got a warrant to go with them questions, Miss Iona?" Stu asked.

A little bit of silence.

"I have reason to believe you might be aiding Sawyer Grant. He's wanted for questioning."

Her voice was muffled but firm from behind the door.

"Again, that's all well and good, Detective Iona, but I ain't seeing no warrant."

No pause.

"Look, you can let me in and we can talk, or I can come back. And if I do get a warrant, and I even see the slightest bit of contact with the preacher, you're gonna be put away quick. You and the office girl, you hear it?"

Stu glanced over at Elaina who was wider-eyed than ever before. He also glanced down at the plate and glass of water the preacher had left there and motioned to it with his eyes. Bandage too.

Elaina got up quickly to grab the stuff. Stu was relieved she followed his cue.

As soon as she got behind the sink, Stu turned back around and opened the door.

There she was. This beautiful, or what could be, a beautiful native Hawaiian lady. She couldn't hide her beauty. Her features were soft. But she was broken.

Her lips were cracked. Her eyes had bags under them. Her hair was thrown back in a ponytail. She looked rather crazy.

"Well, Detective Iona, don't take it as meanin' anything offensive, but you look like you're just coming out of the other side of a bad night."

"Is Grant in here?" She was not moved.

She had a pistol already drawn. Stu didn't typically get nervous about—well anything. But her frenzied look and that firearm made him feel a little uneasy.

"Nah, just me and church administrator, Miss Elaina." He opened the door wider so that the detective could see Elaina at the kitchen sink.

Stu was glad for his open floor plan. He didn't want this

woman to think there was something more she needed to see.

But there was the hallway.

Detective Ani Iona scanned the room, Elaina, and the hallway.

Come on, now. Let this be enough.

"May I come in, Mr. Gentry."

He opened the door all the way now and motioned in with his arm. Different kind of game now.

The woman scanned the room again. This time a lot slower. Elaina was making a career out of washing those two dishes. Acting almost as if there wasn't a cop with a gun in the middle of the living room.

"Live alone?"

"Not by choice, but yeah," Stu said.

Ani Iona turned and faced him completely. "No girlfriend?"

"I'm too old for you, detective." Stu said. He smiled the best and brightest. She was less amused by his charms than he'd hoped.

Elaina had finished scrubbing the dish. She returned to her seat at the table.

The detective stared at her for a moment, then back to Stu.

"Neither of you were at work today. I was there earlier."

Elaina lifted up her hands. Man, she wasn't gonna help Stu in the smoothness department.

"Both thought better not to be there. I can clean the church whenever. Miss Elaina can do a lot of her stuff from home. But after that break in and after our candidate Rev being involved in some sort of police trouble, didn't think church was the place to be 'til this stuff cleared up a little."

Iona shook her head slowly up and down. She was still holding the gun, but Stu was certain she had relaxed.

"Anything from you, Elaina?"

Elaina just shook her head.

Smooth as silk, Miss Elaina.

"One more question, then."

Stu felt relieved.

"Anything, detective."

She walked over to the table and to Elaina who didn't move and pointed to the table. "What's with this massive bandage on the table?"

Oh, Miss Elaina. You forgot the only part that mattered. Anyone could have eaten a peanut butter sandwich.

"I got old bones, detective. Sometimes I put—"

Stu was cut off by Sawyer Grant interrupting.

"Stop," he said from the hall with his hands up. "I came here, they didn't aid me."

Stu didn't have time to react too much because before he could even try to explain, the detective bolted, charging right at Grant.

SIXTY-THREE

The thought of extinguishing one of the lights in the room made Janeen want to pass out. But she had to chance it.

She wished she could just see her mom's face. She remembered the times her mom would tell her that the dark only conceals what you've already seen and known.

If only she could think that way now.

She pulled the light off of the wall from the side closest to the refrigerator. She kept the refrigerator door open as she did so, spilling a little more illumination into the room. The little nine-inch light was framed inside the black sound proofing foam so tightly, that it took every bit of her concentration to pry it off.

She wasn't sure how long she'd been in this dungeon. The smell was still putrid but she was used to it. So she knew it was long.

Her mouth was dry, but she didn't want to drink any more of her kidnapper's providence because she didn't want to pee in the bucket.

She didn't suspect anyone would find her. So she had to figure out a way out on her own.

After wiggling the light for what seemed like forever, Janeen finally popped it off the wall. She sent a silent prayer to God that the light remained lit. Any more darkness in the room would have crushed her, even though she felt as though she had memorized every square inch of her comfortable prison.

Janeen set the light down on the ground, taking a moment to glance at her makeshift toilet with shame.

She felt around the hole that was left in the sound-proofing on the wall and found only one drywall screw sticking out. That was it. The soundproofing was either glued or securely stapled because it wasn't coming off easily.

Janeen took a deep breath. Deep as she could take with the smell and her nerves. She thought about the note. Thought about peeing in a bucket. Thought about the food in the fridge.

So she began to go at the drywall screw. It was tight in the wall, but it was moving. With every twist, her fingers became even more sore.

She decided to enlist the aid of her dress. Janeen had hated that dumb dress anyway, but was glad that she still had it. She tore strips out of the bottom of the fabric. She wrapped the pieces around her fingers.

This would guard from sweating and it would enable her to protect her fingers.

Janeen went at the screw again.

How long was this? It felt like it was a mile long to pull out.

But something else was happening to Janeen inside that room.

For the first time since waking up in the prison, she felt hope.

SIXTY-FOUR

I came out of the room with my hands raised. Armed with nothing but Aloha.

The detective stared at me, as if in shock.

I couldn't let these people that I'd known for seventy-two hours face a police interrogation for me. And risk lying. I'm not good, but I'm not *that* bad.

"Detective, please, I came—"

I didn't have time to finish. She ran toward me and kicked me hard in the stomach.

I hit the ground like a toddler on an ice rink. My insides felt like they'd just gone through a meat grinder. I didn't want to resist. I didn't even want to fight back.

She pulled me up by my hair and I slumped against the wall of the hallway.

I started seeing red. I wanted to fight back but I knew she'd kill me. This was confirmed as she pushed the cold barrel of the gun into my face.

And hard.

The detective had tears in her eyes. They were swollen.

She almost looked strung out. Pretty as the day was long, but a hot mess, as the kids say.

This wasn't police work she was doing. This lady was going to freaking kill me dead.

I remembered her from before but couldn't quite place it.

"Did you kill him?" Her voice was shaky.

"I didn't—"

"Did you kill that cop? At the hotel? Did you kill him?"

A flash came through my mind.

I did remember her.

She was at Dickenson Street. She was also at Janeen Hargrove's school on Saturday. And I remembered her doing something. Throwing something at another cop.

She threw a badge at him.

They were *partners*. It was her partner that I—or somebody else had killed at the Aston.

Yeah, she was going to kill me for sure.

"I didn't kill your partner, detective. I promise."

Gun pressed harder. I felt my skin tear under the pressure.

"Detective, I want to find them. I want to find who did this. That's why I went to Dickenson Street."

Elaina chirped in from the background, "Detective, he's telling the truth. I brought him to Dickenson Street. Please."

I kept my eyes on hers. Tears had started falling. But uncertainty rolled across her face, as well.

Good, maybe I wouldn't die just yet.

"Detective Iona," Stu said. He sounded as calm as a digital customer service representative. "Everyone's allowed due process. Now how 'bout we get some tea, have a sit at that table over there, and get to know what we all know. Don't want no dead reverends in my house. Got a strict policy about that, you dig?"

He paused for a moment. Iona seemed to be softening, but the pressure on my face still felt pretty heavy. Her eyes went between squinting with tears to widening with rage.

It was pretty unnerving.

"Don't want no cops making mistakes in my house, either. We all in this thing now. Far as I could figure, the four of us is better than just one. You don't like what he has to say, take him to county. But you killing him ain't getting justice for your man. And no one knows where that missing girl is yet."

I felt her loosening the gun from me and backing away, bringing a little relief to my money maker. I kept my eyes on her. Until finally she pulled back all together.

I stood up and braced myself for another rumble, but it didn't come. She put her gun in a holster she had at her back, and sobbed.

"That's right, Detective Iona. You chose right. And we got some smart people in this room."

I looked at Stu. He had that look on his face that made me want to be his best friend again.

Lord, I hoped I didn't have to go back to Pittsburgh. I also didn't want to have more crimes pinned on me, either.

Iona sobbed and Stu came over, putting his arm ever so gently around her shoulder. "Come on. Let's have a sit. I got a feeling you gonna bring more to the table than just restraint."

As he was walking her over to his table, and Elaina, who'd still remained very mannequin-like, Stu glanced back at me.

"Come on, Rev. You're the only connection to all this. Better pop an Motrin, say a prayer and put your thinking cap on."

SIXTY-FIVE

Of course, the plan had to change again. That's all this thing had done since he signed on.

Bob was furious. He was tired. He was beat up. He wanted nothing more than to drink and smoke and eat all the fruit on Maui.

He felt like he had been living in this jumpsuit. He knew he stank. But he felt his job was almost done.

Bob also wanted to go on a date with the preacher's girl-friend. He had things in mind that were not church appro-priate. And after all this was done, he planned on doing just that.

He wanted to quit worrying about cars. Worrying about cops. Worrying about churches and he wanted to be done.

But it was all futile thinking.

He walked down the steps of the Maui Sewage Facility. In one hand, he had a couple black bedsheets that he'd picked up from Wal-Mart under Robertson's direction.

In the other hand, he held a gun.

He descended down to where the room was.

It stank so bad in there. Like he was in the world's toilet

or something. After he got done with the deed, Bob was going to demand that he get more money. This was not what he'd signed up for.

Robertson had done nothing but throw Riggins off a cliff. Bob had to provide the muscle. The fear. Bob's the one that had to do the two parents on Dickenson Lane or whatever that street was called.

Yeah, he was getting more money. If Robertson didn't pay up, then maybe he takes this Janeen girl with him and does a little side hostage thing.

He came to the door. Bob jiggled his key a little bit to give the girl a bit of a warning. It would be awkward if he caught her going woo woo. He didn't want to do that. He also didn't want to see another gross thing. It already smelled like human filth in here. He didn't need to watch a teenager straddling a bucket to loose her loins.

Bob slightly tapped on the door.

"Wakey, wakey princess."

He slipped the mask on his face. This was going to be unpleasant but he had to get it over with.

The door stuck a little, so he pulled it pretty hard until it came open.

He stared inside a room that looked empty. The fridge was closed, the bed had clothes on it, and only three of the four closet lights he'd installed remained intact.

But no girl.

"You got—" He couldn't even think.

Bob stepped into the room, letting the sheets hit the ground. That's when he felt a pain in his left eye.

It wasn't a pain. It was a popping.

He screamed. howled, and began swinging in the direction of the pain.

He couldn't open either eye. Something had been stuck in his eye. His right eye was remaining closed in sympathy.

He swore and swung and caught a lucky shot. He felt the girl's head meet his fist.

"You coward," he said to her. Eyes still closed.

Then he started swinging the barrel of the gun. He missed her the first time. He heard her scream.

One final shot.

Boom. It was a lucky hit. He felt the metal do its work as it connected with this bold little witch's skull. He wanted to do more to her. A lot more.

And even though he didn't see it, Bob heard the thud as Janice or Janeen or whoever she was hit the ground.

SIXTY-SIX

I don't know that I had ever tasted coffee the way Stu made it. He said it was a Hawaii thing, but I was starting to get a feeling that he tinkered around with more than just cap guns. He seemed to be an expert in all things.

I talked the most, because like Stu said, I had been to most of the places in question. I explained the Audi. Elaina chimed in that she'd noticed it at the hotel and that's why she came back to get me.

Stu didn't really add much. Occasionally he'd ask a point of clarification. He'd also ask if any of us wanted a refill on coffee. We were all starting to get a little hungry. Dinner was an afterthought until we all realized it was close to that time, and we hadn't eaten. So Stu called a pizza in.

Elaina had her laptop up and open, clacking notes. Asking similar clarifying questions to Stu, but more granular.

The detective said very little. I could tell how destroyed she was over the other detective's death. While I never claimed to be a psychologist, I would go out on a very short limb to say that she and the deceased detective had more between them than a professional partnership. It was a moot point. But it certainly explained her rage and the fact that she was close to killing me.

While we were eating pizza, I dodged some questions from Ani regarding my past. I spoke in generalities. It irritated her and it caused some glances between Stu and Elaina.

It wasn't relevant now. My stuff was mine.

After pizza, the discussion shifted into kidnapping and robbery at Resurrection Church. That's where we bogged down. None of us could tie everything together.

And this was where Elaina spoke up.

"Okay, I do have a little information. But I don't want to, like, indict myself." She glanced in the direction of Ani. We had started calling her Ani during the pizza.

Ani did not give Elaina a reassuring glance, but stared at her with ice in her eyes. It was the kind of look that said, "If you don't talk, I'm going to kill you." That kind of look.

"So, I did get a chance to talk to Malia, Janeen Hargrove's classmate, the orphan."

None of us said anything.

Elaina continued. Her shoulders seemed to relax at the idea of being given permission to throw in. "She was crying for her parents for sure. But on Dickenson Street, she also said something about being horribly guilty because of what she did that caused Janeen's disappearance. Apparently, both of her parents had asked her to do what she had to do to get Janeen Hargrove outside during the formal."

Collective silence again. I felt a bridge being built here. My stomach started to churn a little. Part of it was probably the fourth piece of pizza.

"So," Elaina continued, "Malia picked on her, caused Janeen to run out, and she was taken."

"What did her parents offer her? Money?" This was from the detective. Ani's eyes had softened a little bit.

"It was to let her go to some sort of concert or some nonsense. You know, like how kids do."

"Be careful," Stu snorted, "You ain't much older than that girl."

Elaina rolled her eyes. Ani chuckled a little at this. It was a sweet sound, honestly. Stu had that effect on the tension.

"The most interesting part about this situation is that both of her parents work at the Maui Sewage Treatment Plant. They're—they *were* lower level. But it's interesting that they worked there."

I chimed in. "Yeah, this is what prompted me to make Elaina take me to Dickenson Street. At the school while the children waited, I caught a snippet of a fight between Malia and her dad. He was really putting the pressure on her to zip it. She was pretty shaken."

I thought of how that orphan girl probably wished she could see her dad's face again, under any context.

"There's something else," Elaina added. "I went over to the Sewage Treatment Plant—"

"What?" Ani asked. "You followed up on a lead? Without involving the police?"

Elaina looked down at her MacBook with shame. "I know, I know, but I just wanted to see if it was even worth looking into. But the plant was closed. Couldn't even get in. And there was a guy there, but he was pretty unhelpful."

"Who's the guy?" Stu asked.

"Bill Robertson. Said he wasn't an actual employee of

the place, but some sort of contractor for a short-term thing. Don't know much about him but that he had trouble giving up smoking, had to resort to—"

"This is all you got?" Ani asked. "And you're wondering why you shouldn't have involved the police?"

Shame came back to Elaina.

"Moment he would have seen a detective, don't know that he would have said anything," Stu said. He was looking down, too. No shame, just concentration.

"Maybe," Ani said, quietly, and she picked up her coffee mug to take a swig.

"One thing," Elaina raised her finger, "he did offer to take me inside to get a look at the personnel files, but that was right when Stu texted me that Pastor Grant had woken up. Plus, to be honest, I didn't wanna go in there with him alone. Guy was a little scary. Like really handsome, well-dressed."

Stu laughed. "Wow, sounds terrifying!"

We all laughed at this. And Elaina waved us off. Even Ani had a good chuckle.

"It's not that. It's that, I don't know how to explain it. He just seemed out of place."

We all got back into silence again. I felt just as bogged down and useless as before.

"You're something, Miss Elaina," Stu said as he gathered our pizza plates and took them to the sink. You followed a potential murderer up Highway 30 to a lookout. Then you up at Maui Sewage looking into stuff. Sounds like you might need to live at Resurrection and open up a P.I. business."

She shook her head. "Didn't even get in. Wish I had now."

I added, "I wish I could have gotten a chance to see that overlook. I feel like they might have missed something there."

Ani glared at me as I spoke.

"I mean Detective Kyle Kekoa has such a crush on me that I think he wouldn't look too closely at anything unless it had my fingerprint on it. I don't know. Maybe Black Audi guy threw a weapon out up there or something like that."

Ani nodded.

No doubters there.

Stu was standing at the sink when he spoke. "Well, I got a bit of an idea, but it's gonna require that same spirit of cooperation that's kept this brain trust from breaking out into fists."

We were captive.

"Think maybe you should go up to that overlook, Rev. Nothing else to do. Might even be something that Det Kyle missed. You right. He sounds like he got your scent. You and Elaina can head up that way, if she's willing to drive you, that is."

He switched off the light to the kitchen, leaving just the dining area on. He must be ready to go ASAP.

"I think maybe the sewage company might be worth a look. They closed all day for bereavement, but I think maybe we could get in there. I might be of the type that knows how to sidestep some locks."

Ani stood up. "This is where I gotta draw the line. I can't let you do this. Can't let you break into a place without any knowledge from the police. It doesn't work like that, Stu. I'm sorry."

Stu smiled. Bigger than the moon. His white perfect teeth revealed a confidence I aspired to.

"Thought you'd say that, Detective Iona. That's why

you and me are going together. That way if things get hairy, you can have my back."

I looked at Ani's face waiting for her to shoot Stu, but she said nothing. She was in.

We had a plan. And it was time to start executing it.

SIXTY-SEVEN

Back in Elaina's car. I felt like I was in a permanent Uber from Hell. Stu probably could have rigged something to turn this rickshaw into a convertible.

But I was happy about her company.

That was until she told me the bad news about Wednesday night's speaking engagement.

"You're kidding," I said.

"I'm sorry. I'm really sorry."

She breathed out. I smelled the perfume she was wearing waft over to me. If I wasn't in such distress, I'd have a mind to tell her how beautiful she smelled.

I suddenly became super self-conscious that I hadn't really showered much in the last forty-eight hours.

I shifted back into conversation. "Someone put a Facebook ad promoting my speaking."

Elaina winced. "I'm certain it was Moani Wong. He gets super possessive of the pulpit. Super possessive. And I think he thinks you'll bomb—"

"Well he would have been right," I interrupted.

We were on Highway 30 approaching the overlook.

Clouds loomed ahead but I still didn't get a sense of rain. According the radio we had been listening to, it was coming.

My shoulder and back were starting to hurt again. I hadn't had ibuprofen in about five seconds so I was a little uncomfortable.

Elaine went on. "But the bigger problem was right after Moani made the ad, that's when news broke of your attempted escape from authorities. The two things came together for a perfect storm of people morbidly curious."

I couldn't believe what I was hearing. "Alright, so some jerk makes a Facebook ad about me preaching some amazing message. Then a news story breaks where I'm a potential murderer and what—"

"And I had to turn the church's call forwarding off. I was getting so many questions about who was going to speak in your place. So many questions about how the church was going to handle employing a felon. And what statement we'd make."

When I put the picture of all this together in that Honda that couldn't be worth much more than the suit I'd bought and ruined, I couldn't deal with it. I thought Pittsburgh would kill me, but Maui was giving Pittsburgh a run for its money.

Elaina said, "Look, of course when I get back I'll make an ad to say that we aren't having the event—?"

"You think? Do you want me to preach in an orange jump suit?"

She giggled.

"Let's just track this killer down first. Then we'll get to —whatever it is that you wanna call this."

"Right, Pastor Grant."

Geez. I should have stayed in the bar.

SIXTY-EIGHT

The smell coming from the basement was over the top. Ani had smelled a lot of nasty things on her various assignments, but the basement of the sewage treatment facility was at the top. This couldn't be normal.

"When we figure all this out, I'm citing them."

"For what, detective?"

"For making me wanna puke, that's what."

Stu snickered.

They had checked, double checked, and triple checked the perimeters. Stu even had a device that made surveillance equipment go on the fritz.

This was a guy she'd like to have around in the force. But he'd rather be a janitor at a church.

Ani looked around. Machinery, equipment whirred with heavy motors. The files that they had found on the employees were empty. Someone had literally taken the documents out of them.

While Ani found that troubling, Stu had said that he expected nothing less.

"What are we doing here, Stu."

He smiled at her. "Not sure. I figured this was a place Miss Elaina wanted to get into, it was probably worth a look, you know."

They had searched around the different crevices and work areas and found nothing. The closer they got to the whirring machines, the worse the smell became.

And the angrier Ani got.

This was all frivolous. A dumb use of their time. No one was here. And no clue was here, either.

"One last corner, detective," Stu said as he pointed to a door that looked like it was going to some sort of utility closet.

Of course, the putrid stench of waste got worse and the machines grew louder as they stepped to the door.

The door was shut. Pretty tight. It was odd. It looked like the door had almost recently installed. The other puzzling thing about the door was that it had a very, very expensive heavy-duty-looking lock on it.

She pointed at the lock. "You ain't getting through that thing, Stu."

He shook his head and took a moment to touch the little gray patch on this chin. "I think you're right, ma'am. But one thing I realize is the door that's closed the hardest is usually the one you need opened the most, you dig?"

She did. She knew that he was right.

"If I could get a guarantee of leeway from if I were brought up on destruction-of-property charges, I might be able to find a workaround for that lock."

Ani couldn't believe this was her life right now, but she found herself nodding to Stu.

When she tossed Lulani his badge, she tossed her career with it. Who cares?

Stu fiddled for what seemed like an eternity. He used

tools that Ani had never seen before. She meant to ask him when they were done with this business if he had invented them.

Finally, the monstrous-looking deadbolt on the door clicked and Stu threw a fist in the air. Ani wanted to as well, but thought the better of it.

Stu pulled on the door. It wouldn't budge. Ani also took a shot. Nothing.

Stu kicked it, fiddled with the lock, kicked some more, and fiddled with the lock.

Finally, the door gave a little in their direction. Emboldened by the hope, Stu planted his feet firmly and pulled.

The door opened.

It was... a room. No, not a room. A cell.

Stu gasped and put his hand on his head at the sight.

Ani's stomach felt like it was going to come up. She stared at the small refrigerator in the corner. The little makeshift closet lights that made up all the illumination of the room. But what made her want to throw up was the bed in the corner. There was no one in the bed. This room was empty.

But on the floor just through the door were pieces of Janeen Hargrove's formal dress.

The torn fragments were covered in blood.

SIXTY-NINE

Elaina and I stood at the Papawai Point Overlook. My goodness, her perfume. That jean jacket. Would this woman really be working with me?

No, Grant. You're going to jail for potential kidnapping and murder. This isn't gonna work.

We stood in the lot. It was empty of visitors because clouds were looming over the horizon. The view was still breathtaking, but in a minute we were gonna be wet. The wind was hitting pretty hard. My Aloha t-shirt simply wasn't warm enough. I should have brought a hoodie or something.

Elaina hugged herself as we looked around.

"So what are we exactly expecting?" I asked.

"He parked here. I promise."

"I'm not doubting it. But I just don't know what we ought to do."

"This is hot bed for visitors. Maybe he hid something."

I was puzzled. "Hid something?"

"I don't know. Maybe he left us a clue or something."

"Elaina, this isn't Hansel and Gretel. I mean, we're talking about a stone-cold murderer here."

I could tell she was getting embarrassed.

I looked left and looked right. I was shocked that Maui didn't invest in more than the flimsy little guardrail to keep visitors from attempting to climb the rocks to get a more unobstructed view.

"What are you doing?" Elaina asked. I felt her grab for my arm but didn't realize that I was advancing toward the guardrail.

"If this guy isn't afraid to take out a cop or kidnap a girl, I don't think Maui heights are going to do it for him."

"Grant, what—"

I stepped over the guardrail. As I did, the first clap of thunder made both of us jump. The clouds seemed to be accelerating in their approach to the overlook. I could smell rain in the air.

On the other side of the guardrail, my shoulder ached because I was tensing every muscle. The wind didn't add to my confidence and when I looked down it was pretty unbelievable.

Death was only one step in the wrong direction away.

"Pastor Grant, please, come—"

"Elaina, there seems to be a little bit of a footpath here. Let me check this out. Stay on the other side of the guardrail, and if I go in the drink, call an ambulance. But don't let that Moani guy do the funeral. I'd rather have Stu."

I looked ahead, taking my steps. Stu's tennis shoes were a little loose, and I was regretting not lacing them tighter.

There seemed to be a natural cleft into the rocks—a shelter even. It looked as though there was ample room to stand. If the murderer was hiding something, it was here for sure.

A few more steps and I was there. Thunder clapped once more, but I didn't jump this time.

"Elaina," I yelled. I was only about twenty-five feet away. "There is something here."

"What? What is it?"

I could tell by the sound of her voice that she'd stepped back a little bit. I was fine with that. It was getting windier, and I wasn't paying attention to the type of shoes she was wearing.

On the ground, in the corner there was a rectangular object. I reached down and picked it up. It was a little warped from the weather. I couldn't tell what it was. It looked like a torn-up piece of cardboard. No clue what it was. It looked like a box top or something.

I stood up and turned around and noticed something else closer to the edge. I had to get on my knees to get close enough to the edge. The wind was giving me hell. It actually started to sting. My arms and legs were covered in gooseflesh.

I reached down and picked up the object of interest.

I knew it all too well. It was a swizzle stick. A nice one. I saw them in the Phone Booth growing up. It was the classy way to stir a drink. The new ones were all disposable and plastic. You put these thick ones into drinks when you were trying to impress someone.

This one was plastic and it had grooves in it. Looked like teeth marks.

An animal?

Yeah, man. A raccoon uses these to stir its martinis.

Cardboard, or what looked like cardboard. And a swizzle stick. Wow. Nothing of use whatsoever. Perry Mason couldn't even build a case with this.

I prepared to stand up but stopped. I squinted and

looked down on the jagged rocks. The waves were thrashing against them with the weather's vengeance. Which also meant that the tide was going out further before it pulled the water back.

I stopped breathing.

There was a body down there. I couldn't see the face, but I saw the legs caught on the rocks. The boots were sticking up out of the water. The body moved up and down like a buoy. Arms flailing in reaction to the current. Lifeless and horrifying.

My mouth tasted like I'd swallowed vinegar all of a sudden.

Another murder.

I had to call someone. This was bigger than me. I had to—

Detective Kyle Kekoa. I had to call him. He'd answer. He'd know it wasn't me.

What are you thinking? He's going to throw you in jail faster than you can say Aloha.

It didn't matter. How many more people were going to die? I didn't do any of this.

I opened my burner and dialed his number.

"Grant," he answered in one ring.

"Detective listen—"

"Where are you? I'm going—"

"Please, there's been a murder. Another murder."

"Who'd you kill this time?" He had that venom in his voice.

The wind was getting uncompromising and I started to feel the spittle of the rain. It was gonna come down.

"In that space that Elaina, the secr—administrator told you about."

"I checked that—"

"Kyle, did you actually go over the guardrails or did you just go to the overlook."

Silence.

Yeah, that's what I thought.

"Get here, now. Papawai Overlook."

"I know where it is, but you better be there when I get there."

I started to move back toward Elaina, one cautious tread at a time. "No promises, bro. But get here."

I broke the call, put the cell in my pocket with the swizzle stick, and clutched the cardboard.

"Elaina, you hit the nail—"

I stopped ten feet from the guardrail. Elaina stood there with her hands in the air. Behind her was a man in a ski mask.

He was pointing a revolver at her head.

SEVENTY

Thunder cracked above. That darkness that seemed so uncharacteristic of any brochure I'd ever seen of Hawaii began to settle down upon us.

Me, Elaina, and the masked gunman.

I had nothing on me but a decade-old t-shirt. This was the worst kind of situation.

But, I had my mouth.

"Hey man, you don't wanna do this."

Cliché. Best I could do.

He swore and shoved Elaina forward. Her head jerked backwards.

She had the most hopeless of looks on the prettiest of faces.

"Okay, okay." I raised my hands above my head. Still had that stupid damp piece of cardboard in my hand. As I lifted my hands pain shot through my shoulder and I felt the invasion of raindrops on my skin.

"This is it. You've screwed this up enough. You should have been dealt with at the church."

"Look, seriously. I'm not gonna lie to you. I called the cops a moment ago."

He held the gun up to Elaina's head.

"I know, I know, please," I pleaded. My voice was completely divorced from control. "The cops want to pin this all on me, can you believe that?"

"Yeah, what do you think we've been working on?"

He was bitter.

"But honestly, they're on their way here to arrest me. Like at this very moment."

He was silent. I hoped inside his twisted mind the cogs were turning.

"And honestly, we might have a past, you and me, but we could all make out of this alright."

As I spoke, I inched slowly to the guard rail, narrowing the gap. I noticed that this man was relatively tall. He was as broad as a refrigerator and not nearly as cool. He was wearing a dark jump suit. If he had a white mask on instead of the black ski mask that every villain tends to wear, I'd think it was from some sort of scary movie.

"You better back off, Pastor. I know you think you could handle your business, but I will cut this chick down."

Elaina squinted as the masked man pushed the gun to the back of her head.

Back a step. "Okay, okay. But keep this in mind. You can go scot-free. None of us have seen your face. None of us."

Elaina nodded her head. I could see the relief in her face starting to come. I thought this was it.

The man began to laugh. It started as a snicker, but then a bit of a belly laugh. It was interrupted by the thunder and a flash of lightning. It was getting darker with every moment.

Or was that just how close I knew we were to death?

As he laughed, with this free hand, he pulled his mask off.

My stomach dropped into Hell. He had no intention of letting us live.

None.

We were dead.

"Yeah, there you go preacher."

He didn't look like what I expected, but what was worse, was that he had something protruding out of his eye. It looked like a drywall screw or something. His cheek was stained with bruises and blood.

I thought that the bruises may have been my handiwork. The blood was definitely from that screw.

But his other drywall-screw-free eye was filled with rage and exhaustion. He had a slight beard and his face was full.

I shifted my focus from him as he giggled, to Elaina. I could see the terror. She'd die first, for sure. Bullet in the head. Then he'd empty the rest of that clip into me as I fell, most likely dead already, into the Pacific. Worse ways to go, I guess.

But I wasn't going to let it end without a fight.

I stared at Elaina.

Beautiful stranger, there's no way out of this. Please, make some sort of move to get me some leverage here.

"Listen, bud—"

"Not what you expected, did you. Not Prince Charming, but it'll be the last thing—"

The sirens began to break the distant silence. I had never felt more hopeful and horrified in equal measure. The sound startled him, and I saw shock coming from his eyes... eye.

I took a moment to nod in Elaina's direction, focusing all of my mind in an attempt to will her to action.

And then it went fast and slow at once.

She fell backwards into him without looking and threw a clumsy elbow with all of her force. I could see the effort on her face. Lucky for us, she hit nothing but gut. He groaned as she fell down on top of him.

I didn't see much more beyond that because I had already leapt over that guardrail.

Elaina was on top of Cyclops, who'd now reached one of his massive arms around her neck, but not securely. She thrashed left and right and attempted to roll away. With his other hand he was pulling the gun to her head, but not before I drove one of Stu's loose-fitting sneaks down onto the drywall screw coming out of his eye.

He screamed this time. Really hollered, and pulled away to nurse himself. I pulled Elaina away from him and threw her toward the car.

I didn't think I took very long, but I apparently I misjudged, because he came at my face with the side of gun.

Pain exploded in my head and I knew I had a microsecond to get him under control before he made Swiss cheese out of me.

He raised the pistol and—sad to admit it—I caught him in the nuts with another quick kick. I had more leverage this time.

No rules against that, remember?

The weapon dropped along with the one-eyed assailant.

"Though you had enough of me after our last date, Prince Charming," I said, getting my mojo back.

Sirens drew nearer. Ran began to fall faster. And I was standing over top of the man when he kicked my legs out from under me in one blasting attempt.

My legs flew up and I hit the ground. I couldn't find my breath with a GPS and a guide dog. Most I could do was move left and right a little and try to get my shocked system into reboot.

One-eye was up again, standing over me. He picked up the gun with a smile and prepared to give me another cranial hole when he thrashed left.

Elaina was back.

She was screaming as she hit him, and in an instant I realized she overestimated her own strength against this gorilla.

He took the gun like he had with me and cracked her hard across the face. She spun like a top and fell to the ground near me. I went to get up but before I could find purchase, the refrigerator kicked me mercilessly in the ribs. I lifted off the ground and back down again like I was on a see-saw.

I gasped in horror as he picked up Elaina and walked toward his car. It looked like some sort of a beat-up Chevy.

I finally gained my breath and started after them. I was on my feet and pushing. I pulled in air through broken ribs and I wouldn't live and let this buffoon take her.

He had Elaina over his shoulder like a rag doll. He dropped her to the ground, got into the car and fired up the engine.

He's going to run her over. He's going to kill her.

But that's not what he did.

He shifted the car out of park, turned the wheels in my direction and floored it toward me. I turned to retreat, but I wasn't fast enough. I felt the hood lift me up from behind and as he slammed on the brakes, I went flying over the guardrail of the overlook, heading toward the jagged cliffs below.

SEVENTY-ONE

Elaina gained clarity just in time to see Sawyer Grant fly over the guardrail. He was there and then gone.

He was dead. And she was next.

The rain offered a little relief to the pounding in her head. She welcomed its coolness, but she thought that she was going to black out. She tasted blood in her mouth and felt like she wanted to go to sleep. But more than anything, she was terrified.

She didn't want to die up here. And when the now-unmasked man picked her up and threw her into the passenger seat of a junky old Buick, she knew that what was ahead of her might be worse than what had just happened.

"Get cozy, love. This ride isn't much, but we can always pick another one up on the way. Didn't have time to check this one out like I normally do."

The car smelled like mold. Rancid. She kept thinking she was going to vomit. And then he'd be so angry at her that he'd kill her right on sight.

She couldn't die in this car. She couldn't die with this

maniac. Her only hope was the preacher, and now he was dead.

They drove, but he was cautious. He wasn't going too fast. Elaina figured that was to avoid getting pulled over. The dim headlamps made beams through the rain drops.

"This is all gonna work out, girlie. We just have to get the cargo to the boss."

Cargo?

He was taking the bends carelessly, and as they advanced up Route 30, Elaina imagined that she'd be meeting Sawyer Grant in the ocean.

The man looked to be in his mid-fifties. He looked completely insane. The screw in his eye still protruded slightly. Grant had done a real number on him.

"Hope you don't mind I smoke. Nasty I know but can't seem to kick it, you know?"

Elaina didn't respond.

He pushed in one of those ancient car-cigarette lighters. The kind that come out when they're ready to be used to light the cigarette.

Rain was pouring down, but Elaina didn't want to die in this car. She searched her mind with every possible situation. She wondered if the police would find her. She wondered if they'd find Grant's body. Janeen. All of it.

She thought of Katharine Hepburn. Ingrid Bergman. All those classic ladies and how they'd handle themselves. The pain in her head was so sharp. It was exaggerated by the twisting and turning of the nasty injured man's driving up Highway 30. Lights of other cars flooding into sight on the left. The vast darkness of the ocean and cliffs to the right.

He laughed again, and then placed his hand on her leg, moving it up her thigh.

Her breath became shallow and bile rose up in her throat. Elaina pulled away, and the man smashed his hand off the dashboard in anger.

"Princess, you're a bonus to this mission. Do you honestly think it's going to matter if you struggle?"

Elaina felt herself wanting to throw up. She held it back. Tried to center herself.

She imagined Ingrid Bergman. Imagined a strong woman. Self-sufficient.

He repositioned his hand, higher up on her trembling thigh. As he did the car jerked a little out of his control, causing him to grab the wheel with both hands.

The twisting, the turning. The mold smell.

Cargo?

Grant was dead. She was next. She was alone in a car with a kidnapper and murderer. He was going to do what he wanted and kill her.

Then something clicked.

Literally.

The lighter popped out signifying its readiness to be used to light a cigarette.

"Yeah, we could make this nice princess," he said, as he took a cigarette out of a pack in the upper pocket of his jump suit. "You don't—"

Elaina couldn't let this moment pass. She grabbed the cigarette lighter out of its socket, and before the disgusting pig had a chance to finish his perverted thought, she shoved the lighter into the side of his cheek with all her might.

As hard as she could.

Instantly, the smell of burning flesh filled the already putrid car, but she dug in further.

He screamed and the car fishtailed left into the

oncoming traffic lane. She didn't let go of the lighter. She pushed even harder into his face.

If Elaina was going out, it was on her terms.

A truck's lights filled the window with brightness as the kidnapper pulled the wheel right, narrowly missing the head-on collision. But he overcorrected.

Elaina screamed as he tried to bring the wheel steady.

He didn't.

The car plowed through the guardrail on the right leaving Elaina with one singular thought:

She'd be meeting Sawyer Grant sooner rather than later.

SEVENTY-TWO

Pain shot through my hands, and the thin edge of the guardrail sliced into my fingers. I had tried to grab the top of it, but lost my grip and ended up grabbing the section that was driven into the ground.

My shoulder felt like it was going to explode and my stomach was scraped by the uneven rocks as I attempted to gain more stability and not fall to my bloody death.

He had Elaina. He was going to take her and do God knows what with her. I had to get moving.

The rain poured over me, and I felt that any way that I tried pulling up would cause me to lose my grip completely.

But I had to take a shot. I had to get up.

I flung my feet beneath me as gently as I could, trying to find any type of footing. My right foot caught a deep divot in the side of the cliff and I didn't think twice.

I pushed up, at the same time summoning what strength was left in my back, to pull to the upper part of the guardrail. My footing held and as I let go, I caught hold of the rail. Once again, I felt pain shoot through my fingers, but I had a better grip.

I repeated the action, finding a foothold and thrusting myself up until I was able to get my arm over the guardrail completely.

It was just enough time for me to see Screw Eye's car pull back out onto 30. It was an older Chevy. Looked like a Lumina. But it was nothing but taillights and speed.

I collapsed onto the ground and rolled, getting back to my feet. I was hoping I hadn't broken ribs, but it didn't matter now. Everything was on the line.

I ran to Elaina's Civic and jumped in. I took a moment to thank God that she'd left the keys in it. I started it up and threw it into reverse just in time to see Detective Kyle Kekoa's vehicle ride up, blocking my clean exit. The police lights bounced off of the mountainous rocky wall and flashed in my eyes of the rear view of the Civic.

Every moment mattered.

I could see Kyle's scowl also. He already had a pistol out and he was making the decision about whether to fire on me to keep me from running.

I had to make my own decision.

I put the car in drive and floored the Civic toward the guardrail while at the same time turning the wheel as far as it would go. The car fishtailed as I pulled out onto Highway 30, barely glancing behind me to see if I had cut someone off.

It only took a moment to see the lights of the Explorer growing closer and closer.

No matter what happened ahead, my running was over.

SEVENTY-THREE

Elaina opened her eyes. She was afraid at what she'd see. She knew she was in too much pain to be in Heaven. Her head throbbed. She must have hit it off the dashboard.

The first thing she did was look left.

There was the ugly man. The pig. The kidnapper. He stared ahead. Nothing but fear in his good eye. He was as still as a deer.

Elaina followed his gaze and saw it.

Ocean. Just through the windshield. Endless ocean. It looked like a sheet of black ice. Rain pattered off the hood and roof the car. And with exception of the slight leak of fluids and maybe air from the tires making noise, the rain was all Elaina could really focus on.

The weak beams of light from the headlamps seemed to provide not even the slightest bit of illumination into the vast depth of dark. Elaina did notice the raindrops cutting through the beams, though.

She looked right. And there was the confirmation of her fear.

The car had gone through the guardrail on Highway 30.

But only halfway through. The car was stopped. Straddling the edge of the cliff. Elaina sat back a little in her chair and felt the car move with her.

She looked over at the monster. The predator's good eye widened as the car see-sawed on the edge of the cliff.

Elaina let out a couple sharp gasps and in an instant she was cognizant of every single movement. She felt she was one inhale away from slowly seeing this car find its way to the bottom of the sea.

She'd die from the impact of hitting the water first.

"You put us in a bit of a bind here," the kidnapper said through clenched teeth.

Elaina didn't respond. She couldn't quit looking at the vast ocean. She was glad she couldn't see cliffs. She knew if she caught a glimpse of them she'd throw up.

But she wasn't worried about this man hurting her now. They were both on an equal playing field now.

They were both at death's door.

"Really couldn't just let it go, could you?" the man asked. "You definitely have no idea what you did."

Sirens blared from afar. Elaina felt a slight relief, but couldn't allow herself celebration. She was afraid a police officer would accidentally push the car into the depths of the ocean.

"Really, you had to have that reaction to me having a little fun with you? You have no idea what you've done."

"Oh, I do. I know exactly what I've done. You were going to kill me anyway. I had to make my choice. It was mine to make."

Without taking his eye off the ocean, the man smiled. And began to chuckle. It was a low growling chuckle. Then it turned into a bit of a bellow.

Elaina squeezed her fists so tight she knew that her nails had cut into the flesh of her palms.

He settled a little to a quiet wheeze.

"I made my choice." Elaina said.

As the sirens neared closer, another sound invaded Elaina's frightened mind. A sound that she couldn't quite reconcile to the situation she was in.

It almost sounded like it was coming from a tin can. But it wasn't. It was coming from the trunk.

A sound of a young girl. Crying. Sobbing in fact. Weeping. A young girl.

The young girl.

Elaina turned and looked into the back seat.

It was empty.

But Janeen Hargrove sobbed from the trunk.

She not only heard sirens, but the familiar sound of her own car. She wondered if she imagined that. Imagined the familiarity of it. The sirens were upon them; red and blue filled interior of the car with foreign shadows.

Elaina returned her gaze to the captor. This time he was staring at her with his disfigured face looking at her fully.

He smiled hideously. "Looks like you made the choice for her, too."

SEVENTY-FOUR

I stood there staring in horror at the car. It was teetering on the edge of the cliff. Elaina. She was in there.

Kyle was only a fraction of a moment behind me. He threw his car into park and got out with his gun fixed at me.

The rain was coming down harder, and I was soaked to the bone.

"Kyle, please. The girl from church. She's in the car. That's the kidnapper."

Kyle hadn't even noticed the car hanging. He was so fixed on me.

He lowered his side arm and ran to where I was behind the car.

At this point other cars had started piling up just to see.

The wind and the rain kicked up. I felt the droplets and thought about Elaina being in there.

Kyle kept the gun out and was pointing it lazily toward the car.

"Listen, please stay still," he screamed.

The windows were up. I wasn't sure if they were dead or alive.

I had to believe they were alive.

Kyle came near me. He had his phone out. "I'm calling in someone who can fasten on to this car and pull it back."

"By the time they arrive she'll be dead." I saw the nose move downward.

How many more times was it going to teeter before falling?

"She's dead. They're dead. If we wait."

Kyle said, "Shut up. They can fix this."

I knew that time was what we didn't have. The car moved forward once more. It just needed a strong wind and Elaina would be gone in the ocean.

I figured out what I had to do.

"Elaina," I screamed as I ran toward the car.

"Grant," Kyle said. "Grant!"

"Elaina, when I jump on the back I want you to climb into the back seat and get out."

The car was coming back again. The back was coming down almost to the ground. That was my cue.

I ran and jumped onto the trunk of the car. I saw a scurrying inside of the car and then I realized that the one-eyed man was still conscious. He was hitting Elaina.

And there was someone in the trunk. The very trunk that I was lying across.

SEVENTY-FIVE

Elaina reached over and attempted to push the button releasing the trunk. The one-eyed kidnapper laughed and punched her in the head.

"Yeah, this isn't going to be so easy is it? Now you know how everything I've done in this job has been."

Pastor Grant was on the trunk. The rain was pouring hard now. Both darkness and water seemed to be consuming them. The mildew smell in the car was stronger than ever, and the kidnapper had lost his mind.

"I think maybe I'll be the one—"

Suddenly, a light came beaming into the car. Both Elaina and the kidnapper squinted.

A man's voice. Detective Kyle maybe. "Listen to me closely. If you do not allow this woman out of the car and pop that trunk, I will put a bullet in your head."

He wheezed. Elaina smelled his foul breath. "Put a bullet in me. I'll drive this Buick into the unknown, pig. Promise me you'll go light on my jail time if I let them go. Promise."

Detective Kyle didn't respond.

"Promise me, I said. Or you're gonna have some dead bodies to answer for."

Elaina looked back at Grant who was still on the trunk and who seemed to have stabilized the car.

Detective Kyle said, "All right. It'll be noted. With your cooperation we can make the sentence pass like a day at the park. But right now, I need something from you. Let the girl out first while the preacher is on the back.

Elaina watched with anticipation as the kidnapper smiled, unlocked the door and motioned for Elaina to climb into the backseat.

She moved as quick as she could. Trying to avoid touching any part of the man with her body as she dove in between the front seats to get to the back. Elaina opened the door and collapsed on the wet ground as the rain flooded her senses.

"Okay," Detective Kyle said, keeping his light on the man. Now, pop the trunk latch when we tell you."

Elaina moved toward the rear of the car. Realizing how quickly she'd come to her own death. She wanted to hug Grant. Wanted to thank him for what he'd done.

But he was braced on the trunk. Slowly, Grant put one foot on the ground, followed by the other.

Detective Kyle continued. "Okay, now pop that trunk."

Elaina was horrified to hear the clicking of the trunk but no apparent release. Sawyer Grant stood waiting with his arms open. Finally, after the third click, the trunk popped.

Grant slowly opened the trunk. Elaina was next to him. And there she was.

Janeen Hargrove. She was a pretty blond girl. She'd been beaten. Rather badly in her face. But she was far from death. So long as they could lift her out of the car.

Elaina kept the trunk lid open with her hands as Grant reached down to her. Janeen pulled up and into his arms.

Grant squeezed her tight like he was embracing a long-lost relative.

Detective Kyle was ready to offer his next directive.

"Okay, now the girl is clear, I need you to come out, hands up and we'll get you to safety. Understand?"

Elaina was holding Janeen who was sobbing. She was sobbing too. They both were loud.

She looked up at Sawyer Grant as he smiled down at her. Then she turned her attention back to Janeen who was still trembling.

At the same time, the car teetered forward and fell onto the cliffs.

SEVENTY-SIX

Kyle pulled me back to his car and threw me onto the hood.

"What did you just do? Who do you think you are? You let that car go on purpose."

He pulled my hands back like I was Stretch Armstrong. "Detective, I didn't. I was trying to brace it. You saw!"

He slammed my head onto the hood of the SUV. "You did it. You killed that guy. You did it on purpose."

"Detective, I did nothing, but look, he had the girl. He was the perp. He was the guy you'd been looking for. And now he's gone. Did you really wanna make a deal with him?"

Kyle said, "You are going to jail."

"Detective," Elaina said. "He didn't. We both had Janeen. We both were consoling her. He was holding the car and it just lifted up and went in. It could have been the dirt."

Kyle let his hold go a little bit on me.

"Detective, I saw it," she repeated.

Kyle sighed, pulled my hands apart, and pulled me up by the collar on my t-shirt. We were standing eye to eye.

"Grant, this isn't over. I wanna get the truth out of you at least once in my lifetime."

"Detective, you said 'thank you for helping me rescue a girl' wrong."

I was done with this. Now that I was clean, I wasn't going to let this overzealous cop trying to make a name for himself always make me feel like I'd done something wrong. As far as I was concerned, we were done.

There were already other cops on the scene. And Stu and Ani had shown up, too.

Elaina and I were standing by the Explorer and she looked at me with those bright and intelligent eyes.

"Pastor Grant," she said. Her voice was crackly and exhausted.

"Yes," I said.

"I don't like to lie."

PART 4

Moani had never seen a line so long to get into the church. He sat in the front where he always sat. Front row in the sanctuary. He looked up at the massive pulpit. He longed for it. He was wearing a dark blue suit. At a certain angle it almost looked purple.

Like royalty.

The church background music was blaring, but it couldn't be heard because of the chatter among the crowd.

As the church folks always did, they filed into the back of the church first. So many faces. Children. Men. Women. People that Moani had never seen.

Where were you all when I was preaching?

He banished the thought.

Lila, his mother, sat beside him. She looked pretty, too. The color of her dress almost matched his suit. Moani didn't like that much, but it wasn't worth the fight. Not on a night like this.

"They're here for me, Ma."

She shook her head. "No, Moani, they're here because of you. Because you made that Facebook ad. Because the preacher happened to be on the news. Because they connected your ad to the news story and to his exoneration yesterday. As it turned out, he saved the kidnapped girl. So, yes, son, they're here because of you. But they're really here *for him*. Grant."

The thought made Moani clam up. Hearing his name made him itch with envy.

Who did he think he was being on Maui for three days and becoming a celebrity?

More people came in. The board had appointed some ushers to help guide people to seats. Everything was just about filled and Moani was tired of looking at everyone.

Moani bowed his head and began to pray. Jesus said to pray for your enemies. Jesus didn't say how to pray for them. So Moani prayed that Sawyer Grant would do terribly. He prayed that he would have to step aside and allow Moani to take over. Then Moani would be behind the pulpit, where he belonged.

He was really praying hard when a hand tapped him on his shoulder. It was jarring. He opened his eyes and looked up and felt a twinge of recognition. He stood up and shook the hand of his friend.

"So glad you could make it. I wasn't sure if you'd be able."

William Robertson, the visitor from last week, smiled.

"Wouldn't have missed it for the world, honestly," he said.

SEVENTY-EIGHT

I stood in the corner on the stage. The stage was so large no one noticed me. Also, there were a million and a half people in the church.

I dry heaved at the sight.

I still didn't feel tip-top. And my sleep was less than desirable, but after being exonerated and declared a national hero in Maui, I felt that I didn't need to be so on edge.

Until I saw that crowd.

I thought about the people I'd served with in the military. I thought about the faith. Thought about some of the conversations. I clutched my Bible to my chest like it was life support. I had ten pages of notes printed out.

But somehow I still had no idea what I was going to say.

The crackling of the sound system overhead made me feel very distracted. I wish they'd just shut the music off completely.

I'd talk to Stu about that. I glanced into the crowd of people, looking for places to sit. Many had resorted to standing in the back.

Of course, in the front stood Moani. He was the reason why I wanted to go jump off a cliff.

What a jerk.

He and his mother were fawning over some guy in a suit. Some good-looking guy that probably was saying something like, *Oh, Moani, I wish you were speaking instead of this guy.*

Whatever.

I looked to the other side and saw Elaina. Something made my heart skip a beat every time she looked at me from across the room. She smiled at me. Her smile said *you got this.*

The music director started to lead the church in song, but most people weren't singing. First, they didn't know the words. Second, these weren't church people. They were people here to look with morbid curiosity.

Like I was going to stand on my head and spit out plumeria or something.

Ten pages of notes and didn't know what I was saying. I had studied to the best of my ability, which wasn't much at all.

The music was too short, and before I knew it, the music director was reading my type-out biography.

I did a quick dry heave once more. It was a silent one, so that was okay. It really was.

And then the vacant pulpit was mine.

The room was quiet. And when I walked up and took my spot. Applause erupted. Whistles, yells. And before I knew it, people were on their feet clapping.

I was overwhelmed. But I looked through the crowd. I found Elaina again. She had the brightest eyes and smile. I glanced halfway up the pews to see Ani on the end seat, almost pushed into the row. She had a smile on her, too. She looked so much better with a smile.

And finally, in the back, I saw Stu. He was punching the air with his fist and showing every one of those perfect teeth.

Maybe I could do this. Maybe I could.

The applause began to die down and my nerves returned.

Oh no, they are actually going to expect me to say something.

The lights seemed like they got brighter as the crowd got quieter. I was thirsty all of a sudden. I felt like I couldn't breathe.

While the last clappers ceased, I looked down at Moani the troublemaker and his mom. They both had their arms folded and they were scowling.

What a great look.

I then glanced over at Moani's Number One fan. Unlike them, he was smiling. Nicely dressed guy. He was looking right in my eyes.

But there was something about him.

His outfit? No.

His friendship with Moani. Possibly.

But something sticking out.

Stick.

He was chewing on a stick. One of those sticks I used to use to make cocktails. Instead of it being a drink, it was between his—

I froze completely as the last clap happened.

I had found one of those sticks at the overlook.

Someone else involved. The mastermind.

I couldn't take my eyes off him. And his frown started to

form. I looked down at his hands and saw that he had something. A weapon.

I didn't know what else to say. I put my lips against the microphone fashioned onto the pulpit and I screamed, "Everyone in here, get down now!"

As soon as I said it, screams and murmurs began to wave through. I saw the barrel of his gun come out with a silencer attached to it. He fired three shots at me.

SEVENTY-NINE

I thought for sure I'd been hit, but thankfully the gopher wood used to construct the pulpit was bullet proof.

The screams, the shouts, the voices. Everything was blending.

And I was a walking target on a raised platform.

Not much of a challenge.

I poked my head around the corner, and the man was walking toward the back of the church. Moani and his mom were in the front row holding each other like lovers. I jumped off the platform.

Ani was there to meet me.

"Grant, what—"

"There, get him."

The well-dressed shooter turned toward me and popped off another round. This went wide, but it splintered the woodgrain corner of the pew I was standing near.

Ani got into the Windsor stance and prepared to take a shot. I stopped her. "You can't, the people." I managed.

This man wasn't getting away. He wasn't getting away. I

charged toward him through the pew that had almost completely emptied of people.

He was between two other church goers. A man and a woman, frantically walking but getting nowhere fast.

Fear had spread through the people like a virus, and everyone thought everyone was the shooter.

But the calmest in the crowd was most dangerous.

There were three people standing between me and him. He glanced back at me.

"It's over," I screamed. "You lost."

He didn't agree. He turned with his gun and aimed it at point-blank range to my head.

At the point where I thought that this would be my last moment this side of eternity, the shooter nudged forward as if pushed and he fell to his knees. Stu was behind him.

Good hit, Stu.

The people between us cleared. Stu stood ready to engage him in a fight, and I narrowed the gap between me and the shooter.

I landed my first punch right on his chin. It wasn't a very effective punch because he matched it and then some. He punched me so hard in the forehead that I felt like I had just been head-butted. I stumbled backward but didn't fall. Stu was behind him preparing to advance again.

The shooter must have known because he turned around with his pistol to cut Stu down.

"No!" I shouted.

But I wasn't fast enough. Before I knew it, Ani had opened fire and popped one right into the guy's shoulder.

I wanted to rejoice but couldn't. Stunned, but determined, the shooter lifted the barrel and brought it down against Stu's face. Stu spun and fell to the ground like a sack of potatoes.

I grabbed the shooter in a headlock from behind and we both hit the floor. He threw a hard elbow into my ribs, but I squeezed him with all that I had in me.

His legs kicked and flailed as he wriggled his way out of it. Once there was enough distance between us, he caught me in the side of the head with his shoe. Pain exploded all through my brain and I was on my back.

"All you had to do was nothing, preacher," he said as he picked up his suppressed gun. "All—"

And that was it. Ani emptied an entire clip into him. He flailed left and right like a rag doll before finally collapsing into a puddle of his own blood onto the green carpet of the church.

I looked over at Ani who had tears in her eyes once more.

I knew she wasn't thinking about us.

And I was okay with that, because whatever she was thinking had worked.

EIGHTY

Stu sat at the preacher's desk staring at the gun. The repairs had come out nicely. He had all the bullet holes patched up. Scuffs taken out of the wall. He even replaced some of the volumes of books that had been damaged. This place was right as rain.

Hargrove came in and lifted his hands as if showing he wasn't armed. Stu realized it was because the gun was on the desk.

"Mr. Hargrove, no worries. Think this bad boy was a leftover from our other visitor, the one that tried to kill everyone."

Hargrove dropped his hands and smiled. He was wearing a pair of tan khakis and a black sport jacket. He actually looked a little dressed down than he sometimes did when he came to the church office. He took a seat on the other side of the desk.

Stu heard the chair creak and was reminded that he had to swap out those old dinosaurs for something a little more comfortable. Only part of the office Moani's momma hadn't sprung for.

"This place really shaped up nicely, I thought," Stu said.

"Yeah, great work," Hargrove said.

"Shaping up good for Rev Grant, huh?"

Hargrove pursed his lips together. Stu knew this was gonna be the first of two awkward parts of their conversation.

"You really think we should let that guy come be the preacher? We haven't even heard a sermon yet. And he has a pretty sordid past. Got a violent streak. He was more comfortable handling a sidearm than the Psalms, you know."

"Absolutely agree. Boy needs some practice. And I'll tell you, after his show at the church and how quickly he got that situation neutralized—not to mention he pretty much saved your little girl—that all might factor in on the decision."

Hargrove shook his head. "Sure, I'm going to reward him myself when I see him, but honestly, I don't know if I can go along with the decision."

"Don't gotta worry about it, Mr. Hargrove. I already spoke to the board. Told them my opinion. They said they're bending in his direction. Got really enthusiastic about the idea too when I told them that the increase that I was throwing into my giving would more than cover his salary."

Hargrove smiled. "Not many of us can say that."

"Hey, Mr. Hargrove. Never really thought of it as a bargaining chip before, but I think this might be the beginning of making Resurrection a beacon on a hill again. A real lighthouse."

"Yep, sure. And since you already talked to the board

without my approval, it's a moot point. But keep in mind, the brighter the light the more bugs it attracts."

Stu laughed. "Good follow-through on that metaphor, Mr. Hargrove!" He paused. "Owe you an apology, too. Sorry. I hadn't come in much this whole week. But Miss Elaina told me you were trying to get in. Hadn't had a chance to key the lock to our master."

Hargrove lifted his hands. "No problem. I know that you had a lot going on."

Stu smiled. The biggest smile he knew how to give. "You right, Mr. Hargrove. And it slipped my mind about this Cadillac of an office compared to the Rev, that business over at Dickenson Street, and little Miss Janeen's misfortune."

Hargrove looked down at the ground. "Yeah, it's been the hardest week of my life."

"Can't imagine."

There was silence between them for a moment.

"Although, I did find it a little odd how worried you were about this office."

Hargrove still stared down.

"Know what I mean, Mr. Hargrove?"

Hargrove rubbed his smooth head. "No, I actually don't."

"Well, I'll tell ya, I was really afraid of someone coming back to get a hold of one of these fine collectibles. So I did some reinforcements on the windows, as you see.

Hargrove nodded. "Excellent work."

Stu raised a finger in the air. "Also changed that lock, as you said. Put something a little more sturdy there, eliminating anyone but me that had a key."

Hargrove didn't respond but just nodded more.

"And it might have been overkill, but—say, you know I

like to tinker with stuff—well, I actually had some spare camera parts around the office. I just threw a pretty rough surveillance camera up outside the windows and the office door here."

Hargrove's eyes widened.

"Oh, don't worry Mr. Hargrove. It's really energy savin'. It's motion-activated so it only comes on when there's action. Get it?"

Nothing.

Stu continued. He stood up and walked toward he window. He was admiring his handiwork.

"Only action this office has seen is from you, Mr. Hargrove. You been trying to get in here like a sophomore to a senior prom. In fact, you tried about three or four times."

Hargrove doubled down. "Well, Stu, now that you mention it. I did find it odd that it was locked. I kept checking. Like you, I was worrying about the church being safe. And to be honest, you probably should have consulted me."

"That's fair, that's fair. Felt like I was being indelicate, though, on account of your daughter was kidnapped."

Hargrove didn't say anything, but Stu noticed that his stare began to turn rather icy.

"Tell you what, while we on the subject," Stu said, "I was doing a book inventory. Turns out one of the valuable ones at the top is missing. I couldn't quite put my finger on which one, but it was there."

Stu pointed to the center of the massive bookcase at the leather-bound books.

Hargrove glanced at them and shrugged. "All books in here are mostly donated. Only worth what someone's willing to pay."

"For sure, sir. But these ones are especially valuable. And they're a three-volume set. One of them is missing.

Only people been in here is me, Miss Elaina, the intruder that the Rev stopped, and the Rev."

"So, you're getting to—"

"That intruder nabbed one of 'em. Rev even found the back piece of cardboard at the place one of the bad guys almost killed him. So, they brought the book there, on the overlook."

"Again, I'm not—"

"But they didn't get the right one, did they Mr. Hargrove. That's what you were trying to do."

Hargrove didn't nod. Didn't shrug. He didn't do anything. His eyes almost went into a blank state where he stared far off. It seemed like minutes passed, but it probably wasn't that long.

Stu broke the silence, "Look, Mr. Hargrove, I'm not trying to make this a big deal—"

He was interrupted as Raymond Hargrove stood to his feet, picked up the pistol from the corner of the preacher's desk, pointed it at Stu's chest, and fired.

EIGHTY-ONE

Ani and I heard the shot from the sanctuary and came running down to the office. She already had her gun drawn. I had—my Bible.

Doesn't the Bible describe itself as a sword?

She was fast. She kicked open the door to the pastor's office. A small twinge of resentment rose up in me because that was going to be mine and she wasn't very considerate.

We both stopped just inside the door.

There stood Hargrove in one corner. Wide-eyed and full of desperation. I actually was wide-eyed myself. I couldn't believe that I was seeing this man who had just been a victim hours ago, now pointing a pistol at Stu.

Or I should say that he fired the pistol at Stu.

Stu was standing in the other corner. Arms folded. Glaring at Hargrove.

"How?" he asked.

Then he pointed the gun at me and took another shot. It was so loud my ears hurt and I instinctively ducked in hopes of dodging his bullet.

That same shocked look remained on Hargrove's face.

"Alright, that's enough," Ani said as she walked over to him, elbowed the gun out of his hand, and punched him in the temple. He let out what sounded like a yip and she was cussing something awful.

"Careful, Ani. Geez." I said. "This is still the Lord's house."

She cast a salty glare my way and I was okay with it.

Hargrove's bald head, which now had some blood coming out of it, still framed that shocked look as Ani was handcuffing him. First at Stu, then at me.

"How?" he asked.

"Well," I stepped forward, my chest pumped out, "you can't touch the Lord's anointed. I thought you were a church goer, Mr. Hargrove."

Ani hoisted him up, bumping his hip off the desk as she did, and guided him out of the office.

Stu and I were left alone. He looked at me with that smile worth a thousand near-death experiences.

"Well, Rev, ain't you glad I tinker with cap guns?"

Yep. I really was glad.

EIGHTY-TWO

The sun came in through the patio window. It invaded the kitchen like an army of light.

I loved it.

Sitting at the table, with Stu making coffee, Elaina clacking at her keyboard, and Detective Ani texting, this was the first moment that I felt I could take a breath on Maui.

Stu had opened the door so that a fragrant breeze filled the room with Maui. The presence of it. The smell of it. That flower. I prayed to God I'd never get sick of it. It was such a far cry from the mildewy, alcohol-infused aroma of my former place of work.

I did have a nice-looking outfit on today. No more Aloha shirt but an actual suit again. A gray one this time. I had to dress the part because the board formally asked me to be the interim pastor. They didn't offer me anything permanent, but Stu had assured me that it was a no brainer after the big ordeal we'd been through.

Attendance hadn't been that high at Resurrection in decades.

People are sick. Come to see a potential murderer preach, almost get killed, chase down a killer, and then ask said preacher if he would come back and preach again.

Yep, welcome to Maui.

But we had one final bit of business.

"Go," I said. I drank Stu's coffee that tasted like the tears of angels.

"Alright, this is pretty cut and dry," Stu said, running his finger along the rim of his own cup. "So, Hargrove was in money trouble. Big ones. Nasty divorce. Lots of debt. But, as all bigwigs do, he put fake curtains up. Nice cars. Big house on Maui. Lots more debt. You know the story?"

"Following," I said.

"Right. So, Miss Elaina was the one that turned us on to the Maui Sewage Treatment joint. And we did find Billy Robertson, or at least that's what he was calling himself, having a pretty big role there. He was the temporary outfit set to repair the pipes that had fallen into shambles in the plant."

"Don't give too many details on this," Elaina said over the clacking of her keys.

"Me and Miss Elaina are tired of the potty talk, Rev. Gotta excuse us. We studied up enough on bar screens, clarifiers, grit chambers, all that jazz. We are pretty much experts now. Trust me. You don't wanna look into the process. But the Maui plant's been having issues."

Elaina chimed in, "Enter Billy Robertson. He was contracted to take care of Maui's sewage problems for good. And take care of the issue with the smell in that basement. That's where he and Hargrove were in cahoots."

No, this didn't make sense.

"No, you said that Hargrove sat on a lot of boards and

had investments with a bunch of businesses, but *did not* sit on the board of the sewage treatment center."

Big belly laugh from Stu. "Right you are, Rev. Good listener. He didn't sit on a board for any sewage treatment center. But he did sit on a board for a manufacturing company. A rather big one in the area. They were entertaining a patent from a man called Daniel Willis. He had come up with some pretty sophisticated solutions that would save the treatment center millions. Maui Sewage had scheduled a meeting last week to entertain a pretty hefty deal, if he could provide a system that worked and a way to implement it."

"But unfortunately, he didn't make that meeting," Ani said. She still held onto her phone, but had temporarily lowered it. She was over by the patio door. I loved seeing her with makeup on and hope in her face. She looked like a new person.

But I was willing to wager her journey with grief was only beginning.

"Turns out Mr. Willis had some depression issues, or at least that's what he left in his suicide note. A forty-caliber bullet to the brain keeps people from business meetings."

Elaina said, "Enter once again, Billy Robertson. Knight in shining armor. He had been in talks with Maui Sewage for a while. And as it turns out, Billy so happened to be available to offer a solution to the problem. He just had to show them a schematic. Engineered and everything. Something very similar to what the late Mr. Willis had developed and prepared to present."

"And?" I said.

Stu pulled out one of the big theology books from under his kitchen sink. He opened the cover and there it was, taped into the thick jacket. A slender thumb drive. The cardboard leather-bound jacket looked exactly like the one that I'd found at the overlook before Elaina was taken by One Eye.

"Looks like that first fellow you tangoed with grabbed the wrong book, Rev. Poor fellow."

"Okay," I said. I was starting to get a clearer picture. "Hargrove knew about the development of the poop equipment."

Ani made a tsk noise.

I ignored it. I can't cage my funny. "Robertson was an engineer and able to white-glove the installation of the equipment on the faulty Maui center, right?"

"Keep going, Rev."

"And it all went to crap—pun kinda intended—because Hargrove was never able to get that schematic to Robertson."

"Exactly." Stu showed his million-dollar smile.

"Okay. Two questions. I'm sorry. I just, I am confused."

Elaina made that tsk noise this time.

Must've been hard for these eagles to have a turkey in the room.

"First one—who connected Hargrove to Robertson? Did their paths cross? Was there someone else involved?"

Elaina and Stu shared one of their worried glances. That was going to become something that always made me want to puke in my mouth.

"Rev," Stu said, "we gotta file that one under 'no clue.' Coulda been someone else involved. Maybe a lot of people. But we only know the players that played with us. And Robertson is full of holes so, it's hard to ask him the history."

Stu looked at Ani, whose face didn't change at all.

Note to self: never ever really make Ani mad.

Stu continued, "Hargrove sang to the police, just to get

a plea deal. Hoping to do some white-collar time on account that he never picked up a gun."

"Okay," I said. Really starting to get clear. now. "Last thing: Janeen. Hargrove."

Ani looked down at the ground. Stu and Elaina shared that look.

"Well, that was a side deal Billy and Ray worked out," Ani said. "Believe it or not, it had nothing to do with the sewage stuff. According to his confession, and, God forgive me for sharing this with you, Hargrove did it in hopes that he could get money from his ex-wife's family. They're loaded. It was a bit of a retaliation thing. Never pulled the trigger on a ransom, though, because Priority One was getting that schematic."

"No words for that," I said. I really didn't have it. Nor did I want to ask another question. The thought of paying someone to have your own daughter kidnaped to hurt your ex-wife and the in-laws.

Couldn't get my head around it.

Stu added the final clarifying statement. "Hargrove probably already figured he was in bed with Robertson. And once you cross that line, guess you're open to all other horizons."

"Guess so," I said.

Elaina closed her laptop. Ani put a blue blazer on over her pink dress shirt and dark dress slacks.

Stu took the last word.

"You want a sermon illustration on evil, Rev? Look no further than this."

EIGHTY-THREE

Since I almost died in the preacher's office, it was going to be hard for me to reinvent how I felt about it.

Still smelled like urinal cake. The remodeled look of the office still didn't go with the outdated decor of Resurrection Church. Stu had done an unreal job getting all the bullet holes out. I looked up at the bookcase, where the biggest books, the set of three, only had one remaining volume.

I would probably just throw it out. Truth be told, I don't know that I wanted to think about my initiation to Maui life again.

The desk still looked big. It was the size of a small Buick. I didn't even know what purpose it served. I would do all my sermon prep on a laptop. The books were just for show.

My sermon prep. Wow.

I had my bag on me and I was going to sit down and so some studying. Here was as good of a place as any. Since I had become a temporary resident at Stu's place, I felt funny working from home. Besides, the church had grown a lot in the last couple weeks. So what how the people got there. They were there.

And so was I.

Elaina came through the door as I was setting my MacBook up on the massive desk.

"Anything I can get for you, Pastor Grant?"

She was wearing a really nice green dress. Classy. It had big buttons going down the center. She also had on a great pair of hoop earrings. It was going to be distracting working with someone so gorgeous, but I was up to the task.

"Yeah, can you draft a thank-you note to Lila and Moani Wong for this awesome office."

"You're sinister," Elaina said. She smiled.

Yep, this was going to be distracting.

"There is something," I said.

She raised her eyebrows attentively. Smart as a whip. Anything I asked her she'd try to accomplish. And she'd do it better than anyone.

"Can you tell me how you think this is all gonna shake out?"

She smiled again and looked down.

"I heard a pastor say once that if we knew all the details of God's plan, we'd never take the next step. Apply that to this situation and tell me that's not relevant."

I laughed. It was genuine. But what Elaina didn't know is that coming to Maui was the best decision I'd made. What I left behind. Who I was.

It was dead.

She turned around and walked to the door.

"You're a great secre—I mean—administrator."

Elaina turned back to face me one more time. "One thing is for sure, Pastor Grant. You made a lot of waves on the Valley Isle."

"Well, let's hope that this is the end of it. I'm in the mood for boring, to be honest."

I meant it. I really did.

Elaina smiled once more. "Somehow I doubt that's the end. But at least you know this is where you're supposed to be."

She didn't let me respond. She turned, walked out of my office, and shut the door behind her.

THE END

SAWYER GRANT WILL RETURN IN

DEATH ANGEL

ACKNOWLEDGMENTS

Anything I write is laced with the sacrifice of my family. Starting what my wife, and then the children.

As I write this, my kids are sitting in my office watching a Netflix show on my iPad. My writing enables me to be home more with them.

I love that.

I don't need to go anywhere else in the world other than go to the worlds I created.

I write for them. So that I can provide more for them. But also, I want to set an example of a man who pursues his passion.

I want to acknowledge my editors. Josiah Davis has the most rapid turnaround times and patience. And Stephanie. I'm in her debt for many reasons. But mainly, for her time. She reads everything I write. Edits it. And she isn't afraid to break my heart by telling me if something sucks. But since she reads everything, I've taken her time. And she'll never get that back!

And speaking of time, thank you for giving me yours. You could be doing anything, but you chose to read my words. I want you to know that my number one priority is to have fun as a write. My second priority is to make sure that I transfer that experience to you.

With that being said, let's do this again sometime!

Meanwhile, a detective is hellbent on exposing Grant's past launches into a mission of his own.

Realizing how dangerous Angel Carlisle is, Grant runs into the center of an evil plan that has the potential to bring Maui to its knees. Will Grant defeat the Death Ange, or will we lose his new life, and the lives of his friends in the process?

If you like dangerous villains, witty characters, and page-turning suspense, then prepare to lose some sleep being glued to the pages of the latest installment of Drew Cole's *Sawyer Grant* series.

Grab your copy of *Death Angel* today and buckle up for the ride of your life.

https://books2read.com/deathangel

JOIN MY COLE STORIES CLUB

Cole Stories Club members get free books, free behind the scenes updates, and unique items to accompany the books.

Signing up will get you access to an exclusive short about Sawyer Grant's past: *Deadly Revelation*

Go to subscribepage.io/nSANdx to join today!

PLEASE LEAVE A REVIEW

Enjoy this story? You can make a really big difference.

Please leave a review. Reviews really help readers discover authors like me. Since you've read this far, please consider helping me.

Finding more readers like you fuels me to write more. Thank you again for your review.